LONGING TO BELONG

A novel by
Judi Bergen

Lost Lake Folk Art
SHIPWRECKT BOOKS PUBLISHING COMPANY

IN®
DIE

Minnesota

Front cover photo by Judi Bergen
Back cover photo, cover and interior design by
Shipwreckt Books

To my husband, Dick.
His constant love and support has made it possible for me to spend so much time on my writing.

Longing to Belong
Contents

1. The attic

Your grandfather hanged himself in the attic ... of this house. It's true." Aunt Ethel, who always pulled back her gray streaked hair into a tight bun, reached out and stiffly patted six-year-old Amanda's arm without looking into the distraught girl's eyes, wide with dismay and raw from crying. "But Rebecca Nelson had no business telling you," Ethel fumed. "Furthermore, she lied when she said he was a thief. People believe he took money from the bank, but no one could prove it. The money was never found." Her chapped hands trembling uncontrollably, Ethel reached into the pocket of the patched bib apron she always wore to protect the faded cotton housedresses she also always wore and pulled out a spotless, white handkerchief. "Wipe your tears," she said. "Your father was only fourteen when he searched the house, every inch of it, looking for the money. I knew there would be nothing to find, but I had to let him search." Emotion overwhelmed Ethel. She must stop thinking about the past, get a grip on herself, and focus on the child. How could such a horrible thing happen on Amanda's first day of school?

"I ... hate ... Rebecca," Amanda sobbed. "Tomorrow ... on the playground ... I'm going to trip her!" She rubbed her eyes hard with the handkerchief. "I hope she ... falls flat on her face."

Ethel scowled. "It's a sin even to think such awful thoughts." Her voice gathered strength, confident Amanda needed to hear what she had to say. "Beg God's forgiveness or you will be punished." Her immediate duty to the child done, she reached for a tray filled with warm cookies. "I just took these out of the oven. Why don't you have one."

"I don't want a dumb cookie." Amanda shook her head, dark curls flying every which way.

"They're chocolate chip. I baked them just for you."

"I'm not hungry," she whimpered, slowly reaching for a cookie and sitting at the table.

Ethel, wishing her hands would stop shaking, carefully poured Amanda a glass of milk.

The grotesque image she could never erase from her memory suddenly appeared again—the worn soles of her daddy's black shoes, the legs of his gray wool trousers darkened with urine, his warm body gently swinging back-and-forth his broken neck crooked in a noose made from a thick rope spiked into an attic beam.

How she wished she had come right home from school that day. He wouldn't have taken his life is she had been there. Why did she stop at the drugstore to look with longing at classmates having sodas together? She knew something was wrong when she found the front door wide open. Her daddy's black derby sat on the chair by the door, the hat he always wore when he left the house because it covered his bald spot. She had wandered through the house, wondering why he came home early, calling out, "Daddy, why did you come home so early? Where are you, Daddy?" Finally, she climbed the creaking steps to the attic. She could never forget how she screamed when she saw his body. That scream was still inside her.

Amanda nibbled the cookie. Ethel forced calm into her voice, picked up the phone and asked Helga, the phone operator, to connect her to her brother's office. The receptionist answered. "Mary, I know how busy Doctor MacGregor is, but we need him to come home." Ethel would say no more because she knew, as certain as she knew the sun rose every morning, that Helga was listening-in to every word.

"I'll get him for you," replied Mary briskly.

After what seemed like an eternity to Ethel, Carlton answered. "Yes, Ethel, Mary said you need me at home? What …?"

"… it's Amanda." Ethel drew a deep breath, slowly exhaled and said firmly, "Amanda needs you now."

Carlton sighed, "I swear everyone in Turtle Creek has come down with something today. I'll come as soon as I can."

Ethel hung up, straightened her shoulders and sat down across from Amanda. "I want to hear all about your first day of first grade. You know, I've always thought Miss Williamson looks like a soft, plump teddy bear."

Amanda smiled. "I like her. Today she asked me to stand up in front of the class to recite the *Pledge of Allegiance* with her." She searched Ethel's eyes for approval. "I'm the only one who knows it by heart. School's good, but I'm never talking to that dumb Rebecca again."

"Forget about Rebecca, Amanda, and don't call anyone dumb. I hope you didn't show off in class. Remember what I told you. Just pretend you don't know how to read. The other kids won't like you if they think you're acting like you're better than them." Ethel took both of Amanda's slender wrists in her chapped hands. "You don't have to play with Rebecca, but you must be nice to her in school. After all, her father is the president of the bank." She abruptly let go of Amanda's wrists. "I have to start supper. Your father is going to try to come home early."

"I want him now. Why does he have to take care of everybody else?"

"He's the most respected man in town, Amanda. People come from all over the county to doctor with him. You must always be proud of him."

"But you told me never to be proud."

"You know what I mean. Why don't you finish that book you started last night?" Flustered, Ethel marched to the kitchen to start supper muttering loud enough for Amanda to hear, "I need to talk to Carlton about that child. Of course, he won't see the problems caused by the sin of pride in Amanda. He is too trusting. For goodness sake, he thinks it's a good idea for a black man to play baseball on a white man's team. 1947 is not a good year." Scrubbing carrots with a vengeance, Ethel prayed, "Dear God, I hope that more bad things don't happen to that child."

Amanda snuggled into the overstuffed armchair in the living room and lost herself so deeply in her book she didn't hear her dad enter the room. He leaned down to her level and softly said, "Sorry I couldn't come sooner. How was the first day of school, precious?"

"Good, except for that dumb Rebecca." She quickly put her book down. "Will you pick me up and twirl me around?"

3

Carlton stood up and swept his faded blond hair out of his eyes. Then he gently picked up Amanda, hugged her, grabbed her small wrists and began to twirl her.

Watching from the doorway until Carlton eased Amanda's feet back to the floor, Ethel said, "I'm so glad you're home. I've made your favorite dessert, and ..." Her voice trailed off as she realized he wasn't listening.

Carlton lowered himself into the overstuffed armchair, reached for his child and sat her on his lap facing him.

Amanda looked into his eyes and asked, "Is it really true that grandfather killed himself in our attic?"

Carlton responded in a low voice, "Yes, sweetie." He gently rubbed her back. "It's really true."

Amanda buried her head in his chest. "But it's not true that he was a thief, right?" She burrowed deep.

Ethel pulled one of the straight-backed dining room chairs close to them and sat down. "You'll understand this better when you're older. Your grandfather was very sad because he was accused of doing something he said he didn't do. Nobody believed him." Ethel rose to her feet, straight as an arrow. "Will this town never change? I'm calling Mrs. Nelson to tell her to stop spreading malicious rumors that started twenty years ago."

"Just let it be," admonished Carlton. "You'll only stir things up again. There is no proof that Dad took the money, but there's no proof someone else took the money either. We just have to live with this."

Ethel hurried into the kitchen. "It's time to eat."

Amanda lifted her head from Carlton's chest, shoving her nose against her dad's. "What money?"

"Your grandfather was president of the bank a long time ago. Money went missing from several accounts, and he was the last person in the bank the night the money disappeared."

"Aunt Ethel says you looked for proof he took it."

Carlton answered softly, "It's never been found. We have to put all this behind us, forget about it."

"But what should I do about Rebecca? Auntie says it's sinful to think of ways to hurt her."

Carlton eased Amanda down. "Just hold your head high when you see her, sweet one, and ignore unkind remarks she or anyone else makes about your grandfather. It probably won't happen again."

"You know it will, Carlton," snapped Ethel as they sat down together at the heavy dining room table. "I'll never forget how everyone would stop talking when I entered a room. Reverend Swenson's refusal to bury our father in the Lutheran cemetery made things even worse."

"I focus on people's kindness after his death," he replied.

Amanda played with her food, lining the carrots and peas in neat rows. "How were they kind?"

"I was seven when he died. Auntie was fourteen. People brought us food for months after the funeral. They would just show up to help with major projects like painting the house. Their kindness made it possible for us to stay in our home." He turned to look at Ethel. "But of course, without you here I would have gone to an orphanage. I don't know how you did it." He directed his gaze back to Amanda. "She worked at the grocery store, finished high school and managed to run this big house. She gave up a lot for me, Amanda, and still is taking care of us."

Ethel cleared her throat. "Amanda, dear, eat your potatoes."

"Why Ethel, I think you're blushing," Carlton teased.

The air felt lighter to Ethel by the time they finished eating. She gathered plates and started doing the dishes. Carlton took Amanda's hand and led her back to the big chair. "Let's see how many great school smells we can come up with."

"Paste," Amanda said as she settled herself on his lap, "and my favorite is new crayons."

"That's a good one. What about the smell of varnish?"

"I could almost see myself in the varnish on the floor in the hallway. It smells good, but chalk smells like dust. You know what? I was the only student who got to recite the *Pledge of Allegiance* with Miss Williamson today. I love school."

"And so did I. You know, people in Turtle Creek helped me a lot with college expenses. I wouldn't have been able to go to medical school without their help. Don't ever forget that."

"Is Auntie Ethel happy here, Daddy?"

"Of course, sweetheart."

"But she never smiles."

"She's a very serious person, but you, young lady, think way too much. Now it's time for me to read the paper." Carlton gently lifted her off his lap.

Ethel rinsed the soap bubbles off of each dish with scalding water. She didn't understand why they could waste time talking silly. She always had work to do.

That night, it stormed. The air filled with strange noises. Branches clawed against the house, wind smashed against window panes and rain pummeled the roof. Ethel couldn't sleep. She finally drifted off when the storm stopped, only to awaken just before dawn, sensing something, or someone, was staring at her. She sat up straight.

Amanda stood in a patch of moonlight framed in the doorway. Ethel's voice quivered. "What's wrong?"

"I want Daddy. I'm afraid."

Ethel felt the surge of maternal longing she used to feel when Amanda was an infant and she had wished Amanda was her baby. "I'm glad you remembered that you're not supposed to bother your father during the night. He needs his sleep," she said in a loud whisper. "I'll go upstairs with you, there's nothing to be afraid of."

Amanda raised her voice, "But I hear noises in the attic."

Ethel replied, "It's just the storm, probably tree branches hitting the roof."

"No, it was footsteps on the attic floor, not branches," Amanda insisted.

Ethel got out of bed, shivering, feeling clammy all over. She had to regain control. "You have an overactive imagination, Amanda MacGregor," she half-scolded. "Now I'm taking you up to your bed, and you will sleep." She grabbed Amanda's arm and pulled her up the stairs. Amanda whimpered as she buried her face in the pillow. Ethel pulled the cover up around her, and in a softer voice said, "You need your rest. Think about *Winnie the Pooh* stories. They're your favorites. You'll be asleep before you know it."

Ethel, however, could not go back to sleep.

Carlton found Ethel scrubbing the kitchen floor in the morning, her hands red and raw.

"You work too hard," he told her.

Ethel cleared her throat. "I'll be fine. I can rest this afternoon. I need to wake Amanda." She briskly walked up the stairs. Amanda was sleeping with the quilt pulled over her head. Ethel gently removed the quilt, saying, "You have to get dressed."

Amanda rubbed her eyes. "I don't want to see that dumb Rebecca. She'll poke fun at me."

"I know Rebecca was mean, but kids quickly forget the horrible things they say." Ethel hesitated. "Maybe today she'll want to be your friend."

"I don't want Rebecca. I have a friend who is better than she will ever be."

"And who is that?" Ethel laid out a long-sleeved cotton dress she had sewed, for Amanda to put on.

"Joey Oscarson. I knocked him down when I was running away from Rebecca. He scratched his elbow on the sidewalk. At first I didn't see the blood because I was crying, and because he has so many freckles." Amanda pulled her slip over her head. "He didn't care about the blood. All he cared about was me. When he walked me home he said he lives close by. Joey's my best friend."

Ethel started to talk fast. "He lives in that tarpaper shack on the end of our street. I'm glad he helped you, but he can't be your best friend. For one thing, he's older than you."

"Only two years," Amanda said as she put on her white anklets. "His house looks fine to me."

Ethel sat on the bed and asked Amanda to join her. "This is hard for you to understand. His mother doesn't act like the other ladies in town. Besides, Joey's a boy. You'll find girls in your class to play with."

Amanda grabbed her dress and tried to pull it over her head as Ethel helped her find the sleeves.

When it was time to leave for school, Ethel put on her new, wide brimmed hat. She planned on walking with Amanda, but Joey was waiting by the front door.

"Good morning, Miss `." Joey brushed a shock of carrot red hair out of his eyes. "I thought I'd walk with Amanda. If anything bad is said about her grandfather, I'll deal with it."

Ethel was both pleased and displeased. "If you're sure it's not too much trouble. The lies really upset Amanda."

"I know, ma'am. Rebecca had no business talking like that. You have a good day now." He took Amanda's hand. "That's such a pretty hat you have on, ma'am."

"Why, thank you, young man." Ethel tucked a stray strand of hair under her wide-brimmed hat. "You come right home after school, Amanda."

Joey and Amanda took off, Amanda skipping.

Ethel decided to take a little walk, as long as she looked so good in her new hat. Besides, it was a nice day, and she hadn't visited her daddy's grave recently. When she passed the tarpaper shanty on the north side of the street she looked closely at the weathered shingles desperately hanging on to the roof. Joey's mother, Daisy hung clothes on the line, singing, "'I'm forever blowing bubbles, pretty bubbles in the sky. They fly so high, they reach the sky, and in my dreams, they fade and die.'"

Ethel walked by without stopping to greet the petite blond. She wondered why she was hanging out the wash so early. Of course, I should have thought of that, she muttered to herself. It is because Daisy has to work at the grocery soon. She wouldn't be that industrious if she had a choice. Ethel reached the cornfield on the edge of town, annoyed when she realized she was singing the end of Daisy's song. "'Fortune's always hiding, hiding everywhere, 'cause I'm forever blowing bubbles, pretty bubbles in the air.'"

She thought about Turtle Creek, the only place she'd ever known. Ethel approached the cemetery just beyond the cornfield. All sizes and shapes of houses were mixed together in Turtle Creek, but only Daisy's house had no siding on the exterior walls. Her husband had died when Joey was five. Ethel remembered that well. He was working as a hired hand on a farm when a bull charged him. He was a foolish dreamer, Daisy's husband, with big plans that never worked out. He never should have taken that job. He knew nothing about bulls.

When she got to the cemetery she paused for breath, and then walked around the fence on the north side to a small patch of land, where there were three graves. One had fall flowers planted by the gray tombstone. She knelt and traced her finger over the lettering. Here lies Donald Wallace MacGregor, Born January 28, 1883. Died November 4, 1929. God have mercy on his soul.

"Well, Dear Daddy, here I am again. I'll always take care of you." She carefully pulled out some of the weeds around the tombstone.

"I don't know what to do about Joey Oscarson. He seems nice, but I don't think Amanda should spend much time with him." She searched for more weeds. "However, he did defend you. I know you didn't take that money." She vigorously pulled out the last weed. "Reverend Swenson's death from cholera was God's punishment for his refusal to bury you in the church cemetery. And for that horrible sermon at your funeral, all that talk about your lost soul. How could he be so self-righteous? Pride is one of the worst sins."

Ethel gathered weeds in her apron and carried them to the ditch at the edge of the road. After she threw them away, she hurried to the cemetery entrance. When she came to her mother's grave, she stopped to read the beautiful inscription carved into rose colored granite noting of the death of Elizabeth Anne MacGregor when Carlton was born.

She looked into a gray cloud hovering overhead and begged in a plaintive voice, almost childlike, "Mother, how I wish you hadn't left us so early. Life would have been so much easier if you had stayed. Ethel straightened her spine. It's so sad that you never even saw him. Carlton was a beautiful baby. I know you would be proud of your son, and I'm doing the best job I can with his daughter. "Time to leave," Ethel muttered. "Best go home and scrub the kitchen floor again."

2. Turtle Creek Sunday

On Sunday, after a peaceful week, Carlton, Ethel and Amanda attended services, as they always did, at Saint Olaf Lutheran Church. Ethel wore her wide-brimmed hat, a long-sleeved dress and gloves despite the heat of Indian Summer, the kind of day Iowa often gets in the early fall. She insisted Amanda put on the fancy new dress that had just come by mail from Sears Roebuck & Company, the most expensive girl's dress in the catalogue, pink, with rows of white ruffles, like a fancy cake buried in layers of frosting.

Amanda looked at it, wrinkled up her nose and announced, "I don't like this dress."

Ethel pulled the hem down over Amanda's head. "You'll see how pretty it is when it's on," she replied. "You don't like it because you didn't get enough sleep last night. Now raise your arms."

Amanda refused to lift her arms. "It's itchy on my neck. It feels like your hands, Auntie."

"You're a naughty girl. How can you talk like this on the Lord's day?" Ethel rubbed her hands together, feeling how rough they were. She lowered her head because she didn't want Amanda to see the tears forming in her eyes, but she couldn't hold back two tears that trickled down her cheeks.

Carlton entered the bedroom. "What's going on here? We should leave soon."

Stiff white ruffles bunched around her neck, Amanda ran to her daddy and threw her arms around his waist. "I don't want to wear this dumb dress."

Ethel stiffened and took a deep breath. "She won't even try it on. I know she'll like this beautiful new dress once she's worn it."

Carlton knelt down to Amanda's level. "Let me slip it over your head. It means a lot to your aunt. Now please raise your arms."

"Oh, okay." With a pout, Amanda reluctantly complied.

"We should be at the church right now," said Ethel, grabbing Amanda's white straw hat and gloves, because that's what she wore every Sunday from Easter to October. The hat hid Amanda's dark curls, which made Ethel secretly glad. If Ethel could have everything the way she wanted, Amanda's hair would be straight and blond like most of the other girls in Turtle Creek. Ethel would braid it daily.

"Amanda, you look lovely," said Carlton with a bright smile.

Ethel couldn't believe her eyes when they entered the church five minutes before the service was to start "Someone is sitting in our pew," she hissed, hoping that the young lady and her husband would hear her and move.

Thor Olson and his new bride occupied the church pew. Thor had brought her home from Italy the year before, and Ethel was convinced that the bride never knew what she was supposed to do. When she was asked to bring a hot dish to the Ladies Aid meeting, she brought long spaghetti with a spicy red sauce. It was very hard to eat, and several ladies who tried it had coughing spells.

They didn't move, so Ethel directed Carlton and Amanda to sit in the eighth pew with her. "I hope that Reverend Olafson realizes we are here today," she muttered. "He always looks for me in the second pew."

Several women fanned themselves with church bulletins, folded accordion style, which Ethel felt was beneath her. After the opening hymn, Amanda kept turning her head left, then right, until Ethel pinched her. "Sit up straight and pay attention."

Reverend Olafson ascended to the pulpit and cleared his throat. The theme of the sermon was Judge not and ye shall not be judged. How perfect, Ethel thought. I hope Thor's wife is listening. She's sitting in our pew. This is a judgment against us. How can she think she's better than us? We have sat in pew number two for as long as I can remember.

Amanda leafed through the pages of a new red hymnal during the sermon, something Ethel had never seen her niece do before. She put her hands on top of Amanda's and applied firm pressure, convinced that the new red hymnals were too distracting, and that good hard-earned money should never have been spent for them. The black hymnals worked just fine.

When they got up to sing the last hymn, Amanda kept shifting from her right foot to her left to the beat of *Praise God from Whom All Blessings Flow*. Ethel's patience was worn thin. She jabbed Amanda in the shin, discreetly.

Amanda yelled, "Ouch!" Carlton grinned. Ethel stood stiff as a board and looked straight ahead, trying to pretend another child had made that noise.

After being ushered out of the church, Ethel pulled Amanda firmly and directly to the car instead of visiting with other people. "Amanda, I'm very disappointed in you, acting like a two-year-old instead of a first grader. Why couldn't you sit still?"

"I tried to, but this dress makes me itch all over."

"It was really hot, Ethel," said Carlton as he stooped into the car. "Don't be too hard on her."

"If we'd been sitting in our pew we would have felt the breeze from the window. That Italian bride insisted on taking our place. Thor Olson lets her do whatever she wants. She'll never fit in."

Amanda, seated between Carlton and Ethel in the front seat, looked up at her aunt. "But she looks like me. Do I fit in?"

"Of course you do, dear. You're a MacGregor, and I didn't mean her looks as much as I meant that she doesn't know the good manners and customs of our country."

"I'd like to try her spaghetti sauce. Thor told me it's delicious," Carlton said as he started the car.

"Oh hush. You're just teasing me now, Carlton MacGregor." Ethel rolled down her window to get some fresh air and noticed Mrs. Nelson and Rebecca walking past. She turned away from the window, but it was too late.

Mrs. Nelson stopped beside the car. "Isn't it a beautiful day? We decided it would be good for us to walk."

"It is a nice day, but it is awfully warm." Ethyl turned to Amanda. "Look who's here. Say hi to Rebecca."

Amanda kept her eyes on the floorboard. "Hi," she said in a monotone.

Rebecca replied in the same tone. "Hi."

Rebecca's mother said, "That's a very fancy dress, Amanda. Rebecca doesn't like to wear anything that fussy."

"I'm sorry, but we have to go," Ethel said, rolling up the window. "I have to check on the chicken in the oven." Carlton started the shiny black Ford and pulled onto the street for the drive home six blocks. "It's so nice we don't have to walk in our good Sunday clothes," said Ethel.

As always, they ate Sunday dinner in their good clothes, and Ethel worried the entire time that Amanda would spill something on her new dress. It wasn't a relaxing meal. As soon as they finished, Amanda said, "Can I put on my play clothes?"

"Of course, dear. We don't want to get your lovely dress dirty. Everyone in church was admiring it. I won't mention any names, but I think that some people were a little envious. Envy is a terrible sin."

Amanda ran upstairs to change. Carlton said, "Ethel, I think that kind of talk is very confusing to a six-year-old."

Without responding, Ethel got up to do the dishes. Whenever she felt hurt, Ethel busied herself in house chores. That worked best for her. She washed the dishes, admiring how they shined as she rinsed off soap bubbles with scalding water. Amanda came downstairs and told her dad she was going outside to play. Ethel heard the front screen door slam.

"That child has to learn not to slam the door." The dishes were finished and Ethel sat on the sofa. Carlton looked up from *The Des Moines Register*. Ethel continued in a half-whisper. "We have a problem. Joey Oscarson has been walking with her to and from school every day."

Carlton laid the Sunday paper on his lap. "What's wrong with that? He's a good kid. I should think you'd be glad you don't have to walk with her. You're always so busy."

"I don't think it's normal for those two to spend so much time together." Ethel rubbed the edge of her apron. "Amanda never plays with the beautiful doll we gave her for her birthday."

"You worry too much. Anyway, Amanda's a bit of a tomboy. Not all girls like to play with dolls." Carlton resumed reading.

Ethel got up to change out of her Sunday dress and take a nap. She was exhausted, but her busy mind wouldn't allow her to rest.

When at last she forced herself to stop thinking about her daddy's body hanging from the rafters, she started worrying about Amanda. She got up and washed the kitchen walls.

Amanda came home to find Ethel rearranging the spice rack. "Can I have a drink?" Amanda asked.

"Your clothes are wet. Where have you been?"

"Running through the sprinkler at Joey's. It was really fun, Auntie."

"Go upstairs and change into dry clothes right away. You know it's dangerous to get chilled. How many times have I told you that's how you get polio?"

"But the whole neighborhood was there. Joey's mom made popcorn and strawberry Kool-Aid.

"Daisy Oscarson doesn't take her parenting responsibilities seriously. She's too busy playing."

"But she doesn't play. She was taking care of us."

"When you're older you'll understand what I'm talking about. You are not to run through the sprinkler at Joey Oscarson's. Ever!" Ethel nudged Amanda out of the kitchen. "Now go upstairs and change into dry clothes before you get sick."

Ethel knew what she had to do. She poked her head into the living room. "Carlton, I'm going to get some fresh air." She walked briskly to the Oscarson's home, the tarpaper shanty, and knocked on the screen door. Visible inside through the screen, Daisy folded clothes on a wood table in the center of the room, which appeared to Ethel to be the room where they did everything but sleep.

Ethel noticed a doorway covered with a curtain, and a narrow door closing off another area. She couldn't believe what she saw lying on the table, the underwear, the handkerchiefs, the slips all folded in neat little piles. "Why," Ethel muttered under her breath, "she must not iron a thing. "And look at that worn linoleum. It has never seen wax. No polish on that worn table either. Everything looks used.

Daisy looked at Ethel checking out her home and smiled politely. "What a nice surprise. Please come in."

Ethel cautiously entered, careful not to let the screen door slam behind her. The air had a lightness that the air in the big

MacGregor house didn't have, and there was something else, some elusive quality Ethel couldn't put her finger on.

"Please sit down." Daisy motioned to a worn sofa. "Can I get you something to drink? Iced tea perhaps?"

Ethel took charge. "No thank you." She remained standing. "I can't stay. I need to talk to you about the safety of our children."

"The safety? What do you mean?"

Ethel stepped closer. "I take my responsibility of raising Amanda seriously."

"You must be doing a good job. She's so sweet, and so smart."

Ethel's face turned red. "Yes, I can't take credit for her being smart. She takes after Dr. MacGregor, you know." Ethel stood up as straight as she could, looking down at Daisy Oscarson from her full height. "I'll get right to the point. Amanda can't run through sprinklers. The risk of catching polio is too great."

"I offered her dry clothes," Daisy replied. "She wanted to keep on the wet ones."

"A six-year-old doesn't know what's best. Of course, with her dad being a doctor, I'm very aware of the importance of good health practices."

"Oh?" Daisy looked puzzled. "Please tell me, what does Doctor MacGregor say about the danger of catching polio from a sprinkler?"

"He doesn't need to discuss it with me. Everyone knows you're just asking for polio to strike when you allow kids to play in the sprinkler, getting soaking wet, catching a chill."

"I'm sorry I upset you, Ethel," Daisy replied. "Next time I'll insist Amanda put on dry clothes when they're done playing."

"You don't understand. I don't want Amanda playing in the sprinkler."

"You're right," said Daisy. "I don't understand. Kids should have fun, and there are so many things we can't control. It doesn't pay to worry too much."

"I don't want Amanda spending time here," Ethel said sternly. "I forbid it. Joey should be playing with kids his own age – boys."

Daisy walked to the door and opened it. "I think you should leave now."

Ethel stormed home mumbling to herself, "Carlton is going to hear about this. He has to talk to Daisy."

Amanda sat on Carlton's lap holding a book open when Ethel returned and marched over to them. Carlton look up and said to Amanda, "Read that paragraph for Auntie Ethel. You did such a good job."

"I want both of you to hear what I have to say," said Ethel, her feet planted defiantly in front of the father and daughter. "Amanda, you cannot play at Joey's house anymore. It's not safe."

Amanda's book fell to the floor. Carlton leaned over to pick it up. "What are you talking about?" he demanded.

"Polio. Amanda came home soaking wet. Everyone knows that's how you catch polio. That little Daisy doesn't take parenting seriously. Who knows what else goes on at that house?"

"You worry too much, Ethel. Joey's a fine boy."

"He seems okay. It's his mother I worry about. She lets kids do whatever they want."

Amanda got down from her dad's lap. "Joey's mom makes us share, and if she sees some kid being mean, she makes him sit out. Please let me play there." Amanda put her arms around Ethel's waist.

Ethel removed Amanda's arms and knelt down eye level with her niece. "I don't want you to get polio. You would have to spend the rest of your life in an iron lung because you couldn't breathe on your own."

Carlton got up from the chair. "Ethel, that is enough foolishness. Infantile Paralysis is an infectious virus disease of the central nervous system. The largest percentage of polio victims who receive proper care recover with few, if any, permanent aftereffects. You may have several good reasons why you don't want Amanda to get her clothes wet, but wet clothes do not cause polio. I think it's foolish to forbid her to play at Joey's."

Tears streamed down Amanda's face "I promise I won't run through the sprinkler ever again. Please let me play there."

Ethel wiped Amanda's tears with her dress. "You really should play with kids your own age. You could give tea parties for your dolls. I never had a doll as beautiful as the one you got for your birthday," said Ethel referring to the blond-haired, blue-eyed doll from the Sears Roebuck Catalogue that arrived wearing a blue satin dress, very suitable for tea parties.

"I don't like that doll. She's boring, with that smile pasted on her face."

"But I thought you liked smiles."

"Not fake ones."

"I don't know what I'm going to do with this girl." Ethel gave Carlton a long-suffering look.

Carlton grinned. He took Amanda's hand and pulled her toward the door. "Would you like to play catch?"

Ethel couldn't decide what to do. It was too late to start a major cleaning project. There were clothes to be washed, but she always did laundry on Mondays, ironing on Tuesdays. She wished she had some of Carlton's freshly sprinkled shirts, nice and damp in plastic bags waiting to be ironed. Ironing was Ethel's favorite task, especially her brother's shirts. When she moved the hot iron slowly back and forth over the white cotton shirts, steam rose from the fabric, adding to her trance-like state.

She went to the bureau in Carlton's bedroom to make sure that there were no undershirts or boxer shorts that got wrinkled when he grabbed something to put on in the middle of the night, when he had to deliver a baby. Everything was neat as a pin. Ethel decided instead to work on a cable sweater she was knitting for Amanda's smiling doll. Maybe come Christmas, if there were several new outfits for her blue-eyed doll, Amanda would play with her.

Seated in the chair by the screen door knitting, Ethel listened to Carlton and Amanda chatting while they played catch with a softball. After missing the ball for the third time in a row, Amanda sat on the front steps. "I want to stop. I can't catch that dumb ball," the child complained.

Carlton sat next to her. "I appreciate how hard you try. It'll get easier as you get older."

"Daddy, can I tell you a secret wish? Will you promise you won't laugh at me?"

Ethel stopped knitting and leaned close to the door to eavesdrop as Carlton said, "Of course you can, and I would never laugh at a secret wish."

"You know what Daddy? I wish you and Daisy would get married. She would paint every room in our house a different color. My bedroom would be periwinkle blue, the kitchen dandelion yellow like my new crayons. Daisy is always happy. And Joey would be my brother. His room would be apple green to match his eyes."

"Slow down partner. I can't keep up with you. Sure, it's hard not to have a mother, and of course it would be nice for you to have a brother or sister." He paused. "I don't know what we would have done without your Auntie Ethel. She's been like a mother to you." Ethel's heart swelled with pride. She leaned even closer to the door. Carlton said, "You know what? You can have Joey over here as often as you like."

Ethel resumed her knitting with increasing speed, talking to herself. "Carlton doesn't realize how dangerous it can be for boys and girls who aren't related to spend too much time together. He's naïve about some things. He never would have ended up with Sarah tricking him into marriage if he weren't so gullible. What am I going to do?" She tore out several botched stitches. "At least I can watch them closely if they always play here." She knitted some more. "If I see or hear anything suspicious, I'll report it to Carlton immediately." Ethel stopped knitting to admire her work. "How could Amanda not love this beautiful sweater?"

3. Her own typewriter

Ethel opened her front door the following morning to find Joey waiting for Amanda on the sidewalk. The boy smiled. "Good morning, Miss MacGregor."

Amanda bounded out the door and skipped down the steps. "Hey, Joey!" She glanced back over her shoulder to say, "Bye, Auntie Ethel."

"You have a nice day, ma'am," said Joey, joining Amanda.

Ethel smiled stiffly, watched the happy children and called out before they disappeared, "Be sure to come right home after school, Amanda!"

At ten minutes after four, Ethel heard Amanda open the front door. "Come on in. My dad said it's okay if you play here after school." She let the screen door slam.

"You should close the door quietly," Joey said. "My mom says it's hard on doors when they slam." Then he whispered, "Are you sure this is okay with your aunt?"

"Auntie," Amanda yelled. "Can Joey play with me? We want some cookies and milk." Then she turned to Joey. "I'll try to remember not to slam the door."

Joey smiled at Ethel when she stepped out from the kitchen. "Good afternoon, ma'am," he said. "I can't stay for long. My mom expects me to be home when she gets home from work."

"You mean your mother leaves you on your own until she's off work at the grocery store?" Ethel's stern voice deepened with disapproval, thinking about how Carlton would not approve of such an arrangement.

Joey politely responded. "Yes, ma'am. When I was in first grade I had to go to the store right after school. I waited there till she was done. But in second grade we decided I could go home, or to a friend's, as long as I was home by five. I didn't mind being at the store. I would color or read in the back, but I like this better."

"If you sit nicely at the dining room table, you can have freshly baked peanut butter cookies. I always have something nutritious waiting for Amanda when she gets home."

"Thank you," Joey said as he sat down. "This is such a big house. It must take a lot of work to keep it up."

"It is a lot of work to keep a proper house," boasted Ethel proudly. She poured two glasses of milk.

When they finished, Amanda asked Joey, "Would you like to see my books? They're upstairs." Amanda started to get up.

Ethel said, "Why don't you bring some books down here?"

"But I want him to see all of them."

"Proper girls don't take boys up to their bedrooms."

"If Daddy were here, he'd say it's okay."

Joey stood up. "We can look at some books on the front steps. You go get them."

Amanda ran upstairs. Ethel offered Joey another cookie.

"These are delicious," he said. "Thank you, ma'am."

Ethel had a pot roast in the oven for supper. She was glad that she didn't have to be in the kitchen. She hovered by the front door, knitting, eavesdropping on the children. Joey and Amanda talked about their favorite *Winnie the Pooh* stories. Ethel was bored, but she remained faithfully at her post until Joey left.

That night, after Amanda went to bed, Ethel joined her brother in the living room. Carlton sat in his usual chair reading a medical journal.

"Joey played here after school." Ethel sat on the sofa with her knitting. "Did you know that his mother lets him be on his own to wander all over the town till she comes home from work?"

Carlton looked at Ethel and calmly said, "Joey's a good kid. I'm sure he won't get in trouble. I thought you wouldn't mind when I told Amanda that they could play here. How'd it go today?"

"Well, Amanda wanted to take him up to her bedroom to see her books, which I forbade of course."

"You worry too much, Ethel, about things that aren't important."

"How can you say that girls and boys playing together in a bedroom isn't important?"

"It depends on what they're doing. Amanda's very proud of her book collection, and it is fine with me for Joey to see it."

Ethel stood up, letting her knitting needles and yarn fall on the floor. "As long as I live here, I'm not allowing any boys in her bedroom. It was fine for them to look at books outside." She picked up her yarn and needles and lowered her voice. "But I was surprised at how much Joey liked *Winnie the Pooh*. Isn't he a little old for that?"

"I still love *Winnie the Pooh*," said Carlton with a big grin.

Ethel marched out of the room. "Carlton MacGregor, you're impossible."

Lying in bed that night, Ethel prayed hard. "Help me keep my guard up, Dear Lord. I know the devil is helping Joey Oscarson present himself as a wonderful boy who wouldn't harm Amanda. But I also know that when I consider where he comes from, especially how irresponsible his mother is, that he is a wolf in sheep's clothing. Both Carlton and Amanda are under his spell. I know that you will continue to show me the wolf hiding just beneath the surface. Your faithful servant, Ethel." She tucked the covers under her chin, then folded her hands in prayer under the blanket to add a postscript. "Please help me deal with Carlton's blindness. I know I was put on this earth to take care of him. He will always be too trusting. Your exhausted, faithful servant, trying to do her best, Ethel."

During the next three months Ethel faithfully reported to Carlton each wrong thing she caught Joey saying or doing. Once, she told Carlton, "Joey said 'golly' again. I'm afraid Amanda will start taking the name of the Lord in vain."

"Golly isn't a swear word, Ethel," Carlton replied.

Another time, Ethel said, "Joey had a spot on his shirt. I'm sure he went to school that way because it looked like egg yolk." Then: "Joey didn't want a cookie today. It's not normal for a child not to be hungry after school."

Some days, hard as she tried, Ethel could find nothing to report. She remained vigilant, however, throughout the fall. Then, in late November, in response to Amanda saying that she hated her hair as she brushed it out of her eyes, Joey told her that she was the prettiest girl he knew.

When Carlton walked in the door that night, Ethel reported what Joey had said, adding, "That is inappropriate for an eight-year-old boy to be saying. He should be out playing war with other boys. He's seducing Amanda."

Carlton studied his sister sternly. "Ethel, I don't want to hear another negative thing about Joey. Give the poor boy a chance. You're being unfair, and if this continues I'm going to tell Amanda and Joey to play at his house after school."

Carlton's remarks, of course, hurt Ethel deeply. How could he call her unfair? And how could he say that they should play at Joey's house? He had had a hard day at his office. He wouldn't really tell them to play at the tarpaper shack. But how could she be sure?

Kneeling beside her bed, because she wanted God to know that she was very serious, she prayed, "Dear God, I beg you to open Carlton's eyes and ears. How can it be that he doesn't understand the dangerous road we are taking by allowing Amanda to play with Joey?" She paused for emphasis, then added, "I would worry, of course, if she was spending that much time with any boy, not just Joey. You know, Lord, that I don't have anything against Daisy Oscarson. In fact, I pray for her to see the alarming path Joey and Amanda are on. But I fear there are no prayers strong enough. She would have to become a completely different person. I'm giving you a big enough order when I ask you to open Carlton's eyes. You know how hard I have tried the past three months. I know you will find a way, for you are all powerful. Meanwhile, Lord, I want you to know that I will report to you daily. I know you wouldn't give me this big task if you did not think I could handle it. Thank you, Dear God, for your confidence in me. Your humble servant, Ethel."

When Ethel turned the job of opening Carlton's eyes over to God it helped her relax a little. She still worried, but didn't feel it was totally her responsibility to solve the problem.

T he first week in December in Turtle Creek, it was time to start thinking about Christmas. Snow fell quiet as cotton the afternoon Ethel decided to shop at the Mercantile downtown where she always bought dress shirts for Carlton. Hoping she would run into someone, anyone, Ethel wanted to brag about Amanda being chosen to play an angel in the Christmas Eve program at church put on by children in grades one through three.

Ethel thought she would burst with pride. Usually only second graders were picked to be angels. Third graders always played Mary, Joseph and the three wise men. But Amanda, a first grader, was going to be an angel.

There were no other customers in the store, so Ethel walked up to the second floor of the Mercantile, to the telephone operator's office. She poked her head in the door and saw Helga reading a magazine. "I thought I'd say hello since I was downstairs anyway."

"Glad you stopped by. Have you heard the big news?" Helga removed her reading glasses. "For the first time ever a first grader has been selected to play Mary in the Christmas program. Everybody's talking about it."

"Are you sure? You can't believe everything you hear on the phone you know."

"I heard it from Rebecca's mother herself. Rebecca's going to be Mary."

"I don't understand."

"The rumor is that her father gave a one-hundred-dollar bill to be used for decorating the church. Can you imagine that? We'll buy glass ornaments to put on the tree, and have wreaths on every window."

Ethel straightened her shoulders and inhaled deeply, but still didn't feel like she was getting enough air. She peered down at Helga. "But we must remember the most important thing of all, to focus on the true meaning of Christmas, not to get carried away with fancy decorations." Well-satisfied with how she had handled that, she added. "In my opinion, which is based on the Bible, Mary should have dark hair and brown eyes."

"But she never has, not in Turtle Creek anyways. Where does it say in the Bible that Mary had dark hair and brown eyes?"

"I can't tell you the exact chapter and verse. I think it's Matthew." Ethel got out her handkerchief and wiped her forehead. "It certainly is warm up here. How do you manage?" She put the damp handkerchief back in her purse. "I really have to run. I have lots of shopping to do." She walked slowly down the stairs, her shoulders hunched forward. When she got outside she realized that a bully wind had turned the beautiful snow into harsh crystals, which bit her face and crashed against her body. She bent her head down, leaned into the wind and walked home.

Christmas Eve, getting out of the car in front of the church, Amanda tried to catch snowflakes on her tongue. "Look at the snow dancing in the sky!"

"It's a perfect Christmas Eve," Carlton added. "The soft snow is falling in a cleansing peace."

Grabbing Amanda's hand, Ethel pulled her young niece roughly toward the door. "We've got to put your wings and halo on. I don't know what I'm going to do with that hair."

The service seemed to go on forever for Ethel. She refused to look at Rebecca.

After the service, Carlton said, "You were by far the prettiest angel I've ever seen."

Ethel walked in silence to the car. *How could Carlton say that?* she groused. Amanda certainly stood out, being the only child with dark hair. He must have thought her mother was pretty too, otherwise Sarah wouldn't have been able to catch him in her web.

In the car after the program, Amanda swayed back and forth in the front seat, knocking her shoulder against Ethel. "I hope Santa brought me a real typewriter, just like the one in Sears."

"Sit still. That typewriter is foolishness. I'm sure it doesn't really work."

Three packages waited under the tree for Amanda when she got home, all wrapped in white tissue and tied with red ribbon. She opened the two smallest packages slowly and carefully. The first was a cable knit sweater for her doll. The second was also for her doll, a white nightgown that matched the one Ethel had made for Amanda. Then she tore off the wrapping from the third package, the largest. Amanda got excited when she saw "Sears" in big letters on the box. Inside, she found a red corduroy coat, also for her doll. Amanda looked at it without saying a word.

Ethel started talking, fast. "See, the coat is like the red one you wear. You can be dressed alike when you take your doll downtown. Santa knew what you really would like, and of course I helped him by making the sweater and the nightgown."

Silence hung in the air until Carlton said, "Your aunt did a lot of work making the beautiful clothes, and the coat from Santa is nice."

"Thank you, Aunt Ethel," Amanda said in a flat voice.

Silence dominated until it was shattered by a steady pounding on the back door. "Who could be coming at this hour?" Carlton groused. "I hope it's not another emergency." He got up, a mischievous smile on his face. "I'll go see who it is."

Ethel strained to hear low voices by the door. Then, loud and clear, Carlton said, "Thanks so much, Santa, for making this special delivery. Merry, merry Christmas." He hurried back to the living room, carrying a big cardboard box. "Something else just came. Santa said it's for you, Amanda."

"Let me see, Daddy." Amanda tore open the box. "Just what I've always wanted, my own typewriter!" She picked up the heavy typewriter and placed it on the dining room table. "Look Daddy, every letter of the alphabet is here. Can I have some paper? I want to type. I want to be a writer like my mother."

"Where did you hear that your mother was a writer?" Ethel's voice sounded sharp, even to her own ears.

"Daddy told me. He also told me she was pretty, and that I look just like her."

"We didn't really know her. She was only with us for a few months before she died," Ethel complained. "I didn't know she was a writer."

"I want to know more about her," said Amanda. "We never talk about her."

"That's because it makes your father sad, and this is Christmas."

Carlton walked over and put his arm around Amanda. "It's good to talk about your mother. I will always love Sarah. Very much. When she smiled, my whole world was brighter. Everyone who knew her loved her. When she interviewed people for a story for the school newspaper, they told her things they'd never told anyone else, and the articles she wrote made a difference."

"What kind of articles did she write, Daddy?"

"We were at the University during World War II. The Nazis persecuted the Jewish people. Several students had relatives who had been sent to concentration camps ..."

"That's enough, Carlton. This isn't the time to be talking about that. We are celebrating the birth of Christ."

Frustrated, Amanda asked, "Auntie, is it okay to ask how Daddy and Mommy met?"

Carlton squeezed Amanda and smiled. "Sarah was a senior, very involved in politics. She felt strongly that we should have entered the war sooner, and I think history has shown that she was right. At the end of the war we found out that all the horrible rumors we heard about what happened to people in concentration camps were the truth."

"Carlton, please, she's too young to hear this."

He took a deep breath and slowly exhaled. "I guess you're right. Anyway, I fell madly in love with your mother and we married in the spring of my last year in med school. Sarah grew up in New York. It was hard for her to come to Turtle Creek that summer," he smiled sadly. "She wasn't used to small towns. Then you were born, a month before America entered the war."

"It was very sad that your mother died when you were a baby." Ethel walked over and awkwardly patted her niece's back. "She wasn't a strong woman. When she left to visit her mother, I told her I didn't think she was strong enough to make the long trip back to the East Coast. I offered to take care of you because you were colicky, which I think made her happy. She never would have been so careless as to step in front of a car if she had been stronger and thinking clearly."

"Amanda was a good baby, Ethel."

"You're right," Ethel conceded, "but she was colicky those first months." Ethel started picking up the wrapping paper and boxes. "I do know that it's God's will that Sarah's gone. She would never have been happy here." Even Ethel knew she had gone too far when she noticed her brother's intentional frown.

Carlton made a big fuss over showing Amanda how to put a sheet of paper in the typewriter and pick out keys. He then retired to his bedroom without even saying goodnight to Ethel.

"See, Auntie? The typewriter really does work." Amanda showed her the first sentence that she had laboriously typed.

Ethel firmly replied, "That's nice, dear. I hope it will continue to work for a while. If it breaks, we are not going to keep it around just to gather dust."

Carlton poured his first cup of coffee the next morning. "Ethel, I'm glad Amanda is still asleep," he said. "We need to talk. I understand that it is best not to talk about Sarah all the time, but when Amanda has questions about her mother, it's only fair to answer them."

Ethel stood at the sink scrubbing some potatoes. She didn't look Carlton in the eye. "If you insist, but the concentration camp horror stories will give Amanda nightmares."

Carlton grimaced. "Maybe I did say too much, but it upset me when you said Sarah would never have been happy here. I never realized how deep your prejudice is against Jews." He gently touched Ethel's shoulder. "You aren't alone in Turtle Creek. Many are uncomfortable with people of different backgrounds, different races. You never had the opportunity to meet people different than you, like I have. But I'm certain that everyone would have liked Sarah, given a chance to get to know her."

Ethel scrubbed a potato harder, removing most of the skin. "Now look what happened. I wanted to leave the skins on and bake the potatoes. Now I'll have to change the menu." She lifted her shoulders and sighed before she said, "I'm sorry, Carlton, but I still believe Sarah would have had a hard time fitting in here, and I think she felt the same way. Besides, I don't think it's healthy to live in the past. You are the most respected man in town. That's enough for me. Why isn't it enough for you?"

Carlton stepped back. "Ethel! Amanda is half-Scot and half-Jew. If you can't accept that, she and I will have to leave."

Ethel wiped her hands on a towel, left the potatoes in the sink, and collapsed onto a kitchen chair. Didn't he realize that he was her reason for living? "I don't want you to leave. I will do whatever you think is best."

In a gentle voice, Carlton said, "Then we must let Amanda know that I will always love her mother, and we must talk about the many wonderful things people of her mother's race have done."

"If you insist," Ethel said, pouring herself coffee from the pot on the table. She didn't realize until she felt scalding coffee drip onto her leg that she had gone over the rim of the cup. Ethel put butter on her leg to soothe the burn. Amanda skipped into the room. "Dear Lord," Ethel prayed under her breath, "I really need your help now. The people who persecuted your Son are going to be glorified in our home. How can I tolerate this? Please give me strength."

Amanda stood beside her dad. "Come with me, Daddy." She took his hand and pulled him into the dining room, her typewriter still sitting on the table. "I want you to see the first page of my story about a bear filled with magic." As she was reading the first three sentences, Ethel came into the room.

Look, look Joey. Look what Mother gave me for my birthday.

Oh, oh, oh, a yellow bear.

A magical bear. He can talk.

What can he say?

I love you, the bear says.

Oh my. Your mother must love you a lot to give you this wonderful bear. What is his name?

His name is Boo.

"Boo is a wonderful name for a magical bear," said Carlton. "And you know what else? I'm so pleased that you like to write. Your mother was a very good writer. Many talented writers have been Jewish. I want you always to be very proud of the fact that she was a Jew."

"But Aunt Ethel says that the Jewish people didn't love Jesus."

Ethel couldn't resist adding, "It does say that right in the Bible."

"It's true that some of them didn't accept Jesus, but you must remember the most important thing of all. Jesus was a Jew."

"Okay," replied Amanda. "Auntie, I'm hungry. Can I have some pancakes, please?"

"Of course, dear. What a perfect breakfast for Christmas morning."

Stirring the pancake ingredients, Ethel felt almost as light as the batter. Amanda wasn't that interested in her Jewish heritage. Carlton could say what he wanted, but she'd continue to tell Amanda all the wonderful things she should know about the MacGregors.

4. Boo, Ivan and Star

Amanda woke up excited for the first day of school after Christmas vacation. She slipped on the long sleeve wool dress Ethel had laid out and ran down the stairs. After gulping down a bowl of hot oatmeal Ethel dished up, she went to the dining room and carefully removed from her new typewriter a page she had finished typing the night before.

"What are you doing? We must get your snow pants on." Ethel held out a pair of heavy, dark wool trousers. "It's freezing this morning."

"I want to show Miss Williamson my story. I have one whole page typed." Amanda held up the sheet of paper proudly.

"She doesn't have time to look at things like that, Amanda," scolded Ethel.

"But she told us before vacation that we should bring something from Christmas to show the class today."

"Here, then. Fold it like this and put it inside your book bag." Ethel creased the paper and handed it back to Amanda.

After reciting the *Pledge of Allegiance* that morning, Miss Williamson asked her students to tell the rest of the class about the most exciting thing they did over Christmas break. Robert Knudson, a large boy wearing bib overalls, waved his hand back and forth. "I helped deliver a baby calf," he shouted.

Several classmates wanted to hear more about what it was like. "Was there lots of blood?" one boy asked. "Did you have to pull the calf out?" asked another.

"Boys, you can talk more about the calf at recess," interrupted Miss Williamson. "Who wants to be next?"

Both Rebecca and Amanda raised their hands. "Rebecca, why don't you go first?" said Miss Williamson.

"I got to be Mary in the Christmas program," Rebecca announced proudly. "Everyone said I was the best Mary they'd ever seen." She turned from side to side, clearly looking for her classmates to admire her.

Robert shouted out, "Everyone knows about that. I've heard about it each time I seen you for the past month."

A chorus of other students complained. "Robert's right!" And, "I want to hear more about the calf!"

Miss Williamson said, "Robert, you should raise your hand and wait to be called on before you speak, and remember to use correct grammar. Never say I seen you. What should you say?"

"I saw," Rebecca interjected. "Robert talks that way because he doesn't know any better. He's just a farmer."

"You should never look down on others, Rebecca," Miss Williamson admonished. "Farmers are very important people. They grow the crops and raise the livestock so that we have good food to eat."

Rebecca slumped in her seat. "Is it still my turn?" she mumbled.

"If you have anything else you'd like to say," Miss Williamson replied.

"No, I'm finished," said Rebecca firmly.

Miss Williamson surveyed the class. "All of you have to remember the rule about raising your hand," she said, focusing on Amanda. "It's your turn now. You've been waiting patiently."

After Rebecca, Amanda suddenly had second thoughts about sharing her story. What if everyone poked fun at her too? She stared at the typed page lying on her desk. Then she searched Miss Williamson's face for help.

"What do you want to tell us about?" Miss Williamson gently urged. The first-grade teacher, her gray hair pulled into a tight bun walked to Amanda's desk and studied the neatly typed page a second. "Did you type this yourself?" she asked, her voice swelling with amazement.

"Yes, yes I did. I got a real typewriter for Christmas, delivered Christmas Eve. It's smaller than the one in my Daddy's office, but it really works." She held up the paper for all to see, and was pleased when she heard murmurs of excitement.

Several students raised their hands. Miss Williamson called on Suzy, who responded, "How hard is it to type?"

"It takes time to find the right keys," Amanda explained. "But it's getting easier the more I practice."

Raised hands slowly descended. Apparently, those students had wanted to ask the same question.

When the bell rang to announce the end of the school day, everyone except Amanda rushed out the door. "Would you like me to clean the blackboards, Miss Williamson?" She walked to the front of the room.

"That would be very helpful. I can start correcting papers right away."

"Oh! I have to tell Joey not to wait for me." Amanda abruptly turned around and hurried out of the classroom. "I'll be right back."

When she returned, a bucket of water with a rag draped over the rim sat on the floor below the blackboard. Amanda fell into the rhythm of dipping the rag into the water, ringing it out and gently swiping the board. The smell of the classroom, eraser-felt dusty with chalk, peppermint-scented paste, and varnished woodwork comforted her.

When Amanda finished, Miss Williamson said, "You did a nice job. If you'd like, I'll read your story now."

"Yes, please." Amanda retrieved the unfinished story from her desk and handed it to Miss Williamson, watching anxiously while the teacher read about Boo, the magical bear. Finally, Miss Williamson smiled brightly and said, "You are a good writer, young lady. That typewriter was the perfect gift for you."

Amanda grinned so broadly she could feel her cheeks almost touch her ears. "Thank you! I was afraid to read my story to the class."

"I understand. It's hard to show others something you put your heart and soul into." She patted Amanda's arm. "I would love to read your stories anytime you want to show them to me."

"They're about Boo, I'll bring the stories for you to read."

All the way home, Amanda tried to step only on the patches of snow crusting the sidewalk. The sun sat low in the sky, everything still but for the crunch of ice in the soft twilight. Amanda didn't notice Ethel walking toward her until she heard Ethel's voice. "My child, I've been so worried about you."

"Auntie," said Amanda, half startled as she rushed forward and threw her arms around Ethel's waist. "I stayed after school to help Miss Williamson."

Ethel patted Amanda's shoulder. "When I saw Joey coming home, I wondered why you weren't with him. I knew you wouldn't have to stay after school for misbehaving. You're a good girl. I should have realized you stayed to help your teacher."

"I got to wash the blackboards. It was fun."

They walked, hand in hand, the rest of the way home.

Amanda spent a lot of time that long, cold winter typing stories about Boo. Her typewriter sat on a little table Ethel had brought down from the attic and placed against the wall next to her bed. Ethel gave her an embroidered white handkerchief to keep the dust off the typewriter when she wasn't using it.

Amanda loved school. Miss Williamson sometimes asked her to help another student, Ivan Christopherson, a quiet boy, small for his age, who seldom smiled, when she was finished with her assignments. He had trouble reading and writing. At the blackboard, Ivan wrote *d* instead of *b*. Amanda would help him sound out words, emphasizing the unique design of every letter, especially the letters he had trouble recognizing. She printed letters on a piece of paper and had Ivan copy them. Miss Williamson placed two chairs in the hall right outside the classroom so they wouldn't disturb the other students while Amanda and Ivan read to each other and worked on letters.

Toward the end of the last period on the last day of the school year, Miss Williamson asked Amanda and Ivan to go out to their reading spot in the hallway. "Ivan's reading has improved so much, Amanda, I'd like him to have one last session with you. Rebecca," said Miss Williamson, "Would you help them take chairs out please?" Amanda and Ivan dug into their desks for their worn copies of *Fun with Dick and Jane.*

Rebecca's pale ice eyes glared at Amanda. "Yes, Miss Williamson." She skidded a chair noisily from the back of the classroom into the hall. "You think you're so smart, Amanda MacGregor," Rebecca hissed, "but you're really stupid."

"I am not!" Amanda countered.

"You are so! You're the only person in town who doesn't know that your mother ran away because she couldn't stand you."

Amanda hissed back, "You're a liar."

Ivan chanted, "Liar, liar, pants on fire, nose as long as a telephone wire!"

"You're stupid too," Rebecca half-shouted.

Miss Williamson poked her head into doorway. "What is going on here?"

"Rebecca called me stupid," said Ivan.

"You must never call anyone stupid, Rebecca. Go to your desk and put your head down on your arms until the bell rings."

"But Miss Williamson, I didn't mean it. I'm sorry. Ivan, you're not really stupid." Tears formed in Rebecca's eyes. "Please don't make me put my head down on my desk. I'll do anything else. I'll stay after and clean the blackboards."

"No Rebecca, you must put your head on your desk." Miss Williamson took her hand and led her back to the classroom.

Amanda closed the door just as Rebecca pulled her hand free and lifted her head defiantly high.

Ivan had already opened his book. "I can read the whole thing to you. I'm not stupid."

"No, Ivan, you're not stupid," Amanda said softly. "You just get a few of your letters mixed up."

When the bell rang again, Amanda got up. "Ivan, you did a great job. I have to go now." She pulled her chair through the door as other students started gathering their school supplies. "Joey will tell me it's a lie," she repeated to herself, still stung by what Rebecca had said about her mother. She collected her papers, crayons, pencils and paste, and rushed out the door, but not without noticing that Rebecca hadn't moved from her flattop desk, her head buried in her arms.

Joey waited at the front door. "Hey, we're free now till September," he said, holding the door open for her.

Amanda refused to look at Joey and said nothing. She kept her head down and walked so fast she almost ran home.

Joey hurried to keep pace. "What's wrong?" he asked.

"I can't talk now. Let's get out of here." When they reached her

37

house, she abruptly stopped, turned and said, "I hate Rebecca. She lies." Amanda started to cry so hard she couldn't talk.

"Rebecca?" Joey took her school supplies and sat on the grass. He grabbed her hand and pulled her down next to him. Then he sat there, waiting for Amanda to explain.

"What ... do ... you ... know ... about ... my ... mom?" she finally asked.

He didn't respond right away. Finally, Joey said, "What's there to know? There are things that people say about my dad that are lies so big I don't know how people can even believe them."

"Rebecca said my mother ran away ..." Amanda hung her head. "... because she couldn't stand me."

"Amanda, didn't your mother die? We know for sure she didn't run away. That's a big fat lie. Rebecca's jealous because you're smarter than she is."

"Auntie said Mommy went to visit her family and was hit by a car. Auntie wouldn't lie." Amanda defiantly shook her curls.

"You're right. I can't imagine your Aunt Ethel lying to you. Rebecca lies all the time."

"Why doesn't God punish Rebecca for lying?"

"I don't know. My mother says some of the pillars of the church are really not good Christians."

"What are pillars of the church?"

"I had to look it up the dictionary. A pillar is a freestanding vertical support."

"That doesn't make sense, Joey."

"You're right. Let's forget about pillars until we're old enough to figure it out."

"Let's get a cookie. I'm hungry." Amanda picked up her things and started for the back door.

"Me too," said Joey, brushing red hair out of his eyes and smoothing it down before he entered the house.

Joey and Amanda spent almost every day together that long, lazy summer, sometimes playing games with other kids and sometimes, just the two of them, having long discussions about the books they were reading. When school started in

38

September, they were both eager to return. Soon, it was December again, time to think about Christmas. Amanda kept hoping Santa, whom she only half-believed in, would give her a puppy, or maybe a kitten, since she already had a typewriter. She and Joey seriously discussed Santa's existence, more than once, and mutually agreed that there were many different Santas. Everybody couldn't have the same Santa. It didn't make sense. Both of them wondered, What was Santa really like? Was he more than just a hope?

During the Christmas Eve service, Amanda felt very grown up. Things had changed. There was no manger scene at church. Instead, each Sunday school class recited verses in unison from Luke, chapter two, while Reverend Olafson lit an altar candle. Amanda loved the rhythm of the words she recited. "And Joseph also went up from Galilee, out of the city of Nazareth, into Judea, unto the city of David, which is called Bethlehem." She didn't understand why the sound of the words up, out, into and unto was so soothing, she just loved the music of the four words in the order they were written in the Bible.

When the eighth-grade class recited the final verses, Reverend Olafson lit the last of twenty candles glowing on the altar for the remainder of the service. The ushers turned all the lights off before the closing hymn, *Silent Night*, was sung.

On the way out of church, Amanda listened to the opinions being voiced about the new service.

"It's a shame we're not using the perfectly good costumes we have stored in the basement, and I've got another old bathrobe I was going to donate for a shepherd this year," the president of Ladies Aid said.

Another lady chimed in, "We've gone to a lot of work through the years. Remember how long it took to make all those angel wings out of coat hangers and cheese cloth?"

The young Italian wife, Maria, remarked to Thor, "The children sounded like the angels must have on the night Christ was born. Their voices were so sweet and pure."

Amanda looked up at her to ask, "And didn't you like all the candles?"

"Yes, I did very much," said Marie with a smile.

Amanda rushed ahead, eager to get in line for a brown paper bag filled with a shiny, cardinal red apple, unsalted peanuts in the shell, sticky ribbon candy and chocolate drops covered in foil. Aunt Ethel never bought store candy. Amanda opened her bag as soon as she got in the car. She peeled the silver foil off a chocolate haystack and popped it in her mouth.

"Be careful not to get your pretty new dress dirty," Ethel warned as Carlton backed out of the parking space. Everyone from church hurried home to open their gifts tucked under and spread around the Christmas tree. Amanda bounced up and down in the back seat as the long line of cars wound its way down the street.

She ended up getting another outfit designed by Ethel for her doll, and a goldfish. Ethel attempted to apologize for the goldfish. "I know you wanted a puppy, but I also know I would be doing nothing but vacuuming up dog hair everyday if we had one. I'm sorry, Amanda."

Amanda immediately liked the goldfish, which surprised her. She named it Star and placed its bowl on the table in her room formerly reserved for her typewriter. Amanda would gaze at Star peacefully, dreamily gliding through the water. "You're all alone, just like me. Do you ever get lonesome, Star?" she often asked the goldfish before falling asleep.

"Yes-I-do-but-I-just-keep-swimming," she heard Star once say, Star's tail slowly swishing back and forth, back and forth.

One night, when the wind was howling through the trees, Amanda, unable sleep, watched Star swim in the pale moonlight streaming through the bedroom window. "Don't you miss your mommy?" Amanda whispered. "Don't you need her? Do you even know who your mommy is?" She rested her cheek against the cool glass of the fish bowl. "I wish my mommy was here. Rebecca, who is full of lies, says my mommy ran away because she couldn't stand me." Amanda watched Star swim around and around in the bowl. "You're right. I don't believe her either, and Auntie, who never lies, said Mommy had to leave because her mommy was sick, and then she died. Sometime I want to go to New York, where she lived. I wish I could meet her mommy and daddy. I want to see where Mommy is buried." Amanda sighed. "Why do her mommy and daddy have to live so far away? Why don't they like us? Why don't they love Jesus? Everybody knows we're supposed to.

T he next few years passed peacefully and quickly. Amanda liked Joey's little house better than her own, a huge house by comparison built by her great-grandfather. Her house was a lonely place. The air clung to thick, cream-colored walls and heavy furniture. Auntie Ethel kept it spotless, but she never opened windows nor let the breeze through the screen door like Mrs. Oscarson did.

Sometimes Amanda felt guilty for not telling Auntie Ethel about spending so much time at Joey's. She'd tell white lies, say she was going to the library, making sure to stop there first, to return books. Amanda loved books. She and Joey often spent time reading together. And when she was alone, you could bet she was reading.

In fifth grade, Joey got a paper route. Amanda usually tagged along delivering *The Des Moines Register*. "Joey, what new words did you learn last night?" she'd ask as they walked down the street because Joey had the habit of reading a page in the dictionary every night before he went to sleep.

"Feckless. It means to be weak, irresponsible, and worthless," he told her once. "And fecund, which is being prolific."

"What does prolific mean?" she asked.

Joey wrinkled his brow in concentration. "It's like when there are lots of children in a family, then the parents are prolific."

"I wish I were in a prolific family. Don't you?" She grabbed his arm. "Don't you wish we were in the same prolific family?"

"You nut," Joey laughed, swatting her with the rolled newspaper before gracefully throwing it on someone's front stoop.

"I really mean it. I wish I had lots of brothers and sisters, and that they all looked just like you. You're the only kid in town with hair the color of carrots, and with so many freckles everywhere. We need more kids like you."

"You really think so?" Joey smiled.

"Yes, because you can't tell a lie. You blush when you tell a little fib." Joey started to laugh out loud. Amanda added, "It's true. I know you better than anyone else does."

Joey made Amanda feel like she belonged to a group when they played with other kids.

At dusk on summer evenings, neighborhood kids gathered to play called *Spotlight Tag*, a game Amanda and Joey invented. Any number of kids could play. All you needed was a flashlight for the kid who played detective. Everyone else would hide. The detective would shine the flashlight on kids he found, calling out their names. Kids who were caught had to sit in jail, which was the front steps of Amanda's home. Other kids could sneak up to free prisoners by pulling them away. But if they got caught freeing a prisoner, they had to sit in jail too. The last person caught got to be the detective for the next round.

Every time they played *Spotlight Tag*, Ethel would stick her head out the front door at least once and yell, "Do not go in my flower bed. Do not even go near it!"

Amanda eagerly anticipated the excitement of the darkness on summer evenings, the smell of the moist, heavy air. She could almost feel the corn growing in the rich, thick soil. She loved things about all four seasons in Iowa, but fall was her favorite, because school started.

5. Wink'em

One morning before school in the seventh grade, Amanda rummaged through her book bag and found a permission slip for a field trip to Ames her dad was supposed to have signed. "Auntie?" she asked, "can you sign this for me? I forgot to ask Dad."

"I suppose so." Ethel grabbed a pen and killed a perfect facsimile of Carlton's signature.

Amanda held the permission slip up to the light. "You're so good at this."

Ethel smiled modestly. "I've always been good at copying others' creations. I'm not much of a creative person."

"But you have real talent," Amanda insisted.

"Well, I always got A's in art class my junior year," Ethel boasted.

Walking to school, Amanda thought about how easy it was to make Auntie feel good. "I need to do that more often," she told herself.

That spring, eating super one evening, Amanda announced that she intended to do a paper on the meanings of names. "Did you know that MacGregor means 'Son of the watchful one'?"

"I've always loved our name," Ethel beamed. "It sounds so majestic."

"Don't put too much value in names," Carlton replied with a grin. "From 1617 to 1661, Scots who insisted on keeping the MacGregor name were executed because the MacGregor clan had acted against the crown."

"No kidding, Dad. That's cool. I bet Joey'll have to look it up." She smiled smugly. "But since I didn't find that fact, he probably won't either."

Hearing Joey's name darkened Ethel's mood. She fidgeted. Why was it that whenever she heard good news, it too often turned out to have a bad side? How could anyone from the MacGregor clan be the enemy of the Scots?

"Do you know what your name means, Dad?" Amanda asked,

43

then continued without waiting for her father to respond. "It means, *from the land between the streams.* Amanda means *worthy to be loved.* And, Auntie, Ethel means *noble.*"

Ethel brightened. She sat up even straighter than usual.

"Dad, do you know what Sarah means in Hebrew?"

"Yes, I do, Amanda. It means *princess.* In fact, I used to call your mother my princess."

Ethel jumped up. "Amanda, would you please help me clear the table? My knitting club meets here tomorrow. I have lots to do."

"Yes, Auntie. Oh, and I'll be going to the library after school tomorrow to do more research on names."

"You spend too much time at the library," scolded Ethel. "You should be doing things with other girls."

"It's a good thing to love books, Amanda," said Carlton, passing his dinner plate to Ethel.

Amanda didn't come home from school the next day until after the six o'clock whistle blew. As soon as she entered the house, Ethel demanded, "Where have you been? I've been worried sick. The library closes at five."

"Can't I walk around town without upsetting you? I'm old enough to walk down Main Street by myself." She also had been at Joey's house, but she knew Ethel would have a fit if she told her.

"It's time to eat. Your father's been worried sick too. Come, sit down and say grace.

"How was school today?" Carlton asked.

Amanda snapped, "I hate this town. Can't wait to get out of here."

"What happened at school?" Ethel's hands shook passing a platter of pork chops to Carlton.

"School was boring." The seventh grader's voice cracked. "I'm mad at Miss Kittelsen, the librarian."

"Were you doing something you shouldn't?" Ethel demanded, stabbing a pork chop from the platter.

Amanda looked into her dad's blue eyes. "Can we talk about this later, Dad? Alone."

"Ethel didn't mean anything, honey," said Carlton in an attempt to smooth over Ethel's rough response. "She worries about you."

"Maybe she should worry more about what this town thinks of us," added Ethel. "Miss Kittelsen told me that Turtle Creek used to be called MacGregor's Landing until grandfather stole the money from the bank."

"She actually said that?" The old rage inside Ethel rekindled into a blaze. "Anyone who spreads lies shouldn't be allowed to work in a public institution."

"Is it true, Daddy, that the town name was changed?"

"Your great-grandfather was a hard worker, and a man you could trust. He donated land to start the village in the mid-1800s. When traders started coming here, Carlton Lewis MacGregor encouraged them to stay. He even gave away land next to his store to other merchants." Carlton hesitated, then softly said, "The name was changed to Turtle Creek after a large sum of money went missing from the bank."

"Your grandfather, Donald Wallace MacGregor, was also a man you could trust," Ethel interjected. "I know Father didn't take that money." She leaned forward and grabbed the bowl of mashed potatoes. "The food is getting cold," she muttered, passing the bowl to Amanda. "We have to eat.

"I'm not hungry." Amanda looked at her father. "May I please be excused?"

"No," said Ethel. "If you refuse to eat supper, just remember, you'll get nothing to eat until tomorrow morning. We can't force you to eat, but I insist that you sit here until your father and I are finished."

"Ethel, Amanda is upset," said Carlton. "Let her be. She can eat later."

"What do you think, Dad," asked Amanda, passing the potato bowl to him with both hands without taking any. "Did Grandfather MacGregor steal the money?"

"I don't know," Carlton sighed sorrowfully, his head bowed. "I do know that he liked to gamble. He often made bets with people about when the first snow fall would come, or which team would win a game, and by how much."

"But that was just for fun," explained Ethel, her face flushed.

"Remember the times he went to Kentucky to buy horses? I'm pretty sure he bet on races while he was there."

"I don't think he did. How can you say that?" Ethel quickly replied. "You have no proof, just as Mister Nelson had no proof when he accused him."

"All I'm saying, Ethel, is that we have no proof he did take the money, and no proof he didn't," Carlton replied gently, turning to Amanda. "In the seventeenth century, some brave souls insisted on keeping our name even though MacGregors were being executed for rebelling against the crown. That's not the case today in Turtle Creek. We aren't being punished for mistakes our relatives may have made."

"Are you saying that changing MacGregor's Landing to Turtle Creek isn't punishment?" Amanda asked.

"That is exactly what I'm saying. It's no big deal, Amanda. We live in a good town full of good people, regardless of the name. Besides, I like the name Turtle Creek. Turtles have peaceful dispositions."

"I wish I had a peaceful disposition and could hide my feelings, like everyone else does here. Miss Kittelsen knew I felt bad when she told me about changing the name. I saw a hint of smugness in her eyes, as if she was saying, 'The MacGregor name isn't so great.'"

Ethel quickly added, "The eyes don't lie, Carlton."

"Most people in Turtle Creek are reserved," said Carlton. "It's hard to decipher how they feel. And when people are uncomfortable, which Miss Kittelsen probably was, they often distance themselves. That's one way humans protect themselves when they realize they've said something they wish they hadn't. Like a turtle, they pull back into their shell."

"You have always been too quick to forgive people." Ethel vigorously cut her pork chop, and speared a mouthful.

"Ethel, you can't be too quick to forgive people. Christ tells us to forgive our brothers not seven times, but seventy times seven."

Ethel chewed without reply.

That night, Auntie Ethel prayed even more earnestly than usual, and in a louder voice. "Dear Lord, You know all, and understand all things. You alone understand me. Why doesn't Carlton? He's naïve, too trusting. Of course, I know we are to forgive our brothers seventy times seven, and I do forgive people every day. I forgive Helga for listening to my phone conversations. I always have several ladies to forgive after knitting club meets. I forgive Amanda a hundred times a month for inappropriate things she says and does. And I know now that I have to forgive Carlton for the hurtful thing he said. He doesn't recognize evil when it's staring him right in the face. It is our duty to rid the world of evil, like Christ threw the money changers out of the temple. You know that I have done what I could to get rid of evil. I was placed on this earth to take care of Carlton, to protect him from himself. It's a big job. I beg your forgiveness for the times I fall short of your expectations. If I do say so myself, I don't think this has happened very often over the years. Your humble servant, Ethel."

Sleep didn't come easily. No more would Ethel start to drift off than she heard Carlton's reproach, "Christ tells us to forgive seventy times seven."

She dreamed of her father's hand, and wondered why she could not see his face? He kept saying, "I just want to touch you. It won't hurt, I promise." Auntie Ethel woke up gasping for breath.

Ethel made egg coffee that morning. Her hands shook. Her mind raced. "Why that horrible dream? Father was a good man. I had no reason to be afraid of him." She cracked an egg with so much force the shell shattered. She cried, picking pieces out of the coffee grounds. "I have to shape up, get control. What is wrong with me?" She paused. "This is the work of the devil. Satan planted that horrible dream in my mind. As soon as Carlton and Amanda leave I've got to do some serious praying." Feeling calmer, she removed the last of the shell fragments from the coffee grounds.

A untie Ethel spent a full week preparing for Amanda's eighth grade Confirmation. First, she made sure to tell Carlton to invite his secretary and her family over for Confirmation dinner. Then she gave the whole house an extra hard scrubbing and even changed the furnace filter. She baked a confirmation cake that looked like it came from the town bakery. Ethel's copying skill came in handy for quoting the Bible in frosting, each verse surrounded with a fancy sugary border. She insisted that Amanda practice walking in white heels, new shoes she would wear for the first time to church. She bought Amanda a garter belt and a pair of beige nylons at the *Ben Franklin* five and dime. "Once you're confirmed, you can wear nylons instead of white anklets with your good dresses," she told her fourteen-year-old niece.

Amanda sounded very serious during Confirmation when she told Reverend Olafson that she renounced the devil and all his works and all his ways. Ethel thought Amanda, with her brown eyes and dark hair, actually looked quite pretty in her white Confirmation robe. The rest of the class looked a little pale.

After the service, Ethel aimed her camera, a *Kodak Brownie*, at Amanda standing on the front porch and took a picture of her squinting into the sun, holding the ornate Confirmation cake. Once inside, Auntie removed Amanda's white carnation, carefully wrapped it in wax paper, and put it in the fridge to keep it fresh.

When everyone was finally seated at the dining room table for Confirmation dinner, the guests said grace. Then Ethel promptly and proudly announced, "You can start attending Lutheran Teens Fellowship League next week, Amanda," before passing the platter of carved roast beef to Carlton. She didn't say it out loud, but Ethel hoped Amanda would begin dating a good Lutheran boy her age at Lutheran Teens Fellowship.

Indeed, the following week, Amanda attended her first Lutheran Teens meeting. And the following evening when Carlton came home from work, he discovered Ethel banging pots and pans around the kitchen. "What's wrong?" he asked.

"Nothing I can talk about now." Ethel opened a can of fruit cocktail and added it to miniature marshmallows in a yellow mixing bowl.

"You don't need to stir those so hard. You're pulverizing those poor little marshmallows and turning the fruit into punch. Sit down a minute. Tell me what's upset you." Carlton put his hand over Ethel's hand. She stopped stirring and sat stiffly on the edge of a chrome-plated chair upholstered in red vinyl at the matching kitchen table.

"Well," Ethel exhaled, "it's Amanda. Thelma Knutson called me this morning. Her daughter Evelyn told her about a scandalous game played at Lutheran Teens Fellowship meetings.

Evidently, the new, highfalutin Sunday school superintendent taught the kids how to play it." Ethel took in a deep breath. "I can't even begin to tell you about it."

"It couldn't be that bad, Ethel. Most likely, Helga was listening on the line when Thelma called. The whole town probably knows about it, so you have to tell me," he teased, "or I'll be the only person in Turtle Creek who doesn't know."

"What is going on in the church basement is no laughing matter. I hope Helga has told the whole town." Ethel took another deep breath. "The game is called Wink'em. The girls sit in a circle with a boy standing at the back of each chair. One boy has an empty chair in front of him. When he winks at a girl, she tries to go to his chair." Ethel raised her voice. "Then the boy behind her chair tries to grab her and hold her to his chair!" She paused, all the more frustrated that Carlton didn't appear upset. "Who knows where the boys will grab the girls? He could choke the poor girl if he grabbed her neck, and worse yet, if he is tempted to grab her further down, he will break his Confirmation Vow to renounce the devil and all his works and all his ways." Ethel stood up. "The person you really need to talk to is Reverend Olafson. No one should play that indecent game."

"Ethel, I'm not going to talk to the Reverend. Wink'em sounds like a harmless game. The boys probably just touch the girls' shoulders." Carlton smiled. "If I ever treat any injuries incurred at a Wink'em game, I'll talk to Reverend Olafson. I'm going to read the paper."

"You go ahead. I'm sure you've had a hard day."

Ethel hurried upstairs to Amanda's room. "I'm going to forbid her to play Wink'em," she murmured. That child needs to realize what such an innocent seeming game might lead to. If they want excitement, they should play musical chairs, or blow marshmallows across the table in a race." She found Amanda doing homework at her desk. "Amanda, I must talk to you." Ethel sat on the bed and cleared her throat. "It's about that game called Wink'em you played last night at Lutheran Teens Fellowship."

"That dumb game? I hated it."

Ethel breathed a sigh of relief. "Oh really? What didn't you like about it?"

49

"It's stupid. The popular girls get the wink while the rest of us just sit there."

"You don't have to play if you don't want to. You could…"

"… but if I refuse to play," Amanda interrupted, "everyone will wonder what's wrong with me."

"You could offer to help set out the date bars and Kool-Aid," Ethel said, satisfied that she came up with a good alternative. Then Ethel shared one of her deepest beliefs with Amanda. "When you keep busy being useful, all things go better."

"But Auntie, I can't go to the kitchen to set out treats every time Wink'em is played. I'd rather not go to Lutheran Teens at all. The games are silly."

"Oh my, you shouldn't stop attending Lutheran Teens. What will people think?"

"I don't care what people think. Joey never goes to church, and people don't say bad things about him."

"Joey's situation is totally different than yours, Amanda," Ethel said firmly. "Everyone understands that Joey's family is not normal, so people don't expect him to do the things the rest of us do." Ethel stood up. "I have to set the table now." She put her hand on Amanda's shoulder. "You and I have a burden of responsibility in Turtle Creek. More is expected of us because your father is the only doctor. He's the most important man in town. There are times when I'm not in the mood to go to Ladies Aid, but I do my duty," adding on her way out, "That is, when I'm feeling well enough." Ethel fumed all the way back to the kitchen. "She is half Jewish. She has to be extra careful. I wish she understood."

That night she prayed about Amanda. "Dear God, this is your faithful servant, Ethel, reporting to you again. I need your help. How can I tell Amanda that she will have to be extra careful her entire life because her mother was a Jew? It is hard for Christians to understand how the Jews could have crucified your only Son. They will hold that against her. Of course I realize, because I am more perceptive than most people are, that somehow it was all in your plan for the Jews to reject Christ. He had to die for our sins, therefore someone had to hate him enough to kill him. Because I know this, I can accept that Sarah was a Jew. But most people aren't as open minded as I am. Amanda needs to know that. Help me find a way to discuss this with her. I don't want her to be rejected. That would break Carlton's heart, which would break my heart. I know you will help me find a way. I hope I won't have to encourage her to play that awful game so that she can fit in. Your exhausted servant, Ethel."

Amanda came downstairs for breakfast wearing a cinch-waist circle skirt she had recently bought in Carson City. "You look so nice," Ethel said. "Green is a good color for you."

"Thanks," said Amanda. She sat in front of a bowl of oatmeal and opened her history textbook.

"Are you reading an assignment for today?" asked Ethel, taking a chair at the table. "Can I discuss something with you? That is, if you have time now."

Amanda closed the book and gave Ethel her full attention. "Go ahead."

Ethel cleared her throat. "You know the O'Connors. Their son is a year ahead of you. I know he gets teased because he can't eat meat on Fridays, and he has to go into a dark little booth at the Queen of Angels Catholic church every week to confess his sins to Father Riley. Some people are critical, but I'm not prejudiced. I greet Mrs. O'Connor when I see her on the street, just as if she was normal."

Amanda interrupted Ethel. "Why are you telling me this?"

"I want you to know that I understand how difficult it can be for you at times."

"What do you mean?"

Ethen cleared her throat again. This was harder than she thought it was going to be. She'd been so proud when she came up with the idea of talking about how the O'Connors struggled to fit in. She had to be more direct. "O'Connors are tolerated in our town, but they will never really belong. Because your mother was also of a different faith you have to go out of your way to show people that you are a good Lutheran. I want to emphasize that you have to faithfully attend Luther League." Ethel searched Amanda's face for any clue that she understood and accepted what was being said, but saw none. She didn't want to, but said,

"Maybe you should even occasionally play Wink'em, so that you can fit in."

"Auntie, I will never fit in. Don't worry about me. I'm getting by. I don't need a lot of fake friends because I have Joey."

This was definitely not going the way Ethel hoped it would. "But you need to be accepted here. Do it for your father's sake." She took a deep breath. "Please." She took another deep breath. "And Joey can't be your only friend. It's not healthy." Ethel saw that Amanda was getting upset, her face actually turning red. "I'm trying to give you good advice. I've learned a lot about how to fit in. When you are older you will understand," she begged.

Amanda jumped up, grabbed her book and headed for the door. "I'll never understand," she said as she left.

Ethel sipped cold coffee. "I don't like what is happening," she mumbled. "I wasn't born yesterday. I wish Amanda would listen to me. To get such poor results, even after I said she should play Wink'em occasionally, is very discouraging."

Ethel gathered up dirty cups and bowls and placed them in the sink. There was work to be done. The Knit and Purl club was meeting that afternoon at her home. She was glad to be busy.

6. Best friends

Ethel continued to point out Amanda's Scottish heritage at every opportunity. She focused on the superiority of the Scots to the Norwegians, a job Ethel often found difficult in the large Norwegian community of Turtle Creek.

"They're so serious," she once said. "Norwegians only nod, or maybe give a slight grin when you meet them. They think that a quick smile shows insincerity. I keep track, and the only person who really smiles when I meet her on the street is Thor's Italian wife. Of course, she isn't someone you can depend on. I wish I could meet a Scot in Turtle Creek. Then I would get a genuine smile."

Joey continued to spend way too much time with Amanda. Thank goodness sometimes there were other kids with them when they played Spotlight Tag, however, she wished the kids would not trample on her flower bed. How many times did she tell them not to go near it? But they would soon outgrow Spotlight Tag. Amanda and Joey eventually stopped trampling the flowerbeds and took up sitting on the front steps, talking until Ethel called her inside. Amanda could talk to Joey about almost anything.

"I got my locker assignment and was shown my homeroom," she told him one August night. She would be a high school freshman; Joey a junior. "That building is so drab. I want art work lining the halls, like we had in grade school, and I want the varnished wood floors with the warm shades of brown and the good smell. The beige tiles look institutional."

"I know what you mean. That flat roofed building is supposed to look modern, but I think it looks more like a prison than a school."

"Yeah. From now on I'll always refer to it as my prison."

"Oh, I guess it's not as bad as it looks," said Joey. He'd been in high school for two years. "Kids from the neighboring towns go there too. You'll make all kinds of new friends. And you have a choice about which subjects you take. You'll have no trouble with the classes."

"I'm not worried about the academics." She broke eye contact with Joey and looked off into the distance. "I hate meeting new kids. I never know what to say."

"You'll do okay, kiddo, and I'll be there to look out for you." Joey patted her arm.

"But you'll be a big shot junior. I'll never see you."

"We can walk to school together again. I'll meet you at your locker after school and we can walk home, at least until basketball practice starts."

"That'll be great, Joey. You're the best." Amanda lightly punched him on the arm.

The first day of school went fine. Amanda felt very grown up going to different rooms for each class. "I didn't get lost once," she told Joey when they met at her locker.

Walking home the next day Joey said, "You're so quiet. Are you okay?"

"Sure." She didn't want to tell him that she was the last one chosen for volleyball in Phys-Ed. Three times, when she attempted to return the ball, she hit another team player on the head.

"Tell me what you did today. Then I'll tell you my news," Joey said.

"School's boring. Nothing to tell. What's going on with you?"

"Coach talked with me after Social Studies today. He thinks I should go to college. He said I have a good chance of getting an athletic scholarship." Joey stopped walking. "I know I'll need lots of money, even if I'm lucky enough to get a scholarship. Coach told me try to get a job at Hank's Hardware next year. He thinks I'll be able to work out hours with Hank Peterson during basketball season because Hank is a big fan of the team. Our captain works there this year."

"That's wonderful, Joey. I can't wait till basketball starts. The band plays at the home games, but my squeaky oboe won't add much to the pep songs."

Being in the band pleased Amanda because it meant she didn't have to worry about who to sit with. She was so proud of Joey. The crowd didn't seem to bother him. He made basket after basket. Amanda loved the gym on game nights, the smell of sweat mingling with that of fresh popcorn.

It was during the winter of her freshman year she experienced her first menstruation. She wasn't prepared for so much blood. Ethel had given her a very clinical book about how babies are conceived, but she thought something was wrong when she started to bleed so much. "Is this normal?" she asked Ethel the second day of her period.

"Of course. Now that you have the curse that all women have to put up with, make sure you don't fool around with any boys." Ethel avoided eye contact as she vigorously beat cake batter.

Amanda bought her first bra at the Five and Dime with money from her allowance. She felt self-conscious, waiting for Ethel to say something. Ethel never did. Amanda washed out by hand the stiff cotton bra because she was embarrassed to put it in the laundry basket. In Phys-Ed class, she felt more like she belonged when she could hang her bra on the hook with her other clothes before she showered.

A manda became more comfortable at school, and she became less critical of it. Joey continued to be her best friend. Sitting on the front steps talking the week before her sophomore year and Joey's senior year started, she said, "I'm going to work on the school paper. I have to start as a lowly mimeograph machine operator, but I hope I'll be a reporter next year."

"That's great, Amanda. You'll be a good one. I bet you'll major in journalism in college." Joey paused, appearing to concentrate. "I'm not sure what I want to be, but I know I'm going to do everything I can to get to college."

"Joey, you'll go to college, and you can be anything you want to be."

He blushed, and finally said, "I know one thing I want to be … your boyfriend. Will you go steady with me?" He removed his class ring.

The need in his voice made her uncomfortable. There was another long pause. "I can't, Joey. We know too much about each other." She lightly punched his arm. "You know that I sucked my thumb until I was seven. Going steady would feel strange for you and me, not normal." Needing to explain more, she added, "We don't need to date because we're best friends."

Joey stood up, put the ring back on his finger and shoved his hands deep in his pockets. "Can't best friends go steady?"

"Joey, I'd worry that we couldn't still be friends if going steady didn't work. I want you to always be my best friend."

Joey didn't respond. After a heavy silence filled with the background noises of the night, he said, "I have to go."

"See you in the morning, partner?" she yelled as he walked away. Amanda wasn't sure if he replied because a mosquito started buzzing around her ear. She swatted it as it landed on her arm. "He'll be his old self tomorrow," she muttered to herself. "He's my brother."

Amanda sat for the longest time listening to the buzz of dragonflies and moths hitting the porch light glass.

She didn't talk with Joey the rest of that week, refusing to be the first to call, because she was sure he was over-reacting. When she left her house, she looked longingly at the end of the street where his humble home sat all alone.

The morning of the first day of school, Joey showed up at her front door. "Hey Joey. Where you been?"

"I started working at Hank's. Been there every day, learning the ropes. He wants me to work as much as I can now, but he'll have to work alone when basketball starts." Joey looked directly at Amanda for the first time. "I'm lucky to have this job, but I'm really going to be busy. I have to get to the store as soon as I can on school days so that he can go home and take care of his wife. I'm going to work Saturdays too."

"But we can still walk to school together in the morning, right partner?"

"I don't think so. I should work out in the gym before school starts. I need to work hard if I'm going to get a scholarship."

"Joey, you are good enough right now."

"You don't know anything about what I have to do," he snapped.

Amanda didn't know what to say. Joey had never talked to her that way before.

When the first day of school ended, Amanda wished she could talk with Joey. It made her mad that she missed him. She gathered her books and left in a hurry. When she walked past Hank's Hardware she picked up speed, refusing to glance in the window to see if she could catch a glimpse of Joey.

7. Juvenile delinquent

Amanda couldn't decide between the red and the autumn gold *Bobbie Brooks* outfit. Which would look better for the first day of her junior year? She put on the autumn gold skirt and hurried downstairs to eat breakfast, then decided to change to the red plaid pleated skirt and matching top.

Aunt Ethel yelled up the stairs, "You're going to be late."

Giving up on taming her curls, she rushed down the stairs and ran all the way to school, sliding inside the main door just as the bell rang. Her books piled high in her arms, she didn't see the guy in front of her and bumped into him, sending her books crashing to the floor. "Oh shit," she exclaimed, embarrassed by what came out of her mouth after surveying the mess.

"Let me help you," drawled a soft voice she didn't recognize.

"Who … are …you?" Amanda asked, staring at the new boy, and immediately regretted her demanding tone, the way her hair looked and her reaction to dropping the books in the first place.

"You tell me first. Who are you?" he asked in a voice slow as molasses. His light brown hair, streaked blond from sun, fell in his eyes when he bent down to pick up her books. Amanda stood there, unable to move. "Here's your books." His deep blue eyes locked with hers.

"We're going to be late," she said, flustered. "I'm Amanda," she added over her shoulder, noticing that he was standing still, watching her walk down the hall. "Th-thank you for picking up my books," she stammered.

Wearing a tweed jacket, a wispy mustache riding above his lips on his narrow face, Mr. Wessel, the advanced algebra teacher, stopped writing equations on the board that looked like Greek to Amanda. He turned around and glared at her. "Young lady, you get the seat directly in front of my desk because you are late."

Mr. Wessel made Amanda think of a weasel. "So you had to wait," she mumbled as she sat down. Everyone in class stared at her.

"What did you say?"

"I said I'm sorry I'm late."

"And what is your name?"

"Amanda MacGregor."

"Well, Amanda MacGregor, you'll have to get the notes on what you've missed from one of your classmates. I hope you can keep up."

She decided a man who looks like a rodent should never wear tweed, and he shouldn't speak so rapidly. Learning usually came easy for Amanda, but she had trouble keeping up with Mr. Wessel. He might as well have been speaking Greek.

When the bell rang, she hoped to see the new boy who'd picked up her books. She looked for him between classes all day. When the last period ended, she asked Roberta, whose locker was next to hers, "Have you met the new kid yet?"

"The new boy? No. But doesn't he look like he's from California? He reminds me of Jimmy Dean. I saw he ate lunch at a table with seniors, but they paid no attention to him"

"I ran into him on my way to Algebra. I mean, like, I actually ran into him."

Roberta raised her eyebrows, as if to say, "So what?" She put her arm around another girl and said, "Let's get a coke at Swenson's."

Amanda grabbed her books and hurried out of school, walking fast, looking straight ahead. She didn't want Roberta and the other girls to catch up. When she reached the oak trees lining Main Street, she was thankful to be close to home.

Amanda heard a gentle voice ask, "Why do you look so sad?" Then she spotted the new boy leaning against an oak on the boulevard.

Amanda stopped. She could feel her face becoming flushed. "I'm not sad, just thinking. You don't know me at all."

"No, I don't," he admitted. "Well, I know that you're Amanda." He studied her, trying to figure out what she was like. "I'm Gael Delaney," he finally said.

"Do you know what Amanda means? Worthy to be loved," she blurted out, immediately wishing she hadn't said such a stupid thing.

"That's cool. I don't know what Gael means." His soft voice had a haunting, musical quality.

She hesitantly asked, "Where're you from, Gael?"

"California. My parents sent me here to Turtle Creek for my senior year. I live with my Aunt Frieda."

"Frieda and Olav Johansson?"

"Yeah. Aunt Frieda's okay, but this town is hopeless."

"I feel the same way, and I've got two years before I can escape."

"One year's too much."

"Why'd your parents send you here?"

Gael shrugged. A slow, mocking laugh emerged from his throat. "I've been a bad boy." He added, "You don't want to know how bad." Amanda blushed deep red and continued walking. Gael waked alongside her in silence. "Where do you live?" he asked.

"I'm almost home." She pointed to the big red house dominating the street. I'll get us something to drink if you'd like. My aunt always has lemonade in the fridge. She's a pain. Refuses to buy Coke, or any soda." She told him to wait by the big oak just to the left of the front door. "I'll be right back. Aunt Ethel doesn't like to be disturbed during her nap."

Gael leaned against the tree. "Lemonade's okay."

Amanda went inside and stealthily poured two glasses of lemonade, balancing one glass in the crook of her elbow to open the door as she left. She handed a glass to Gael. "Sorry there's no ice cubes." She sat on the grass. "Getting ice out of the tray makes way too much noise. I didn't want to wake my aunt."

"That's fine, really." Gael lowered himself to the grass across from her.

"Everything you do is in slow motion," Amanda said, smoothing the pleats in her red plaid skirt.

Gael made a strange sound. She couldn't decide if it was a groan or a laugh. He smiled. "I think everyone here speaks in monotone, and they don't say what they really mean."

"I hope I don't sound that bad." Amanda felt like she was drowning in his deep blue eyes. Feeling self-conscious, she lowered her gaze and started playing with the pleats on her skirt.

"No, I like that you speak your mind. I hate girls who play games."

Amanda basked in the compliment. Then Aunt Ethel opened the screen door and ruined the moment. "Amanda, what are you doing outside?" she hollered.

"Nothing. Be right in." She jumped up.

Gael stood. "Goodbye Amanda," he said softly, "worthy to be loved." He handed her the lemonade glass, his fingers lightly brushing her arm.

"Goodbye," she whispered. Amanda watched Gael walk away. Back in the house, she held her right arm out, careful not to brush it against anything. Inside she lifted the glass he drank from, circling the rim with her tongue.

"What on earth are you doing?" Aunt Ethel's voice pierced the air.

Amanda slammed the glass down on the kitchen counter. "Nothing. Got a ton of homework already. Must get started." She ran up the stairs, but when she got to her room she didn't sit at her desk. Amanda threw her books down on the bed and paced. She wanted to go to a quiet place to think, a place where Aunt Ethel wouldn't barge in. The door to the attic beckoned, yet repulsed her. She had never been to the attic. Her grandfather had hanged himself in the attic. It scared her.

But her anger at Aunt Ethel gave her courage. Amanda yanked the door open and resolutely walked up the stairs. It wasn't so bad. Sunlight streamed through the attic window. It was pretty. She saw boxes of Christmas decorations neatly stacked in the middle of the floor, remembering how her father always carefully carried them down two flights of stairs the week after Thanksgiving for her and Auntie Ethel to unpack before decorating the tree. She felt bad, because she realized how hard it was for her dad to bring all the boxes down from the attic every Christmas. Feeling brave and very grown-up, she walked around the decorations, vowing she would help him in the future.

She was surprised at how little was stored in the attic. In their house, nothing was easily discarded. Her grandparents had bought the furniture, the dishes, the pictures on the walls and the oriental rugs. Ethel never had the urge to change the dull cream color on all the walls, or to replace the ancient camelback sofa with a sectional or two love seats. She thought it was still the 1940s. Nothing was disposable to her. She even washed the plastic bread bags in hot sudsy water and hung them on the clothesline to dry. The attic felt empty, and that made her think of those plastic bags. "Where are those dumb empty bags?" she wondered. "Auntie's been saving them for years. Could they be up here in the attic?

Out where the roof met the eaves, she spotted a grimy, rectangular trunk covered with canvas that looked like it had been there forever. She crouched, carefully lifted the lid and raised a cloud of dust. Pale fabric printed with small purple violets lined the interior. Amanda gently lifted out tissue paper covering the contents and discovered an ivory colored silk dress she remembered from the wedding picture in her father's bedroom, the only picture of her mother she'd ever seen.

Amanda held the dress next to her body. It would fit her, except that it was too short by several inches above her knees. She laid the wedding dress on the tissue and picked through the remaining contents of the old trunk. There were several tailored dresses with shoulder pads. She removed each dress and examined them. When she had emptied the trunk, she looked with despair at the clothes piled on the attic floor. Was this all that was left of her mother? Amanda ran her fingers over the inside of the trunk.

Amanda picked up a delicate envelope from the bottom corner and set it on the box containing the angel that topped off the Christmas tree. She carefully replaced the clothing, ending with the wedding dress covered by the tissue, trying to make it look like no one had opened the trunk.

Clutching the envelope, she quietly descended the creaky attic stairs, doing her best not to make noise. Back to her room, she stared for a long time at the envelope addressed to Carlton, in a light, flowery handwriting. Afraid to open the envelope, she slipped the letter inside the waistband of her skirt and went downstairs.

She called to Ethel on her way out the front door. "I'm going out."

"Where to?" When Amanda didn't answer, Ethel shouted, "I'm going to tell your father how disrespectful you are."

"Just going for a walk!" Amanda hollered. "I need some fresh air." She hurried down the street past Joey's house, wishing he was there, but he was away at college. Joey would know what to do with the envelope, however, even if he were home, Amanda would have been too proud to seek his advice. She kept walking all the way to Turtle Creek.

She stopped near the edge of the water and studied the small, yellowed envelope addressed to her father. For a split second, Amanda considered throwing it in the creek, but she couldn't. She had to read it.

November 17, 1941
My Dearest Carlton,

I can never love you as much as you love me. I can never be all the things you want me to be — all the things you need me to be. It is best for me to go home. Please, please do not come to New York to try to convince me to change my mind. I'm getting a divorce.

If you really love me, you will let me be. I'm doing what I need to do. You know how hard it is for me to live in this town, and I know that you know deep in your heart that I will never fit in here. People will never accept me.

You and Amanda will be fine, and so will I. I was not meant to marry, nor to be a mother. Your sister will be a much better mother to Amanda than I could ever be. Sarah

Amanda perched at the edge of the creek bank, and began to cry, which is how Carlton and Aunt Ethel found her more than an hour later, statue-like, staring into the water, her face raw from crying.

E arlier that same afternoon, preparing supper, Ethel had placed a serving of strawberry Jell-O with bananas and miniature marshmallows on a lettuce leaf when she heard the back door open. "Amanda?" she called, assuming her niece had just come home from school, "would you set the table? Your father will be home soon."

But Carlton walked into the kitchen. "Amanda isn't home yet? It's almost six," he said.

"I don't know where that girl is," said Ethel. "She said she was going for a walk. That was over an hour ago."

"We all should walk more." Carlton smiled. "She'll be home soon."

Ethel fumed. Carlton always took Amanda's side. "The worst part," she mumbled under her breath, "is that she's just like her mother. What did Carlton see in Sarah?" Ethel grabbed plates from the cupboard. "It's not that I can't set the table by myself, mind you. I'm just trying to train her to be more responsible."

"You worry too much," Carlton said, loosening his tie on the way to his room. "But I know you mean well."

Amanda still wasn't home when suppertime arrived. "Where is that girl?" Ethel complained to Carlton in the living room.

"It's not like her to be this late." Carlton looked at his watch. "If she doesn't come soon I'll go look for her."

"My meal will be ruined. The chicken will dry out in the oven."

"I'll go now. Why don't you turn the oven off? I'm sure the meal will stay warm. If it doesn't, your chicken will still be delicious cold."

Ethel turned off the oven and followed her brother out to the car, still wearing her patched apron. "I'm going with you."

Carlton drove slowly up and down each quiet street in the sleepy town. Except for the Chat and Chew Cafe, there was no activity on Main Street. Ethel pointed out Ivor Olson's truck parked in front of the diner. Ivor's son Thor had married the Italian woman. "It's a shame that since Mrs. Olson passed, Ivor has to eat out instead of at Thor's. I bet his stomach can't take that spicy Italian food."

The library was closed when they drove past. Neighborhoods of tidy homes on empty streets grew dark. "Could Amanda be at a friend's?" Carlton asked.

"I don't think so. Besides, everyone is eating supper, so if she had gone to a friend's, she would have left by now."

Carlton drove back to their house. "I'm going to walk down to the creek," he said. "That's the only place we haven't looked."

Ethel hurried to keep up. When they arrived at the path along Turtle Creek, she leaned on Carlton's arm. "I don't know what this accomplishes. I just thought of where she probably is. That new boy from California staying with Frieda and Olaf Johansson walked her home from school today. Everyone on the party line is talking about having a juvenile delinquent from California in Turtle Creek. Why didn't I think of it before? I bet they are together. As soon as I get home, I'm going to call Frieda. She's probably worried sick too." Just as those words left her mouth, Ethel spotted Amanda sitting under a willow beside the creek, head down, shoulders hunched like a stone carving.

Carlton knelt. "Amanda, darling, what's wrong? We've been looking for you."

Her hands trembling, she handed her father the now tear-soaked letter her mother had written. "Oh my God," he gasped, wrapping his arms around her. "We should have told you about this a long time ago. I'm so sorry you had to find out this way."

"We planned on telling you about the letter when you're older," Ethel interjected. "We thought it was best for you not to know that she abandoned her family and ran away. We were trying to protect you." Ethel stood straight as an arrow. Then, enunciating each word with staccato precision, she said, "Everyone here thinks she left to visit her sick mother. We had to protect you. We did what was best for you."

"Not everyone believes that story!" cried Amanda. "Rebecca told me the truth when we were in first grade. You lied to me. I'll never trust either one of you again!"

Amanda pushed her father away and wiped her eyes with her sleeve. "You were weak. Why didn't you go after her if you really loved her? If you had gone to New York, she might still be alive!"

Carlton reached out for Amanda, tears streaming down his cheeks. His voice trembled. "I've lived with that thought all these years. My deepest regret is that I didn't go after her. I thought I was doing the right thing by honoring her wish. I knew she was miserable here." He put his hands on Amanda's shoulders. "I can't bear you being mad at me."

Ethel stood immobile, watching. She hadn't seen Carlton cry since Sarah left. Her mind racing, she replayed the scene when Carlton found the note. "I told him we should get rid of all of Sarah's things. It broke my heart to see him wrap each fancy dress in white tissue, as if she was planning to come back. Why didn't I burn those dresses? And the letter? He hasn't looked in that trunk once in all these years. How stupid of me. I should have burned it. This is not a good time for Amanda to find out that her mother never wanted her."

Her voice heavy with sadness, Amanda said, "Dad, I don't know what to do. I'm miserable. Auntie never liked her. Maybe Mother would have stayed if Auntie had helped my mother feel like she belonged."

Ethel hesitantly touched Carlton's shoulder. "It's good Amanda knows the truth. She'll get over this." The only response came from a hoot owl in the twilight. After the owl's third mournful cry, Ethel walked back to the house alone muttering, "Carlton needs me. He is so tender hearted. I have to be strong. I knew from the instant Sarah crossed our threshold that she would never fit in. She never wanted to be a mother. I did what I had to then and will do what needs to be done now."

Amanda and Carlton returned much later, neither one of them hungry, which Ethel thought was just as well. Except for the Jell-O salad, their supper was ruined.

Amanda refused to talk to Ethel. She wouldn't even look at her. In a voice cold as steel, she said to her father, "Tell Aunt Ethel I don't want her to come near me; and she has to stay out of my room. She never liked my mother. She was mean to her. This is all Ethel's fault."

"Amanda, you're not being fair!" cried Ethel.

Carlton and Amanda went up to her bedroom where they talked in hushed tones for over an hour. When Carlton came downstairs, he found Ethel was sitting in the living room, knitting furiously. "I'm going upstairs to read," he said.

Ethel stopped knitting and searched his eyes. "I understand why Amanda is upset, but she's blaming me now for everything. What did you tell her?"

"It will take a long time for Amanda to heal," he said softly. "We have to be patient. After finding the letter, she doesn't trust us." Carlton started to walk away then stopped. "I never should have allowed you to tell everyone that Sarah went to New York to visit her sick mother. The web of lies you spread about Sarah's mother suddenly taking ill has tormented me all these years. I don't know why I let you do that. Did you really think it would be easier if people believed a lie?"

"You know this town as well as I do, Carlton!" Ether scolded. "Turtle Creek would have never stopped talking about Sarah and her abandoned child. The town believes lies! They believe the lies about our father! Sarah wanted a divorce. She abandoned Amanda. It was a blessing that she stepped in front of a car and was killed."

"Sarah's death was a tragedy, Ethel! And the tragedy continues." Carlton's voice grew louder. "Amanda is convinced that her mother never wanted her. I didn't believe that then, and I don't want Amanda to believe that now! Lies, Ethel!"

Ethel tried to calm her brother down. "I believe Sarah was involved in some kind of espionage to help her people during the war. She was upset about what was happening to her people in Europe."

"She never said anything to me about espionage."

"Think about it, Carlton. You know how idealistic Sarah was." Carlton slowly nodded his head, convincing Ethel that she had said the right thing. She resumed knitting. "What's done is done. We need to focus on Amanda."

"You're right." Carlton started to sob, just as hard as he had down at the creek with Amanda.

Ethel lowered her gaze to the knitting, picking up speed, missing stitches. All she could hear was the click of the needles. She talked to herself. "He is so tender hearted. He needs me so much. I must be strong. It's good that Sarah's gone. She never loved him, not like I do." Ethel raised her head. Carlton was gone. Amanda must never speak of this with anyone in Turtle Creek. It would only stir up malicious gossip about the horrible scandal. What can I say to make her understand? This is something I have to pray about." Ethel laid her knitting aside. She removed hairpins from her bun, washed her face and knelt on the cold floor beside her bed. "Dear God, I wish Amanda had not found the letter, but I know you work in mysterious ways and even this will turn out for the best. You know that my heart is pure. I've had to live a lie, I know, but I cannot go through the shame of another disgrace like I'm still going through regarding my daddy. Please continue to give me the strength to do what I have to do. Your humble servant, Ethel."

Meanwhile, dream visions haunted Amanda. Her mother appeared wearing dresses from the attic trunk. Sarah's eyes were filled with desire. She wanted to leave her baby girl and the unwelcoming little town of Turtle Creek.

Sometime around midnight Amanda bolted up, breathing with great difficulty. "My mother didn't want me," she cried. "If she cared about me, she would have taken me with her."

Amanda rose from her bed and walked to the window. Below, moonlight bathed the yard. She pulled on some jeans and an old sweatshirt and tiptoed down the stairs. Another thought came to her: Why wasn't Dad worthy of Mother's love? Why didn't he go after her? If he had any guts, he would have brought her home.

She inhaled cool autumn air. It wasn't heavy like the air in her house. She could breathe easier. She walked down the street, not sure where she was going. When she got to the house with the pitched roof and the clapboard walls, at the end of what everyone called Church Street, she stopped at Frieda and Olav Johansson's house and sat on damp grass on their front lawn. "I wonder, which one is Gael's room?" Amanda wished she could talk to the new boy. A cold gust made her shiver. She wrapped her arms around herself for warmth. After a short while, she returned home and went to bed.

8. Tribulation

Amanda went through the motions of trying to be her old self after reading her mother's letter at Turtle Creek. She took copious notes in all her classes, but when she read them back, most made no sense. Going from class to class, she scanned the crowded hallways, looking for Gael. When she finally saw him way ahead of her, she tried to catch up, but stopped because she wouldn't know what to say to him anyway.

A boy in a hurry bumped into her in the hall. "Watch where you're going!" he yelled.

By the end of the school day, Amanda could hardly put one foot in front of the other as she walked to her locker. She counted the fifty-five steps to get out the door where fresh air made it possible to breath with less effort.

On the way home, there he was, Gael, leaning against the same oak tree as she'd prayed a thousand times that day he would be. "Can I walk with you, Amanda, worthy to be loved?" he asked.

"I was looking for you all day," said Amanda. She immediately beat herself up for saying such a dumb thing. Why couldn't she be more like Rebecca and play hard to get? She kept her eyes on the sidewalk and picked up speed.

But when she looked up, Gael was walking beside her. "I know where your locker is. I saw you not ten minutes ago. That girl next to your locker was putting on lipstick. She has this mirror in her locker and had her door wide open. She blocked my view of you. How can anyone spend five minutes putting on lipstick?"

Amanda laughed. "I don't know, but all the guys are crazy about Rebecca."

Gael reached out for her hand. "You look great without lipstick."

"Really?" She took his hand. She felt alive again. "I could barely function at school. It was like all the teachers were talking in a foreign language. I was relieved when I got to band practice seventh hour, but that ended up worse. I played so many wrong notes, and my timing was off. Mr. Mortenson asked me what was wrong." Amanda mimicked Mr. Mortenson by talking through her nose, "I know you can do better than that. Pay attention, Amanda."

Gael laughed and squeezed her hand.

"I hate the oboe. The band doesn't even need it. The only time people hear me is when I squeak, or play a wrong note."

"Couldn't you quit the band?" he asked.

"I wish I could. My life is filled with doing what's expected of me."

"That has to be awful. I always feel like I'm on trial in this town." Gael squeezed her hand a second time.

"I've never fit in. I can't wait to get out of Turtle Creek. I hate this place."

"You're different. Most people here look colorless, with such pale eyes."

"I am?" It felt so good to be holding Gael's hand. Amanda started to feel better. "Why do you say that?"

"Because you are. Your dad is too."

"You know my father?" Amanda's feet felt heavy again. It was hard to keep walking.

"People have to get gas, and I work at the gas station. Doctor MacGregor drives a Ford."

"It's interesting that you say my dad's different. He's not the great guy everyone thinks he is."

Gael stopped in front of Amanda's house, still holding her hand. "What's bothering you? Do you want to talk about it?"

"You wait by the tree. I'll get some lemonade." Amanda hurried inside. Ethel sat at the kitchen table peeling potatoes. Amanda wanted to run but she forced a smile, which was actually more of a grimace.

"How was school?" Ethel asked.

Amanda managed a weak, "Okay." She poured two glasses of lemonade and went back outside as fast as she could.

Gael took one of the lemonades and sat down, his back against the tree. "Thank you, Amanda, worthy to be loved."

Amanda settled herself on the grass, putting her legs to one side. "I don't know where to begin. I'm trying to understand what my life will be like from now on. I've been lied to. I can't believe what I found out yesterday."

Gael lightly stroked her hand. Tears filled her eyes. "My mother died when I was a baby. All these years I thought she loved me. Well, yesterday I found out that she never wanted to be a mother. She hated living in Turtle Creek, and she left." Amanda looked at Gael, his eyes fastened on her. It felt good to be able to talk to him about the letter. "I think people in this town disliked her, and I'm sure my crazy aunt didn't help." Amanda took a deep breath. The air hurt her lungs. "She went back East to her parents. But why did Dad let her go? If he loved her as much as he says, why didn't he try to convince her to come back." Tears streamed down Amanda's face, so she lowered her head.

Gael held her by the shoulders to keep her from collapsing. When she calmed down, he said, "Show me your face." Amanda raised her chin, but kept her eyes down. "Look at me, Amanda."

Amanda looked up, blushing. "I get lost in your eyes."

Gael gave her a lopsided grin. "They're blue, like everyone else's eyes in Turtle Creek …'cept for you."

"No, your eyes are different. I see something in them I can't define." Amanda studied Gael's face. "There is sorrow buried deep inside you."

Gael drew her close and whispered in her ear, "I'm battle scarred." Then he turned her face, lifting her chin so that their lips almost touched.

Amanda inhaled his breath. Then she heard, "Am-m-manda! Come in and set the table."

"I hate Ethel. She ruins everything," Amanda groaned.

Gael leaned back. "It's okay, Amanda. I'd better go." He stood up as her body froze, her face down. He touched her hair, then lightly ran his fingers down the length of her face. He lifted her chin so that she looked right at him. "I promise I'll see you later."

Amanda watched Gael walk away. When his body was just a dot in the distance, she went inside, her cheek still tingling. The heaviness of the big house nearly consumed her.

Ethel stood at the door, her hands on her hips. "What is going on? How could you be so indecent, right in our yard where the whole town can see you?"

Amanda rushed past Ethel without answering, raced up the stairs, slammed the bedroom door, threw herself on the bed and buried her face in a pillow. "I hate her," she moaned. "She will drive Gael away, just like she probably did my mother." She wanted to scream. Tears welled in her eyes. She was afraid that if she started crying, she would not stop. Amanda kept her tears inside, determined to give Ethel no satisfaction from hearing her weep.

Ethel yelled from the bottom of the stairs, "Amanda, come down right now. I need to talk to you. What were you doing with that boy?"

Amanda refused to answer, instead pretending as hard as she could that her aunt did not exist. She shut out Auntie Ethel completely. After a long silence, Amanda heard Ethel's pots and pans clattering in the kitchen. She continued to lie still, wondering if it was worth it to get up, wondering if she'd even be able to move again. She didn't know how much time had passed when she heard her dad pull into the driveway and a car door slam.

Amanda lifted her head when she heard Ethel say, "Oh Carlton. I'm so glad you're here. You look exhausted. I'm sure you've had a hard day, and have been worried sick about Amanda. Sit down. I'll get the paper and a cup of coffee for you."

"She fusses over him like she's his wife," Amanda fumed. "I hate her."

"I'm fine, Ethel. Where's Amanda?" her father asked. "She's the one you should be worried about."

Amanda sat up. "What did he say?" Then she heard Ethel's harsh, jagged sobs. Amanda got up and opened her door. She stood at the head of the stairs.

Ethel begged, "Don't blame me, Carlton. I only did what needed to be done. It's not my fault. Sarah didn't fit in."

"Ethel! This is not about Sarah. We need to help Amanda now." Carlton's voice sounded raw. Was he going to cry? Amanda ran down the stairs. She wanted to hug her dad, but found him rubbing Ethel's back, her head resting on folded arms. He was concentrating on her and didn't hear Amanda come.

Amanda stood in the doorway, disgusted. Ethel said, "That feels good. I have such a stiff neck. Can you rub there?"

"Dammit, I have to get out of here," Amanda hissed. She took a deep breath and ran past them.

Carlton looked up. "Amanda!" he shouted.

She escaped out the back door with no destination in mind; she ran for survival. Amanda heard the door slam again followed by her father's footsteps. She didn't stop until she reached the cemetery. Standing at the entrance, staring at tombstones, she could hear her father breathing hard as he approached.

They both said, "You okay?" at the same time. Then Amanda hugged him long and hard.

"I'm sorry honey, so sorry I never told you about the letter. We were trying to protect you. We planned on telling you when you were older." He let his hands fall from her shoulders, defeated.

"I suspected Mother didn't want me, ever since first grade when Rebecca said I was stupid because everyone in town knew my mother had run away."

"Why didn't you tell me?"

"Because Ethel said it wasn't true. I didn't think Aunt Ethel would ever tell a lie, so I figured Rebecca was lying." Amanda smiled sadly. "I'm sorry. I know this upsets you."

"Oh sweetheart, I wish you had told me. Your mother left because she was unhappy here. No matter how awful the truth is, it's better than a lie."

"I don't know about that. If there was proof that Grandpa stole money from the bank, would people be any more awful than they are now." Carlton visibly shrank before her eyes. She couldn't bear it. "It's okay, Dad, It's okay, but you know what? As long as we're here at the cemetery, I want to see his grave." Sorrow deepen in her father's eyes. Amanda despaired. All I ever do is make things worse, she thought. Why doesn't he want me to see the grave?

Carlton took Amanda's hand. "We should have brought you here long ago," he said softly, leading her from the gate to a field behind the cemetery. Three tombstones sat alone on the other side of a chain-link fence. Two were lovingly cared for, no weeds on either grave, and flowers planted around them.

Amanda stopped and stared. "Why are these people buried outside the fence?"

Carlton shook his head. "Only members of the Saint Olaf Lutheran Church are allowed to be buried in the cemetery."

"But Grandpa was a member, wasn't he?"

"Yes, sweetheart, but he wasn't allowed to be buried in the cemetery because he committed suicide." Carlton put his arms around Amanda.

"I ... hate ... this ... town," she sobbed, her head buried in his chest. He gently rubbed her back until she quieted down. "Ethel takes care of Grandpa's grave. She plants colorful flowers. Many in town believed he should not have been excluded from the churchyard. But the minister at the time insisted that he couldn't allow someone who had taken his own life to be buried next to good Christians. He wasn't allowed to be buried next to my mother." Carlton let go of Amanda and rubbed the tombstone, almost caressing it. "I think your grandfather, despite what old Revered Swenson said, is in heaven with your grandmother, whom he loved very much."

"You really think so, Dad?"

"I have to believe it. I never knew my mother, but Ethel remembers that my father worshiped my mother."

Amanda looked at the other graves, and slowly walked over to the neglected one. "It's sad that nobody cares about this grave." She examined the tombstone. "It has no name on it. Do you know who this is, Daddy?"

"That was a stranger who came to town during the depression, a salesman who choked on a piece of meat at the Chat and Chew. He was a loner. The townspeople had no luck contacting next of kin. When I was a kid, we make up ghost stories about the stranger. I've always wondered what his life was like."

"I never even knew this was here. It's so awful."

"There are churches in other towns that have the same policy, honey." He put his arm around her again. "But you're right. It's not a Christian thing to do. We should have a cemetery in Turtle Creek where everyone is welcome."

Amanda's glance wandered to a third grave, one with white daisies growing around the tombstone. Amanda leaned forward to read the name. "Jack Oscarson? Oh no. Tell me this isn't Joey's dad."

"I'm afraid it is, honey."

"But why's he here? He didn't purposely run in front of the bull, did he?"

"No, of course not. He's buried here because he was an independent thinker who wasn't officially a member of our church. Daisy went to church every Sunday, Joey by her side. Jack came with them a couple of times a year, but he never joined."

"I hate this town," Amanda said again, starting back toward town.

Carlton stared at the ground. "After Jack's death, Daisy and Joey stopped going to church." He lowered his head. "I don't blame them."

Amanda stopped. "Why do you and Ethel still go?"

Carlton took several long strides to catch up with his daughter. "Honey, what your grandfather did was wrong. No one should take his own life. But he did it because he was desperate. He saw no way to save the bank, his pride and joy."

"But was he a thief? If he was, he deserves to be buried here and Ethel shouldn't be putting dumb flowers by his grave." Amanda walked faster.

Carlton caught up with her again. "I don't know if he ever stole money. There was gossip because he did enjoy gambling. I do know that the bank collapsed. But that was because of the Great Depression. Other people in town know it too."

Amanda had never heard her dad talk so passionately about his father. "But then, why are people like Rebecca still talking about him stealing money?"

"I don't know the answer, honey. Rebecca is a very insecure girl, so she needs to think she is better than other people." He stopped walking. "It's easier for humans to blame others for their problems. Accusing our grandfather of stealing the money made sense to many of the people who were frightened by the fact that our country was in big financial trouble."

They resumed walking, but slower, both of them lost in thought. "You are always so quick to forgive people," Amanda said.

"I find, sweetheart, that being unable to forgive others ends up being a heavy burden to carry."

Amanda pondered this the rest of the way home. What she didn't understand was how her father was able to forgive her mother, however, she couldn't ask him to explain. She did tell him that someday she wanted to visit her grandma's grave, and Carlton said that he would take her there soon.

Back at home, Ethel asked, "Are you okay?"

Amanda ignored the question. She walked upstairs with effort, sat at her desk, opened her advanced algebra book and stared at it. The lesson made no sense, so she looked over the copious notes she had taken. She had tried to write down every word Mr. Wessel said. Why were all the sentences incoherent fragments?

Her English notes were no better, but she could make appropriate deductions from the mess. She started to work on the assignment, a short essay on the most important thing she learned over the summer break. Her mind went blank.

Three days into her junior year, Gael again walked her home.

Amanda's hand shook pouring lemonade. Ethel was in bed, not feeling well, which made Amanda feel glad, but also guilty about feeling glad. She decided she would forget about Ethel and concentrate on Gael instead. After school, she found him waiting at her locker. Amanda remembered how Rebecca stared when she saw them together. It made her smile. Gael quietly opened and closed the backdoor. "Thank you," she whispered, careful not to spill the lemonade.

"You're beautiful," he said as they sat down under the Oak tree. Then he said, "I can't stay long today. My uncle told me I should always come to the station right after school from now on."

Amanda rode an emotional rollercoaster. How could she go from being so happy to being so sad, so fast?

Gael reached out and touched her arm. "I have some very good news. There is an old Ford in the back of the garage that Uncle said I can have if I can get it running, and guess what? It's almost ready to go. Do you want to hang out with me Saturday morning, show me a cool park or something? Will you be free? I could pick you up anytime.

"Why don't we meet at nine at the library?"

Gael took a sip of his lemonade before he said, "That would work." Then he gently removed the glass from her hand and set both glasses on the grass. He leaned toward her, putting his arms on her shoulders, and kissed her softly on the lips. "I have to go now," he said.

Amanda sat there unable to move after Gael left. She wished he was still kissing her.

For Ethel, things had gone from bad to worse all day. Stirring pancake batter, waiting for Carlton and Amanda to come down for breakfast, she remembered the morning Amanda ate seven pancakes by herself when she was nine. "What could I do now to make her feel better?" Normally Ethel only made egg coffee for special occasions, but now that Amanda was drinking coffee too, egg coffee would be a special treat.

"It sure smells good in here," said Carlton, entering the kitchen.

"You sit down now and I'll serve you." Ethel pointed to the dining room. "I'm sure Amanda will be joining you shortly."

After twenty minutes, Ethel filled a clean cup with coffee. "I don't want to spoil her, but I'm going to take a cup of coffee up to Amanda. Yesterday was hard for her. I hope she slept okay."

"I'll take it up." Carlton reached for the cup.

Ethel held on. "I'd like to take it to her."

"I think it's best if I do it," he said kindly, taking the cup from her.

In the dining room, Ethel strained to listen to voices upstairs. She heard Carlton softly knock on Amanda's door, then say, "Is it okay if I come in?" The door opened slowly with a creak, then abruptly closed.

Ethel folded her hands and bowed her head. "It's not fair for her to be mad at me, Dear God. Help me to be strong. I know that the just are not always treated fairly. I am being tested as Jonah was."

Carlton finally returned. "Amanda overslept," he said. "She appreciated the coffee. I told her it was your idea."

"Thank you," Ethel replied humbly.

"Where are my car keys? I'm sure I have patients waiting to see me."

"Your keys are where you always leave them, on the kitchen counter." Ethel shook her head.

Carlton smiled. "You take good care of me." Then his expression changed. In a voice wrought with tension he added, "Ethel, Amanda needs time. Sarah wrote that she never was meant to be a mother. It's tearing Amanda apart."

"That's what I've been trying to protect her from all these years."

"I know, I know." Carlton slowly walked to the door, his shoulders bent like an old man.

Ethel continued to sit in silence. Carlton opened the garage door, started the car and pulled out of the driveway. The lonely sound of the car was swallowed by the whine of Ethel's mind racing.

"I've got to be sure Amanda gets to school on time. Maybe she will want me to walk with her today. Yes, I will offer to do that. She needs comfort." Ethel stood at the foot of the stairs. "When should I start pancakes for you? Everything is ready."

Amanda hurried downstairs carrying her books. "I'm not hungry. It's late. I've got to go."

"You should eat something. Can't I make you just one? It will be ready in a minute."

"Didn't you hear what I said? Read my lips. I'm ... not ... hungry!"

Ethel reached for Amanda. "My poor child. I know how you are hurting."

"No you don't. You lied pretending my mother wanted me. How could you do that? I don't know why Dad let you do that."

"We thought it was the best."

"Best? You expect me to believe that? You drove her away and Dad was too much of a coward to go after her!"

"No, no, it wasn't like that at all," cried Ethel as Amanda yanked open the door. "Wait for me. I want to walk with you to school."

"Are you crazy? I'm not like Dad. I can take care of myself."

Amanda slammed the door behind her when she left. Ethel immediately filled a pail with scalding water and floor cleaner. "I'm not crazy," she muttered, scrubbing the kitchen linoleum on her hands and knees. "How could she think I'm crazy?" When she finally finished, she felt a little better and resolved that as soon as Amanda came home from school, they would have a heart to heart talk.

Ethel emptied the pail into the slop sink on the back porch, pain rising up her back, her neck stiff as her scrubbing brush. She sat down at the kitchen table and massaged her neck. It didn't help. She got up and grabbed a handful of chocolate chips from a bag lying on the linoleum countertop next to the stove. They tasted tart, and yet so rich. She grabbed another handful wishing Carlton would come home for lunch. It would be a comfort to talk. How she yearned for him to have more free time. She was certain that he inhaled lunch at the Chat and Chew and that it could not possibly be as good as her cooking.

Ethel's neck hurt so bad she had to lie down. Lying very still, her neck didn't bother her, but she couldn't slow down her busy mind. "I wish I had the energy to get up. What is wrong with me? I wish Amanda understood why I had to lie about Sarah. Carlton is so blind. He thinks Amanda can do no wrong. But he thought Sarah was perfect too. It's a good thing Sarah is dead."

Ethel got up, listlessly opened a can of Campbell's chicken noodle soup and heated it on the stove. The soup tasted flat, metallic to her. She wondered if she was coming down with the flu. She pushed the bowl from the place mat, crossed her arms, rested her head on them and didn't lift her it until she heard Amanda open the back door. "How was school today?" Ethel forced a smile.

"Okay." Amanda took the lemonade pitcher from the fridge and poured two glasses.

"Who's with you?"

"Gael." Amanda pushed open the back door.

"Why don't you sit at the table?"

"It's a nice day. We'd rather be outside."

"Don't be too long. I'll need some help with supper. I'm not feeling one hundred percent." Ethel listened for a reply but only heard the backdoor slam shut. After several minutes, she peered out the window above the kitchen sink to find Amanda and Gael sitting under the oak tree almost nose to nose. Amanda held her arms open to emphasize something she was saying.

Ethel went to the pantry for potatoes and carrots, and started peeling them in the sink, watching Amanda and Gael so closely she nicked a finger with the paring knife and had to run cold water over the cut to stop the bleeding. She leaned close to the window, her forehead almost touching the glass pane. Gael Delaney was going to kiss Amanda! Ethel's neck felt like it would snap in two.

"Am-m-manda! Come in and set the table," she yelled. The pain and stiffness only increased when Amanda refused to answer Ethel's questions when she came inside to set the table for supper. Amanda later refused to eat. "Just as well," Ethel thought to herself, relieved. "I need to talk to Carlton."

While clearing the table, Ethel said, "We need to talk about that juvenile delinquent California boy. He walked Amanda home again. They sat outside for a long time, until I finally called Amanda inside." She stabbed a small potato and lifted it to her mouth. "Mark my words. Nothing good will come of this."

"I haven't heard one bad word about Gael," Carlton replied." He works evenings at his uncle's station, which gives Olav some free time."

"I wish he'd go to work right after school. I don't like the idea of Amanda spending time with him."

"Gael worked on Hank Peterson's Chevy and Hank said it runs like a new car now. I think it's okay for Amanda to spend some time with the boy. She is sixteen after all."

"That boy is nothing but trouble. Everyone knows he got kicked out of school in California. What did he have to do to get kicked out of school in a state as permissive as California?"

Carlton said, "I'm taking some food up to Amanda's room."

Just rewarding Amanda's bad behavior, Ethel thought to herself.

That night, Ethel knelt on the bare floor beside her bed to do some serious praying. "Dear God, what am I supposed to do? I know I was put on this earth to take care of Carlton, and I think I do a pretty good job of it, if I do say so myself. I've also taken care of Amanda as if she came from my own womb, but, as you know, caring for my niece has been a much harder job. I know you wouldn't have given me this task if you didn't think I could do it, but I really need your help now. Carlton's eyes have to be opened. He must forbid Amanda to see Gael Delaney. You are all powerful. I know you can open his eyes."

Ethel's neck hurt so badly she had to rub it vigorously with both hands, which helped a little but interrupted her prayer. She folded her hands again. "If you see fit not to do this, Dear God, I know that you must have a divine plan I don't know about. If that is the case, I need your help to get through this time of tribulation. Help me to endure the next two years until Amanda leaves. I ask this in the name of your dear son, who died on the cross to forgive my sins. Amen."

Barely able to stand, Ethel slowly lowered herself into bed. She pulled the covers up around her stiff neck. Several times during the night, pain sharp as broken glass awakened her to tell her she had moved in her sleep. When morning came, Ethel forced herself to get up.

9. Kissing in public

"Something smells strange," thought Ethel. She scooped grounds into the chrome coffee percolator. "Is this stale?" she muttered. "I just bought it last week. I'll have to talk to the grocer." Ethel collapsed onto a kitchen chair, her elbows resting on the table, her hands supporting her head. "Oh Dear God, it's my body I smell. She lifted her right arm and slowly raised her head, a sharp pain shooting through her neck. The smell of her own skin sent waves of nausea rushing through her. She needed fresh air and slowly made her way to the back door to inhale crisp September air. Her stomach settled. "I need to be strong," she told herself, then started making breakfast for Carlton and Amanda.

After they'd eaten and gone, Ethel left the dirty dishes on the table and rested on the sofa, her head on the back pillow, eyes fixed in the ceiling. She saw jagged lines. Flashing lights filled the room. Ethel cried out in pain when her neck rebelled against raising her head. She lunged forward and fell to her knees.

"Is this the end of the world? Lord have mercy on my soul." Ethel's head felt like it would explode into a million pieces. Flashing lights continued to terrify her when she lay on the thin Oriental rug covering the hardwood floor. "Dear God, what is happening to me? What have I done to deserve this?" Ethel crawled to her bedroom, a club pounding inside her skull, lights flashing, and pulled herself onto the mattress. Eventually, lights stopped flashing but the pounding continued harder than ever. "What is happening to me, Dear God? When is this going to end?" Ethel was still in bed that afternoon when she heard the back door open quietly. "Amanda, is that you?"

"I'm just getting some lemonade. What do you want?"

"I'm not feeling well. You'll have to make supper tonight. Come here and I'll tell you what you'll have to do."

"You're never sick." Amanda poked her head through the door to Ethel's room. "What's wrong?"

"I can't lift my head. It's a headache like I've never had before. I've been praying, and it seems to be better as long as I lie perfectly still."

"Oh. What do you want me to do? Gael's waiting."

Ethel tried to lift her head. She moaned in pain and lowered it back to the pillow. "What do you see that boy? He's nothing but trouble."

"You can't tell me who to spend my time with. He's not like the other boys in town. Gael's seen things people here can't even imagine."

The hammering inside her skull intensified. "I can't argue with you now," Ethel groaned. "Just open a can of soup when your dad comes home. I'm not hungry."

When Carlton arrived, he immediately went to Ethel's room. "What's wrong?" he asked gently.

Ethel managed to lift her head a little. "I've got a bad headache."

"Can I get you something?"

"Thank you for asking. A cool rag would feel good on my forehead."

Carlton returned with a wet cloth, a glass of water and aspirin. "Take these."

"Oh no. You know I never take pills. But the rag will feel good."

He set the water glass on Ethel's bedside table. "Make sure you drink this water."

"I'm sorry I'm not well enough to make supper ... only a can of soup for a meal."

"If you will be okay alone, I'll take Amanda down to the Chat and Chew for a hamburger."

"Don't worry about me. I'll manage somehow."

Ethel felt better the next day, but it took a lot of effort to vacuum and dust the main floor. Amanda came right home after school, and without Gael, which pleased her. Amanda was civil to her for the first time since finding her mother's letter.

"I had a good day at school, Auntie. Amanda actually sounded happy, and she was, but not for the reasons Ethel presumed.

Amanda woke up Saturday morning thinking about Gael. "Every time I look at him, I melt. Can't believe he came into my life, especially after reading Mother's letter. I need him so much. A soft breeze made the leaves dance in sunlight outside her bedroom window. "Don't blow this perfect day," she said to herself. "I'll never forgive myself if I ruin this."

In the mirror above her dresser, Amanda saw that, as usual, her hair was unruly. She sighed, grabbed a pair of new jeans and a black sweatshirt out of the bottom dresser drawer, holding the sweatshirt up against her. She liked the way it looked, not too fancy. She washed up, smoothed her curls down with water and dressed for Gael.

In the kitchen, Ethel fussed with breakfast, almost as if she hadn't spent two days in bed with a crushing headache. "What would you like to eat?" Ethel asked, not looking up as Amanda entered carrying a notebook and a Jane Austen novel.

"Cheerios." Amanda grabbed a bowl from a cupboard and sat at the table. "I'm going to the library this morning to work on my essay on *Wuthering Heights*. She opened the book and started to read.

Ethel poured Amanda a glass of orange juice. "You're going to the library dressed like that?" she asked. "You look like a juvenile delinquent." Ethel shook her head disapprovingly. "I don't think girls should wear jeans. And where did you get that sweatshirt?"

Amanda ate her Cheerios slowly, careful to avoid eye contact with her aunt. "I bought it at the mercantile. Everyone is wearing sweatshirts, even Rebecca," she added, hoping Ethel would shut up. Amanda pretended to read. Ethel clanked pots and pans in the sink. Tension gripped the air. On her way out the back door, Amanda turned to face Ethel. "Don't worry about how I look, Auntie. Everyone really does dress this way, except for at school of course."

"Well, thank goodness they don't allow girls to wear jeans at school."

Amanda found the air outside light and crisp. "Fall is a time to celebrate life," she said to herself. I wonder if my mother loved fall as much as I do." Amanda started walking faster. "Must not think about Mother."

Amanda stood on the library steps at nine, just as Miss Kittelsen unlocked the huge wooden door. "Good morning, Amanda," the librarian said.

Amanda smiled. "I've always loved the carvings of pine trees, mountains and lakes on this door. But it does seem out of character for our prairie town."

"These are scenes of Norway."

"I should have realized that. The artist who carved them probably missed Norway a lot."

"Niles Swanson, a local carpenter, carved the door. He was homesick for our native land." Miss Kittelsen examined the scenes closely. "Niles was quite an artist."

At the first reading table, her back to the door, unable to see Gael enter, Amanda opened her book. At nine-ten, he whispered in her ear, "Good morning Amanda, worthy to be loved."

She jerked her head up. "Gael!"

"Did I startle you?" Gael asked softly.

Amanda blushed. "You move so quietly, like a panther or something. I was listening for your car."

"I parked in the next block." He took her hand and pulled her up to him. "Let's get out of here before Miss Kittelsen tells us to be quiet."

"She's always in the stacks the first hour, making sure every book is in its proper place." They walked out holding hands. Gael's shiny black Ford had a dent in the right back fender that someone had tried to smooth out. "Where should we go?" she asked.

Gael opened Amanda's door. "Wherever you want to take me," he replied.

The worn upholstery had been cleaned and brushed. Comfortable. She ran her fingers along the dashboard. "Did it take a lot of work to fix up?"

Gael started the engine. "Yeah. I've been working on it at the station in between pumping gas for customers." He smoothly pushed the shift lever into gear and pulled out into the street. "Where to?"

"Let's go north." Amanda settled into the seat. "I don't know how to drive a manual transmission. I'm learning on Dad's automatic."

He glanced at her. "Stick's not hard. I'll teach you sometime."

"That would be a challenge for you. I'm not very coordinated."

"I welcome the challenge," said Gael. The vehicle picked up speed and he shifted. "Now where exactly do you want to go?"

"There's a place I've wanted to see, but I'm not sure exactly where it is." Amanda again could feel herself blush as she tried to decide how she could tell Gael about it. She was glad he wasn't looking at her. "It's an abandoned gravel pit off the highway, about five miles north I think. Boys go there to swim. They call it Bare Ass Beach.

Gael looked at her sideways, a mischievous grin on his face. "What do you want to do there?"

A deep laugh escaped Amanda's throat. "I just want to see it. Honest. Rebecca says that boys go out there on hot summer nights and sometimes after games to skinny dip. Girls don't go, but Rebecca and her clique want to surprise the guys sometimes."

"I think she's asking for trouble. Next time her dad gets gas, I'm going to tell him about her plans."

"Don't do that. You'll be the one who gets into trouble. Rebecca always twists things around so that nothing is ever her fault. She'll probably tell them you told her how to find Bare Ass Beach."

Gael searched Amanda's face. "Seems like everybody in Turtle Creek emerges from the same mold. I'm glad you're different."

"How did you figure out Turtle Creek so quickly?"

Gael smiled. "I'm working on Main Street most every day. I know which women shop at the Red Owl and which at Gunder Larson's grocery. And of course, I pump gas, change oil and wash the cars. Some are even asking me to diagnose and repair engine problems. The dads and sons can get chatty hanging around while I work on their cars."

"Wow. I'm amazed that the town people trust you so fast. I think they'll always be suspicious of me." She crossed and uncrossed her legs.

"Why is that?"

"My mother was a Jew," blurted Amanda, immediately regretting she'd said anything. She stared out her side window.

Gael reached over and stroked her arm. "It's so hard when you feel like you don't belong."

"At least twice a year Reverend Olafson rants about how wicked Jews are because they crucified Jesus. Every time he does this, I can feel condemning eyes bore into the back of my skull. It doesn't help that he usually brings this up on Christmas and Easter." Tears filled Amanda's eyes.

Gael pulled the car over to the side of the road and turned off the motor. His eyes filled with tenderness as he slid over, put his arms around her and rubbed her back. "Don't feel bad."

Amanda buried her head in his shoulder and cried. She lifted her head. "Your shirt's all wet. I'm sorry."

"No big deal. It'll dry."

"I'm okay now. We shouldn't park here. Somebody'll think we're having car trouble."

Gael started the car and cruised north toward the road to Bare Ass Beach. "You tell me when to turn."

"How far from town are we?"

"We've gone just about five miles." Gael spotted a rough gravel road. "This could be it," he said, turning onto a corduroy surface.

"Don't get stuck," warned Amanda.

"I'll bet this bad road leads to the quarry pit. Robert Knudson came in to have the front end of his dad's car realigned after driving out to Bare Ass Beach. He said his dad'll ground him if he drives out here anymore, so I told him I would realign it again if needed, no charge."

"That's really nice of you to do for Robert. He's a good kid." The washboard surface got worse. "Maybe we should turn around," said Amanda. "I don't want you to wreck your car."

"Don't worry. I can realign the front end and rebalance the tires. This is fun!" The road turned sharply. Gael stopped in an open area that resembled a parking lot with a tall hill of crushed gravel piled off to the side.

Amanda looked around, regretting she'd ever suggested Bare Ass Beach. "This was a dumb idea."

"Let's look around. The road ends here." Gael jumped from the car and darted around to open Amanda's door with a flourish. "Come, my fair maiden. Help me find Iowa's famous Bare Ass Beach."

A few yards beyond the gravel pile, they discovered a big hole filled with murky water, surrounded by tall corn. "I can't believe this," Amanda exclaimed. "It's so different than I imagined." A scraggly tree with gnarled branches grew near the beach. A huge branch extended out to the water's edge, a thick rope looped around a spike in the tree trunk dangling from it.

Gael tugged the twisted rope. "Be fun to swing out into the water."

"You're not going to try, are you?"

Gael laughed. "My shirt would really get soaked. Then I'd have to go in the tall corn over there and strip." Mischief sparkled in his eyes. I'd toss my clothes to you and you'd have to find a place to spread them out to dry. Might take a long time. I could weave a blanket out of corn leaves so you could come in and keep me company."

"You nut," she said. "What if somebody came and stole your clothes?"

"I guess if I'm going to try it I'd better take my clothes off first. Promise not to look?"

"I'm making no promises," said Amanda, realizing she was seriously flirting.

"You big tease." Gael's eyes smoldered. He threw his arms around her and kissed her long and hard. "I like this side of you," he murmured. Nothing existed for Amanda but the contour of his body as she melted into it. By the time she pulled away, both young lovers gasped for breath. "Let's find a secluded place. We don't want any company." He led her to the car. Once more rattling down the rough road, a throaty laugh, more of a groan actually, escaped Gael's throat. "Maybe we should find a more public place, not more private."

Amanda felt rejected. "I liked what we were doing," she stated simply.

"You don't know what you do to me." Gael shivered, his eyes fixed ahead. "We have to do this right. I don't want you to get hurt."

Gael's words fell heavily on Amanda's heart. She realized they were good words, words filled with respect, maybe even love. "Let's go to Carson City," she said. "It's only five miles further. They have a park where we can go for a walk."

"I'd like that." Gael picked up speed. "We'll have to head back by 11:30."

"We have plenty of time."

Amanda directed Gael to Carson City park where they found two cars parked next to a picnic area where several kids played on the swings and slide. Their parents spread a nearby picnic table with paper plates for lunch.

Gael whispered, "This is like a scene from a Hollywood movie about the perfect American family."

"Shouldn't Spot the dog be here too? And there should be a red and white checkered table cloth on the picnic table," Amanda said as she got out of the car.

"You're right." Gael grabbed her hand. "I know this sounds corny, but I wish this could be my life someday."

"It can be."

"No, I don't think so." Gael led her away from the picnic area towards a narrow trail into the woods.

"Why do you say that?" she asked.

"You don't want to know about my problems."

Amanda stopped and turned around. "Please tell me. I want to know everything about you."

"You're so pure, so innocent." Gael put his arms around Amanda, kissing her gently at first, then with an urgency that she responded to. When they stopped to breathe, he added, "That's why I love you."

"Please say that again, and kiss me a hundred times."

"I love you!" Gael kissed her forehead. "I love you," he said again and kissed her ear, the back of her neck. "I love you, Amanda," he whispered into her hair.

Amanda felt weak, certain she would collapse if he let go of her. "I love you too," she said.

They clung to each other, neither wanting to let go, until Gael said, "Would you like a coke or something to eat?"

"We could go to Bert's Cafe on Main," she mumbled.

"I want to hold you forever; but we should go to Bert's." Gael stepped back, grabbed her hand and walked her back to the car. "You look dazed," he exclaimed.

"I can't believe how happy I am," she said.

Gael kissed her again gently on the lips. "I want to know everything about you."

"You know most everything already. You know what it's like to live in Turtle Creek, and you know that Auntie and Dad lied to me all these years about my mother" She looked off into space on the way to Bert's. "I don't want to think about my mother today. I want to think about you. I've had a life in black and white. Since I met you, everything is in vivid Technicolor." She paused before adding, "You know more about me than I know about you."

"You know that I love you." Gael parked in front of Bert's Cafe. "That's the most important thing."

Amanda repeated to herself, "Gael loves me," and decided that was all she wanted to think about.

They sat on the same side of a wooden booth in the deserted café, holding hands. "Are you hungry?" he asked. "I'm ordering a hamburger."

A stern, middle-aged waitress wearing a dark hairnet took their order. "I'll just have a Coke." Amanda probed the depth of Gael's eyes. "Tell me, what is your earliest memory?"

"My dad whipping my legs with a belt until I couldn't stand up," answered Gael in a voice so low it was barely audible. "The first time it happened I was playing with a toy truck in the street. Please, no more questions about my past."

"I'm sorry, so sorry." Amanda vowed never to ask Gael again about his past.

"Nothing to be sorry for. Let's not talk about me. Let's talk about your mother."

"I know Dad loved her, but she never wanted to be married so she left him with nothing but a baby daughter and a letter. How could he still love her after what she wrote in that letter?"

When the waitress came with drinks, Amanda stopped talking. She took a sip of Coke. "What I wonder about is if my mother ever really loved my dad. I mean, why did she start dating him? He's Lutheran. She probably would have been happier with someone of her own faith."

"Your dad is a handsome man, and he's very smart. I'm sure lots of women are attracted to him." Gael took a bite of his hamburger. "You know what else? People are often fascinated by someone who has a background different from their own. Mystery is a powerful magnet."

"That's true." Amanda knew it was true of her attraction to Gael, and probably of his attraction to her.

Another couple sat in the booth next to them. Amanda wished they had chosen to sit at the other end of the cafe. She nervously looked at her watch. "I can't believe it is 11:15 already."

"That's a nice-looking watch." He reached across the table for her hand and examined the delicate gold, oval face. "*Bulova*. A lot of girls at Turtle Creek High have *Bulova* watches."

"That's what every girl in Turtle Creek gets when she's confirmed." She placed her hand over his. "You sure don't miss much."

"I have to be observant. It's a survival skill." In the car, heading back to Turtle Creek Gael said, "Your wrists are so delicate. I'd like to caress every bone in your body." He reached across the seat and stroked her arm. "By the way, did I tell you that I love you?"

Amanda was frightened by how much she wanted Gael to caress every bone in her body. "All my life, I've wanted to fall in love. It's better than I ever imagined."

Gael headed for the Turtle Creek library, parking in the shade of a side street. He got out of the car and opened the door for Amanda. "I thought the local militia had better see that you have been at the library," he said, grabbing her wrist and looking at her watch, "at 11:38 sharp."

Amanda threw her arms around Gael and kissed him. When they separated, she took an uneven breath. Rebecca's mother drove past very slowly. "Oh shit, Gael," Amanda muttered. "Mrs. Nelson is the queen of the local militia, but you know what? I don't care."

"Tell her I was trying to protect you," Gael teased.

"With Ethel and Dad, I don't need any more protectors. Ethel is an authority on how to protect people."

Gael got serious. "I will protect you in good ways. I love you."

Amanda defiantly kissed him again. Mrs. Nelson slammed on her brakes in the middle of the road.

"I love you too," said Amanda. "You have to go now."

Gael got in the car and slowly drove away as Amanda held her head high and walked proudly past Mrs. Nelson's car.

Mrs. Nelson rolled down her window and sang, "Why, hello Amanda."

"Oh, hello Mrs. Nelson," Amanda replied in a strong voice, trying to show Mrs. Nelson that she wasn't the least embarrassed. She walked to the creek, telling herself she didn't care if Mrs. Nelson told the whole town. "I've always wanted to be loved," she mused, heading for home. "Now I realize, the greatest gift is the capacity to love another person completely."

She found Ethel shelling peas at the kitchen table. "You must be hungry." Ethel ran her fingernail along the inside seam of a pea pod and dropped the peas from it into a large bowl. "You've been at the library a long time. Can you make yourself a sandwich? I want to finish canning these and get them in the pressure cooker."

"Why do you go to all that work of canning peas when you can buy peas?" Amanda wasn't trying to make Ethel mad. She was curious.

"We don't have money to throw around," Ethel responded angrily. "Besides, my canned peas taste much better than any from the store."

"I love your creamed peas on toast." Amanda was determined not to fight with her aunt. She actually did love the creamed peas Ethel served every Sunday night for as long as she could remember. And she didn't want to spoil her wonderful day.

"Why, thank you," Ethel said primly. The phone rang. Ethel stopped shelling peas and started to get up to answer it.

"I can get that," said Amanda. "Has Mrs. Nelson been talking to someone already?" she wondered. Her stomach churned.

"No, I'll get it. It's always for me anyway." The phone rang for a third time. Ethel picked up the receiver. "Why Mrs. Olafson, how nice of you to call."

Amanda got the jar of peanut butter out of the cupboard and started making a sandwich, though all of a suddenly she wasn't hungry.

"What are you saying?" Ethel sounded alarmed. "She's with me right now. I can't believe she would do that. I know she would never do that in public. It must have been someone else Mrs. Nelson saw kissing that juvenile delinquent." Her voice desperate, Ethel added, "Amanda isn't the only girl in town with dark hair. Those O'Connors have all those kids running around town unsupervised. They all have dark hair."

Amanda could hear Mrs. Olafson's strong voice. "The O'Connor girls are too young!"

Ethel quickly responded, "I know the oldest O'Connor girl is in eighth grade. Maybe that Gael Delaney wants to be with young girls he can take advantage of. It must have been that O'Connor girl." Then abruptly she said, "I can't talk anymore. I have to warn Amanda about that Gael Delaney. You know, all the girls at Turtle Creek High think he's something, even Rebecca Nelson."

Before Ethel could hang up the phone, Amanda confessed, "I kissed Gael by the library. That's not a crime … maybe in Turtle Creek it's a crime. I hate this dumb town."

"How can you talk like that?" Ethel looked like she was going to topple over. She grabbed a chair, slumped across the table, her head on her arms, and moaned, "The devil is in you!"

"The devil? You're crazy," Amanda screamed on her way upstairs. She could hear Ethel immediately call Carlton. Amanda slammed her bedroom door, took a deep, shaky breath and sat on her bed, frightened and angry. "Shit! Shit! Got to come up with a plan, but what are my options?" Amanda started to write down ideas. The first: run away. But she decided she would only do that if she could run away with Gael. Second, she wrote that she had to find a way to survive in her house, in her town, because Gael was there. She calmed down. That was her plan, to survive, like Gael.

She heard her father's Ford pull into the driveway and a car door slam. "Where is she?" she heard him say. Footsteps hurried up to her room. He knocked and said, "Amanda, may I come in?" Amanda was surprised at how calm he sounded.

"Yes." Amanda waited hopefully for him to open the door.

"Honey, you need to tell me what is going on," he said, joining her on the edge of her bed.

Knowing she needed to tell him everything, she started at the beginning. "This morning I met Gael Delaney at the library and we went to Carson City. Ethel thought I was at the library studying. She wouldn't have let me go, so I didn't tell her." All her dad did was nod his head, which relaxed Amanda. "The first thing we did was go to the gravel pit where guys go to swim, because I wanted to see it. There wasn't much to see. Then we went to Carson City Park, and then we had a Coke at Bert's. Gael had to be at the station at noon so we went back to the library, where he dropped me off."

She stopped, and then decided she had to tell the whole story. "When I got out of the car, I put my arms around Gael and kissed him. I started it, not Gael. Mrs. Nelson drove by as we were kissing." She searched her dad's face to try to determine if this upset him. He had his professional, doctor look on. She whispered, "I love Gael, Dad."

Carlton studied Amanda in silence. Finally, he said, "I know how all-consuming love is, sweetheart, but we have a problem to deal with now. I'd hoped when we got dial phones gossip would be less of a problem, but gossip still spreads like a wild fire." He opened his arms and lifted his palms in the air. "This is very hard on Ethel."

"I don't care what she thinks. She hates Gael because he's different. Besides, she doesn't even know what love is."

"You're wrong, Amanda. Ethel loves you with all her heart. And me. From a very young age she had to take care of me. Ethel gave up everything to take care of me after Dad died."

"She loves you, but she doesn't love me. Can't you see that?"

"I know it feels that way to you because it's hard for Ethel to

97

accept anything that's different, but she has taken care of you since you were a baby. I will tell her that you must be allowed to spend time with Gael and that if I have any concerns about what is going on with you and Gael I will discuss them with you. There will be a few rules. The first, and most important one, is that you always tell me when you are going out with Gael and where you are going. The second rule is that I will expect you to be back home at a reasonable hour. The third rule is that you must promise me that you will be nice to Ethel."

The first two rules sounded reasonable, but Amanda didn't think she could be nice to Ethel. "She said I have the devil in me, Dad. I don't want to talk to her again. I don't want to be in the same room with her."

"She was upset because she didn't even know you were out with Gael, and you must understand how hard it was for her to find that out from Mrs. Olafson. Sometimes when we're upset we say things we don't really mean. She doesn't think the devil is in you, at least not any more than it is in all of us at times. You did wrong by deceiving her. You have to forgive her for saying the devil is in you, just as she has to forgive you for lying to her."

"I didn't lie. I was at the library studying until Gael picked me up. And I'll never feel that I did something wrong by kissing Gael."

"It wasn't wrong. But I'm sure you didn't intend for the whole town to know about it."

A plan formed in Amanda's head. "When I'm at home, I'll be in my room. I'll eat my meals here too."

Amanda saw a look of desperation on her dad's face. "Don't refuse to eat meals with us. You're my daughter, my life." He added, his voice sad, "You'll be off to college before we know it."

Amanda hugged her dad. "I love you," she said. "When you are here, I'll eat with you. I'll try to be civil to Ethel."

10. The chiffonier

Ethel sat at the kitchen table, her head, as usual, resting on her arms, when Carlton came back downstairs after talking to Amanda. He sat next to her, put his elbows on the table, chin in his hands.

"Ethel," he said quietly, "Gael's a nice young man. Amanda has my permission to continue to see him. I know the gossip is hard for you to cope with, but I also know you can do it. When our father died, what you had to cope with was much worse. If you hadn't been here to pick up the pieces, to take care of me, I don't know what would have happened." He raised his voice. "You can do it, Ethel. You have to do it."

She lifted her head. "I'm worried sick about Amanda. She's being tempted by the devil to do things she shouldn't." In a low whisper she added, "She could end up PG."

Spending a couple of hours with Gael, having a coke at Bert's, is a long way from getting pregnant. What they are doing is healthy. They're teenagers. They're dating."

"Then why did Amanda lie about where she was going this morning? She knew what she did was wrong." Ethel lifted her head high, satisfied that what she said was the absolute truth.

"She didn't tell you she was meeting Gael at the library because she knew you wouldn't approve. You're being unreasonable about Gael, just like you used to be unreasonable about Joey. Think about it, Ethel. Joey's a fine young man who was always a good kid."

"It's a miracle Joey turned out okay with the lack of upbringing he's had."

"Daisy's a good mother. She's done a better job as a parent than some of the people active in our church." Carlton paused. "We need to talk about Amanda, not Joey. She's a good girl. You must forgive her for not telling you she was meeting Gael."

"Of course I forgive her. I will forgive her seventy times seven, but that doesn't mean that I trust her. It will take a long time for me to trust her like I used to."

"You don't need to worry about what she's doing any more. I'm taking over that job, and I trust her completely."

"This is not how I want things to go," Ethel fumed. "How can Carlton say that? He is not realistic. He will always think Amanda can do no wrong. And now that I think about it, I wonder if he hasn't always had a secret crush on Daisy? She's never taken her parenting responsibilities seriously, but he refuses to see the truth. It's pure luck that Joey is such a good basketball player. That's what has kept him out of trouble."

"Ethel?" Carlton asked, breaking her rumination.

"How can you trust her when, according to Mrs. Olafson, she passionately kissed Gael right in front of Mrs. Nelson, who said it looked like Amanda had no self-control? The devil made her do that, Carlton!"

"It's not a sin to kiss your boyfriend. Granted, it would have been better if she had not done it in a public place, especially in this town. Gossip can be sinful too. There are many good people here, Ethel, but even the best of us get caught up in the thrill of spreading gossip. I will talk with Amanda about the importance of not giving people reasons to gossip about her."

"Are you saying that she can do whatever she pleases with Gael Delaney so long as no one sees it? You realize what can happen?"

"Of course I do. I will talk to Amanda about the dangers of getting intimate too fast. I often deal with the problems that result from this." Carlton got up. "I have to go back to work."

"But you're only supposed to work till noon on Saturdays."

"There were two people in the waiting room when I left. I have to take care of them, Ethel."

"I hope that the people in this town appreciate all that you do."

"They do, Ethel."

Ethel continued to sit long after Carlton left, her elbows on the table, her tired hands rubbing the back of her stiff neck. "I can't trust Amanda! What can I do? Can't talk with her. That's hopeless. Right now I would be happy if I never saw her again. It will be so nice when Amanda leaves for college. Just me and Carlton here. Why did he ever get involved with Sarah? What did he see in her? It was so humiliating when he came back to Turtle Creek after medical school with a pregnant wife. I hadn't even met her. I know he didn't tell me about her because he was embarrassed. He, of all people, should know the dangers of going too far with the wrong person." Ethel tried to lift her head. "It's too bright in here," she complained. Then she saw jagged lines flashing. "No, not again. I have to get to bed. Why does the devil torment me like this?"

Unsteady and in considerable pain, Ethel found her way to the bedroom by groping furniture and walls for support. She collapsed on her bed. Closing her eyes and lying very still seemed to help. Thinking about how peaceful her life would be after Amanda left for college also helped. In and out of fitful sleep, Ethel didn't know how much time had passed before she heard Carlton's car pull in the driveway. She weakly called out when he entered, "Carlton, come here."

"What is it, Ethel?" Standing in her bedroom doorway, Carlton appeared to have shrunken to half his normal size, his neck twice its normal length. His head bobbed on his neck like a balloon.

Never so frightened, Ethel screamed, "No! Carlton. You monster. No!" She tried to push him away with her hands as he stepped closer.

"What's wrong, Ethel?" Carlton put a cool hand on her forehead. "You don't have a fever. Can I get you something?"

His voice sounded normal, his touch soothing. Ethel quickly calmed down, but kept her eyes closed. She didn't want to see any evidence that the devil had changed her dear Carlton into a monster. "I have another terrible headache," she moaned. "A cold rag for my forehead would help."

Carlton applied a cool washcloth to his sister's forehead. Ethel opened her eyes. "Thank you, God," she whispered. "My Carlton is normal again. He is stronger than the devil."

"Devil? Ethel, I know this is a stressful time for you. Please trust my judgment in dealing with Amanda."

"Thank you for the rag."

"You need to rest. I'll be in the living room. Call me if you need anything."

As soon as Carlton left, Ethel said to herself, "I can't trust Amanda. But God has shown me that I have to trust Carlton. I can do that. But how I wish Amanda was gone." She'd clenched her jaw and her teeth started to hurt, forcing her to relax. "Dear God," she prayed. "I've been civil to Mrs. Nelson for as long as I can remember. Now give me the same strength to live in this house with Amanda. You must think I am amazingly strong because you are again testing me like Job was tested. I will try to be worthy of your confidence. I realize you don't expect me to drive the devil out of Amanda. She has to want the devil gone before it can happen. Yet, it's hard to have the devil so active right in my own home. I know you will help me survive. Your faithful, but frightened servant, Ethel."

Lying very still, dozing restlessly, Ethel lay in bed until the six o'clock whistle blew. Her head throbbing, she cautiously put both feet on the floor, grabbed the dresser next to her bed, pulled herself up and slowly walked out of the room. After using the bathroom, she went to the kitchen. The house was unusually quiet. She collapsed on a kitchen chair. Then she saw a note from Carlton. "Ethel. I am taking Amanda for dinner at the Chat and Chew. You were sleeping peacefully, so we didn't want to disturb you. I can make something for you when we get back. Please rest until then."

"How ridiculous," Ethel muttered. "He can't prepare a meal. He doesn't even know how to turn on the stove. Why didn't he wake me? This is the second time they have run off without me. People will think my cooking is so bad they prefer to eat at the Chat and Chew." She folded her hands and rested them on the table. "Dear God, I need the strength to keep going. I have to make the meals, keep the house clean, and buy the groceries. If I don't do these things, what will happen to me? Most importantly, what will happen to Carlton? He cannot survive without me. I know you will help me do these things because you are all powerful. I am trusting you, the only one I can trust completely. Your weak and lonely servant, Ethel."

Ethel pushed herself up, palms flat on the table, and groped the wall to a pantry cupboard filled with canned goods: Mason jars of beans, peas and corn. Arrows of pain pierced her neck and shot to her skull. In desperation, she grabbed the nearest jar and pried the lid off. "Corn. I will eat this," she muttered, stumbling to the stove, splattering corn into a saucepan and lighting the burner.

Ethel knifed thick slabs of butter on a slice of *Taystee* white bread. She moved the barely lukewarm canned corn to the table and began eating out of the saucepan, bread chewed ragged lying on the table. She didn't hear Amanda and Carlton come through the back door.

"Ethel, are you okay?" Carlton rushed over to her.

She lifted her head. "I thought I was hungry, but I guess I'm not," she said weakly, pushing herself away from the table. She felt dizzy and braced her arms on the table.

"Let me help you." Carlton guided her to her bedroom, steadying her as she lay down on the bed.

"Terrible headache," she said weakly. "Need to be still."

"I'm getting you a pain killer," he said.

With all the strength she could muster, Ethel slurred, "Don't need a pill, need peace."

"Yes, you do need peace." Carlton placed a cool hand on her forehead. "I'll get you some water. You must not get dehydrated."

"I wish his hand touched my forehead forever," whispered Ethel waiting for Carlton to return with a glass of water.

Supporting her head with one hand, he put the glass to her lips. "Drink all you can," he said gently.

Ethel took two sips before feebly brushing the glass away with her hand. "No more."

"I'll leave the glass on your dresser. Promise me you'll drink it," said Carlton. He placed a washcloth on his sister's pale forehead. "I'll be in the living room if you need anything." He paused at the doorway. "Amanda is here to help you too."

"No, no, not Amanda. Only you, Carlton."

Ethel dozed on and off throughout the night. When morning came, she willed herself to sit up in bed. She was weak, but the pounding hammer in her head had stopped. "God will give me strength to go to church, she thought. I'll make some tea and toast." She cautiously made her way to the kitchen and put the teakettle on.

"It's good to see you up," said Carlton when he came downstairs. "You were asleep when I went to bed. Did you sleep well?"

"I'm feeling better, thank you. I'll start a pot roast and peel the potatoes and carrots before we go to church."

"Amanda can do that. Are you sure you feel well enough to go to church?"

"You know I never miss church. And I prefer to cook Sunday dinner and set the table myself." Ethel pushed herself up from the table and removed a rump roast wrapped in butcher paper from the refrigerator.

"Why don't you let Amanda help? She should do more around the house anyway. When you were her age, you took care of everything, including me, by yourself."

"And I still can, Carlton."

"I know you can, and you do a wonderful job of it. But I want Amanda to learn from you. You do it so well."

"You are in charge of Amanda, but I am in charge of our home," Ethel said firmly. "You'd better tell her it's time to get dressed. We have to leave for church in forty-five minutes." Ethel peeled potatoes under a thin stream of cold water at the sink and prayed, "Dear God, please protect Carlton. I know his faith is strong, but the devil may reach him through Amanda." She arranged the potatoes in a blue enamel pan along with the roast and started vigorously scrubbing the carrots. "You know how hard I have tried through the years to keep Amanda pure, but there was only so much I could do. Your humble servant, Ethel, who will be in pew number two this morning."

Amanda appeared in the kitchen wearing a short nightgown with smocking embroidered across the front. "Good morning. Dad said you're feeling better."

Ethel refused to make eye contact when she poured herself a cup of coffee, but couldn't help notice out of the corner of her eye that Amanda's nightgown didn't reach her knees. "That nightgown is the work of the devil," Ethel fumed. "She knows it is sinful to have that much leg showing. Why won't Carlton say something?"

On her way back upstairs with the coffee, Amanda turned and sarcastically said, "Good morning, Ethel."

"Don't ..." snapped Ethel, then stopped herself. "If Amanda leaves a ring on her dresser from that hot coffee cup, I won't be able to remove it." Ethel scrubbed a carrot so hard it broke in two.

Ethel stared straight ahead through the windshield from the front passenger seat of Carlton's car on the way to church, pretending that Amanda was not sitting behind her. Once inside the church, Ethel relaxed a little because she knew the devil would not have as strong a grip on Amanda, especially sitting where they belonged, in pew number two.

Pastor Halverson entitled his sermon, "Love one another as I have loved you," which greatly comforted Ethel. She hoped that everyone took it to heart, especially Mrs. Nelson. Ethel felt Mrs. Nelson should love her and realize how hard she had worked to keep Amanda pure. But as Ethel thought about Amanda's purity, the more certain she was that Mrs. Nelson held her responsible for Amanda's indecency.

After the service, Ethel was not surprised when Amanda greeted Thor and his Italian wife. But she was shocked and feared the devil's work at play when Amanda said, in a voice that actually sounded warm, "Hello Mrs. Nelson, Rebecca. How are you today?"

Mrs. Nelson apparently recovered faster than Ethel from Amanda's friendly tone. "I'm fine, Amanda. Thank you," she said primly.

Rebecca studied Amanda with suspicion. "And so am I."

Ethel hurried to the car. On the way home, Carlton said, "That was nice of you to greet the Nelsons, Amanda." And when they entered the house, he said to Ethel, "Boy, does that pot roast smell good." Ethel had set the dining room table with their best gold rimmed china before church. "The table looks so nice. We should use our fancy dishes more often. When did you find the time to put flowers from your garden in that vase?" he exclaimed, judging Ethel's recovery by yellow and orange mums.

"It didn't take long to snip a few flowers, nor to use the good dishes from the buffet. Remember when Daddy came home from Kentucky with these dishes?"

"Yes. He won them in a dice game." Carlton smiled. "I was six years old, and tried to imagine a set of dishes stacked like poker chips in the middle of a card table."

"Oh Carlton, I'm sure he bought these dishes at an estate sale. He often went to auctions and estate sales on his trips. One time he told me about a beautiful four poster bed and chiffonier he found. Daddy was going to buy it for me, but when he went to the hotel to get his checkbook, someone else bought it."

"What is a chiffonier?" Amanda asked.

Refusing to look at her niece, Ethel said, "A chiffonier is a tall, narrow chest with many drawers. Please tell Amanda, Carlton. The one Daddy found had a beveled mirror on top."

"Ethel, stop playing this silly game. You're being childish. Amanda did nothing wrong. Gossips like Mrs. Nelson are always hard to endure, but by the end of the week she will be rumoring about a new scandal."

"People still say that Daddy stole money from the bank!" Ethel furiously shook her head. "Gossip never forgets."

"It's not fair to equate Amanda and Gael kissing by the library with people being upset about losing their life savings. Dad was the president of the bank. In the absence of proof to the contrary, people will speculate and conclude that he was responsible."

Ethel stabbed a piece of the pot roast and chewed vigorously. Her mind echoed the same old refrain. "He always thinks Amanda can do no wrong." Ethel swallowed with some difficulty and said, "I have to lie down. My headache is back."

On the way to her bedroom, Ethel heard Carlton say, "We have to be patient Amanda. Ethel will calm down … soon, I hope."

11. Doc MacGregor's

"I don't think Ethel will ever forgive me, Dad, but she's right about one thing, people here will never forget what I did. They will always think I'm a slut because I kissed Gael out in front of the ..."

Carlton interrupted her. "Nobody thinks you're a slut, Amanda. There are lots of good people in this town who remember what it was like to be young."

"You say that because everyone likes you. You hardly had a chance to eat at the Chat and Chew last night, so many people stopped to greet you. 'How's it going, Doc? Good to see you, Doc. MacGregor. Hi Doc, that new medicine works real good.' You're a local hero or something." Amanda was surprised to see her dad blush.

"A doctor heals the sick and wounded, sweetie. It's not so much that they think I'm a great person as they appreciate having a doctor in town."

"I know that, Dad, but I also think you must be a good Doctor."

"I do the best I can. Sometimes I wish I could do more." Carlton ran fingers through his thinning, dust-blond hair. "You know what? I could use some extra help at the office. My secretary is behind on paper work. The phone never stops ringing. Do you think you could come over after school a couple of days a week?"

"You really mean it? I'd love that."

"Why don't you come by the office after school tomorrow? Mary will be pleased to have some help."

"That'll work. Is it okay though if I skip a few days at the end of the month for the school paper deadline?"

"Absolutely. Reporter for the school paper comes first. There's a lot of flexibility at Doc MacGregor's." Carlton got up from the table. "I better check on Ethel."

"She drives me crazy, but I'm sorry she's not feeling well. I'll go with you."

They found Ethel in her bedroom, eyes were closed. Carlton put his hand on her forehead. She stirred, but made no sound. "It's good for her to rest," he whispered in the hallway. "I'm just glad she's not feverish."

"I'm glad too, Dad." Amanda peeked into Ethel's bedroom. "You know what? I wish grandfather would have given her that four poster bed and chiffonier. Her room is so bare and cold. Why doesn't she put some garden flowers in a vase on her dresser next to your high school graduation picture? Or at least a doily on the dresser." Amanda looked closer. "And that pathetic rag rug on the floor. It looks so sad." She immediately went to the dining room and picked up the vase full of yellow and white mums. "I'll put these on her dresser," she said, tiptoeing back to Ethel's room while her father read the Sunday paper.

Amanda took off her Sunday dress and put on jeans and a white cotton tee. She noticed her algebra book waiting for her on the desk. "I'd rather work on anything else, she thought, but this homework assignment has to be done. Wish it came easier for me, the way it does for Gael. Wish he was here now, looking at me the way he does." Amanda opened the book and worked slowly. She preferred words to letters standing for numbers, knowing she had to memorize formulas before she would understand how to do the problems. "At least it's starting to make sense." When she finished her homework, Amanda went for a walk. Ole's gas station pulled her like a magnet. She found Gael outside with his head under the hood of a car. "Hey, what are you doing?" she called.

Gael popped up with a warm smile that wrapped around her. "Changing oil for my uncle. I'd like to hug you, but I'd get grease on your clothes."

"It's probably better if we don't touch each other in public. Auntie heard about our kiss at the library and is very upset. I barely walked in the door yesterday when Mrs. Olafson called to tell Ethel that Mrs. Nelson saw us kissing."

"Sorry I got you into trouble." Gael reached out to touch her arm then pulled away. "Whoops. Greasy hands."

"Don't be sorry. I was the one who kissed you, remember? Besides, we didn't do anything wrong. My aunt is crazy. She thinks the devil made us do it." Gael looked alarmed. "Don't worry. Dad understands. He remembers what it was like to be young. I think it's actually funny."

Gael searched her face. "I don't think that's funny. I think it's Turtle Creek. But it helps that your dad understands."

"You know what else? I'm going to work at his office two days a week."

"Hey, that's great. It's Sunday. We close early. Want to go for a ride after I clean up? I'll pick you up at your house this time."

"I'd like that." Amanda felt like her feet barely touched the sidewalk on the way home. She found her dad still in his favorite chair reading. "Gael is coming over," she said. "We're going for a ride."

"Ole told me about the car Gael fixed up. I'd like to see it." Carlton laid the Sunday paper on an end table. "People are talking about what a good mechanic he is."

"You can see it when he picks me up." She started to go to her bedroom, but after taking a few steps she stopped. "Is Auntie still sleeping?" she asked softly.

"She was the last time I checked. Don't worry. If she wakes up, I'll take care of it. Your friends are always welcome here."

Amanda crept upstairs, combed her hair and looked critically at her tee shirt. She decided to put on a sweater instead, the new red sweater lying in her bottom dresser drawer. She changed fast, leaving the tee shirt unfolded on her bed because she wanted to be ready when Gael came to the door. She wasn't sure what Ethel would say or do if she knew Gael was coming, and she didn't want to find out. Downstairs, she sat impatiently on the sofa. "Dad, I'm so excited about a chance to help out at the office."

"I'm glad, sweetheart. Mary will be too. She's been my secretary for a long time. I forget sometimes, she's ten years older than me. It's hard to keep up with everything." Doctor Carlson handed the front-page section to Amanda. "Would you like to read some of this?"

Both read silently until they heard a car drive up and park on the street out front. Amanda jumped up. "That's Gael."

"He must have worked hard on that motor. It sounds so good," Carlton said quietly.

Amanda raced to the door, opening it as Gael climbed the steps. "Dad wants to see your car," she said excitedly, stepping outside.

"He does?" said Gael with a cautious smile.

Carlton followed Amanda outside. "Good to see you, Gael. Easy to tell you've done a lot of work on Mabel Olson's old car. I remember well what it used to sound like putt-putting around town. I expected it to stall in the middle of Main Street someday."

An easy laugh slipped out of Gael's throat. "Good to see you too, Dr. MacGregor. Like to look under the hood?"

Amanda took a deep breath, scolded herself for being so nervous and listened to the relaxing exchange between the two main guys in her life. She didn't understand much about the carburetor and manifold, brake drums, driveshaft, crankshaft, pistons, sparkplugs and torque, but she was proud that her dad was fluent in the foreign language of cars.

Carlton pulled his head out of the engine compartment and straightened up. "It must have taken many hours to get everything looking and sounding so good."

Amanda took it as a signal that it was time to leave. "We should get going. I'll be home for supper, Dad." She walked around to the passenger side of the car.

Carlton shook hands with Gael. "Thanks for tuning-up my car last week. Runs great."

"Thank you, Doc MacGregor." Gael rushed around to open Amanda's door. "Hey, I like that sweater," he said as she got in.

Amanda felt the warmth of blushing. She hated when she did that. "Where we going?" she asked.

"How about a Coke at Pete's Drive-in?"

"That'd be great!" she said, suddenly realizing she'd clenched both hands into fists. She stretched her fingers.

There were only two other cars at Pete's. They both rolled down their windows and the carhop – one of Rebecca Nelson's disciples, Suzy, came to take their order. "Hi, what would you like?" asked Suzy brightly.

"Want anything to eat?" Gael asked. "Maybe some ice cream?"

"Just a coke," she replied, feeling too happy to eat. At school on Monday, everyone would know that her boyfriend Gale had taken her out on a date twice over the weekend. Suzy would see to that.

Suzy left to get their drinks. Gael smiled and said, "I'm glad your dad approves of me. He's such a nice guy."

"Isn't he? I wish my aunt wasn't so crazy. They're complete opposites. He's accepting and generous. She cold and possessive. She's always been rigid, but I used to think that she had a good heart. Now I don't know."

"It's this town. She'd be a different person if she lived somewhere where she didn't feel she was being judged all the time."

"Maybe so. I can't wait to get out of here. I bet you're anxious to get back to California."

As Suzy approached with their order, Gael quickly replied, "I don't think I should go back to California."

Amanda didn't know how to respond. She sat in shocked silence while Gael paid for the cokes. When Suzy left, Amanda asked, "What are you going to do? You're so smart. Dad told me that Mr. Wessel says you're way ahead of the rest of the class in Physics."

"I don't know, Amanda. I need to get out on my own." Gael continued forcefully, "I never want to see my father again." He slid closer to Amanda and rested his arm on the back seat. "I'm sorry. I don't mean to upset you. I always want you in my life."

Her response was automatic. "I always want you in my life, no matter where you are or what you're doing."

Gael leaned close as if he were going to say something important when a white Chevy convertible, Rebecca behind the wheel, parked in the stall next to them. She had three of her followers in the car, all of them giggling convulsively. Rebecca leaned toward Amanda until she almost touched Gael's car. "Hi," she said innocently. The other girls stopped laughing and leaned forward. "We don't want to interrupt anything going on between you two lovebirds. Just pretend we're not here." The disciples started to giggle again.

Gael reached across Amanda's lap and rolled up the window without saying a word. Amanda leaned her back against her window and said, loud enough for Rebecca to hear, "Isn't the privacy we have in Turtle Creek wonderful?"

"Way to go," Gael said quietly. "Rebecca's leaning over so far, trying to hear us, I think she's going to fall out of the car."

Amanda forced a laugh. The magical spell she experienced before Rebecca showed up was broken. Gael slid back into the driver's seat and studied Rebecca's car. "A '57 Bel Air. Pretty fancy car. They cost over two thousand dollars," he whispered.

"She gets everything she wants." They finished their cokes in silence.

When Suzy approached to pick up the tray, Gael murmured, "Look at her. What a sappy smile."

"Boy, you two were sure speedy," said Suzy. Rebecca and the others giggled again. "What's the big hurry?"

Gael turned the ignition and backed up without saying a word. Out on Main Street, he suggested, "Let's go for a ride."

"As long as they aren't following us." Amanda realized that she had her hands clenched again. She forced herself to open them.

They left town on a deserted gravel road towing a cloud of dust.

"They make me feel so stupid and dirty," she said. "My aunt constantly talking about the devil inside me doesn't help."

"Don't let them spoil what we have." He reached over and gave her hand a gentle squeeze.

"I know they're jealous, but I still feel dirty." She looked behind, fearing she'd see Rebecca's car. All she saw was a trail of dust. "Maybe you should take me home." Gael turned the car around without saying a word. Amanda implored, "Please don't be mad at me."

"I'm not mad at you. I'm mad at Rebecca, and your aunt, and this town."

Parked in front of her house, she said, "Thank you for not being mad. I'll be better tomorrow, I promise." She opened the car door and quickly got out.

Gael rolled down his window. "I could never be mad at you."

Before Amanda could sit down with her dad, Ethel entered the living room holding the flower vase. "Who put these in my bedroom?" she demanded. "I don't like flowers in my room. They make my headache worse."

"Amanda was trying to do something nice, Ethel."

"I don't expect her to know any better, but you should remember, Carlton, that I've never liked the garden flowers anywhere but on the dining room table. In my small bedroom, the sweet smell reminds me too much of almonds." Ethel held out the vase. "Here, take them."

Carlton grabbed the flowers. "I guess I've never paid any attention to the fact that flowers have never been anywhere else." He went to the dining room and set the vase on the table. "I recall you liked flowers in your room when you were a child," he said.

"That was a long time ago. You should throw those out. They'll be dead by morning. I'm going to lie down again."

Amanda walked over to the table, picked up the vase and walked briskly to the back door, letting the screen door crash shut on her way outside. She plucked the flowers out of the vase and threw them in the garbage can. Some of the water from the vase splashed on her new red sweater. Her anger inflamed, she hurried inside and slapped the vase down on the kitchen counter, then ran upstairs and slammed her door.

Carlton raced to Amanda's room two steps at a time just as she collapsed on her bed. "Sweetheart, it was terrible for Ethel to react like that. I don't know where that came from."

"How can I be civil to her when she treats me like dirt? I hate her."

"It has to be a migraine. She refuses even to take aspirin. She needs to see Dr. Olson. I've got to convince her."

"Migraine or not, Dad, you know she's never liked me."

"Ethel's cared for you since you were an infant. I remember many times watching her feed you and rock you back to sleep in the middle of the night. Your aunt loves you."

"Loves me? She took care of me because it was her duty to take care of me the same way it's her duty to scrub the floor on her hands and knees."

Carlton took a deep breath. "I know this is complicated. She has always had a prejudice against Jews. But your mother died, Amanda, and Ethel has been like a mother to you. She's been a mother to me too. She gave up her young life for me, and it's too late now for her to have children of her own. Please try to put up with her idiosyncrasies."

"You're not getting it, Dad. She doesn't love me, she doesn't even like me, and she never liked my mother either."

"Honey, she didn't like the fact that Sarah was the only Jew living in a town full of Christians. Ethel understood how hard it would be for people here to accept Sarah, and she was right. I want to believe that once folks got to know Sarah they would have loved her like I did. If only she hadn't given up so soon." Carlton sighed deeply, almost a groan. "I will never forgive myself for missing the signs of postpartum depression Sarah struggled with before she left us."

Amanda turned her face to the bedroom wall. "What does that mean? Was she depressed because I was born?"

Carlton caressed Amanda's shoulder. "She was happy when you were born. But the responsibilities of taking care of a baby can be overwhelming. It happens a lot, honey. Being rejected by her own parents didn't help. They were very orthodox Jews, kept a kosher house. When Sarah told them we were getting married, they disowned her. She said we had to give them time, that they would one day want to meet their granddaughter, that she knew they would accept me once they met me. You know what? I never even met them."

"You got married in such a hurry because of me. I don't believe Sarah loved me, and I don't know how you can be sure she loved you." Carlton said nothing. In the deep silence, tears ran down Amanda's face. She buried her head in her pillow.

"You're right, Amanda, your mother was pregnant before we got married, she carried you in her womb. But we were deeply in love. I never regretted that you were born. You are the reason I've been able to get up each morning and go on with my life after your mother died."

Amanda listened to her father quietly get up and leave the room without closing the door. She turned her head and stared at the empty space in the hallway where her father had stood, feeling hollow inside. She had never said such a cruel thing to her dad before, and she knew she had hurt him. But she also believed, deep in her heart, that everything she said was true.

Amanda lost track of time until twilight. With great effort, still feeling hollow inside, she slipped out of bed and cautiously walked downstairs. Her dad and her aunt were sitting at the kitchen table when she entered in time to hear Ethel say, "No, no, I don't need to see Dr. Olson. I'm feeling much better now."

Carlton was happy to see Amanda. "Ethel made supper. I didn't want to disturb you so we went ahead and ate. We kept yours warm on the stove."

"I made creamed peas on toast just for you. Come sit down," said Ethel waving her hand over a place setting for Amanda. "I'll dish some up for you."

"Ok." Amanda sat down without another word. She couldn't believe her aunt was being nice.

"I'm sorry I got so upset over the flowers," said Ethel in a brittle tone. The apology surprised Amanda, but she didn't respond. Ethel placed two slices of toast on Amanda's plate then spooned on creamed peas. "You couldn't have known that the smell of flowers in my bedroom bothers me when I have a bad headache."

Keeping her eyes on her plate, Amanda mumbled, "Are you better now?"

Carlton interjected, "She is. Auntie Ethel is feeling much better. She is also pleased to hear that you're coming to work at the office."

Her dad sounded so hopeful. Amanda knew he wanted her to be nice to Ethel so she said with as much warmth as she could manage, "Glad you're feeling better, Auntie."

The next morning, Amanda woke up early. She put on the *Bobbie Brooks* autumn gold skirt and was already seated at the kitchen table reading her American history book when Ethel entered wearing a faded Chenille bathrobe, her coarse gray hair draped loosely around her face, making her look softer and more vulnerable.

In one of Amanda's earliest memories, Ethel wore a similar bathrobe, possibly the same one. Amanda wanted to touch it, rub her cheek against the soft chenille like she used to do when she was little, snuggling in Ethel's lap. Amanda said, "I hope you had a good night's sleep."

"It was adequate," relied Ethel. "I'm behind on my fall cleaning, so I'm going to have a busy day." Ethel's icy response froze Amanda. She got up, grabbed her book and started for her bedroom. Ethel gently added, "You're such a good student, always studying."

Ethel's warmth came too little, too late. Amanda said nothing. She studied in her bedroom until it was time to leave for school and left without eating breakfast. All the way to school, she fretted about the nasty comments she was sure Rebecca would make. How would she respond? Just ignore them? She wished she could hide her feelings better. If she was not embarrassed she wouldn't blush. "I have nothing to be embarrassed about," she kept repeating to herself.

She found Gael waiting for her, nonchalantly leaning his shoulder against the wall opposite her locker. Rebecca primped in the next locker, fussing with her hair in the mirror handgng on the locker door. It looked to Amanda like Rebecca was trying to make eye contact with Gael.

Gael looked at the ceiling until he noticed Amanda and stepped between her locker and Rebecca's. "Hey, you look great," he said softly. "I'll walk you to your class."

"Thanks, I feel great," Amanda replied. She heard Rebecca's locker door slam shut as they walked away.

Gael flashed a crooked smile. "You are the first person in Turtle Creek I've heard say that they feel great. People here always say they feel pretty good." When they reached Mr. Wessel's room, he said, "I'll save a place for you in the cafeteria."

Amanda sailed through her morning classes, even to understanding everything Mr. Wessel said in Algebra, but waiting in the cafeteria line, her heart sank. Gael sat alone at a table on the far end of the room, with nobody seated at the next two tables closest to his. She lifted her chin high and walked to her boyfriend, hoping no one noticed that her hands were trembling. The firmer she grabbed the tray the more her hands shook.

Suddenly, she realized that Ivan Christopherson walked beside her. "Is it okay if I sit with you guys?" he casually asked.

"Sure," she replied, taking a seat across from Gael. Ivan sat next to her.

Gael smiled, almost a smirk, and drawled, "Plenty of room here." Then he solemnly asked Ivan, "How're you doing?"

"Pretty good," Ivan said. He took a bite of hamburger hot dish. "I bet you'd never guess that I actually like English lit now, Amanda. Remember how I struggled with reading? I hated it until you helped me."

"I knew once you caught on you'd like reading. Want to know something funny? Algebra made no sense to me the first week, but now I'm starting to get it."

"If you ever need help let me know."

After her last class, which was band, Amanda hurried to her locker. Gael was there, leaning against the wall, and Rebecca was there, surrounded by her disciples. Suzy blocked Amanda's locker. "Excuse me," said Amanda. Suzy giggled and stepped aside.

"Let's get going," said Gael. "I'll walk you to your dad's office." Amanda threw her books in the locker and they left.

Rebecca practically yelled down the hall as they left, "I wonder what Amanda needs to see her dad, the doctor, about?" Her disciples giggled hysterically.

"Don't pay any attention to them." Gael grabbed Amanda's hand and walked her to Doc MacGregor's office. "I have to get to work," he said at the clinic door. "Can I stop by this evening? Thought maybe we could study together." He wanted to kiss her but squeezed her hand instead.

"That'd be great!" Amanda watched him disappear. Then she entered the waiting room to discover Robert Knudson's dad, wearing bib overalls, sitting in a waiting room chair.

"Hello Mr. Knudson," said Amanda. She approached Mary's desk.

"Why hello," smiled Mary. "How are you, Amanda?"

"Fine. I'm here to help with the office work."

Mary stopped typing and gave Amanda a puzzled look. "I don't really know what you can do. I have a system, and it's not easy to learn." Mary resumed typing, her speed increasing. She looked frazzled, white hair flying every which way, her glasses slipping half way down her nose.

Amanda took a chair, crossed her legs and said, "I'll ask my father what he wants me to do." She picked up *Life* magazine, casually turning the pages. Several times she glanced at Mary, thinking she looked like a nervous bird, afraid that a cat was going to attack her.

Mr. Knudson caught Amanda's eye. "Doc's always so busy. I'm sure you'll be a big help around here."

Amanda smiled gratefully. "I hope so."

Carlton eventually accompanied Mrs. Olafson out into the waiting room. "Thank you, Doctor MacGregor," she said, stopping short in front of Amanda. "What a surprise to see you here," she said, stammering, flustered.

"Amanda's going to help out a couple days a week so that Mary can go home earlier," Carlton said smoothly. "Today's her first day."

"Well then, that's nice," said Mrs. Olafson, briskly hurrying from the office.

"Mr. Knudson, why don't you go into the examining room while I explain what I want Amanda to do? I won't be long."

Mary started talking rapidly. "I like being able to leave early, even though I didn't hear about it until this morning, but I don't know what Amanda could do, other than greet people of course."

"For today, Mary, she can greet people and answer the phone. Down the road, I'd like her to type up reminders for overdue bills." When he saw Mary's deep frown, Doc MacGregor added, "You'll need to approve the phrasing of course before any letters are sent."

"Well, I don't know if it's a good idea to have a teenager sending out bills. It's important there are no typing errors, in addition to the correct phrasing. Certain patients don't like to be reminded about owing money. You know, Doctor, that most of the good people in Turtle Creek pay you what they can."

"Of course. We won't send anything out without first running it by you, Mary."

Mary got up from her desk. "I guess you can ask people to be seated and tell the doctor who is here. Of course, you have to answer the phone too, but there usually aren't many calls this time of day." Mary looked at her watch. "Is it okay for me to leave now, Doctor?"

"Yes, Mary. Thank you." After she left, Carlton whispered, "Mary doesn't like to try new things, but she'll like this change once she has adjusted to it."

"I think I can greet people and answer the phone," Amanda said sarcastically.

"I know you can, sweetheart."

12. Menopause and migraines

Winter came early to Turtle Creek that year and never let up. Harsh winds carelessly tossed biting snow when Ethel walked to the grocery store. She felt like shards of glass were being thrown at her. She only went out to shop when her cupboards were bare. She stopped going to the Lutheran Ladies Aid and the Knit and Purl club because, even when she was feeling well enough to go, she lived in fear that the unbearable pounding and the flashing lights would start during a meeting. Besides, the thought of all the hot dishes made her queasy.

Sometimes, headaches returned after a two weeks' reprieve, sometimes three. The only place she really felt safe outside of her home was in church on Sunday morning. She reasoned that she could lean on Carlton's arm if she felt dizzy, and she knew that the devil couldn't torment her while she looked at the cross above the altar.

Knowing that Ethel's headaches were not going away, in November Carlton insisted that Ethel make an appointment to see Doctor Olson in Carson City. "I really don't think this is necessary, Carlton. I'm sure I'll be fine once Amanda leaves home. It's worry that's causing my headaches." She showed him an article in the *Ladies' Home Journal* about the difficulties of raising teenager girls.

"That may be a factor, but I want you to have a complete physical to find out if there are other problems."

When Dr. Olson asked Ethel to take off her clothes and put on an examining gown, she said, "That won't be necessary, Doctor. I'm perfectly healthy. Carlton insisted I see you because I've had a few headaches. I know the Lord will take care of me." Ethel crossed her arms, clenched her teeth and refused to move out of the chair next to his desk.

Dr. Olson took a deep breath and slowly exhaled. "Can you describe the headaches? When did they start?"

"Just this fall. You know what a headache is like. I lie down until it goes away." Ethel hesitated. "Just before one starts, I see flashing lights and jagged lines, but I know that's the devil tormenting me."

"The devil?" Dr. Olson said, "Tell me more."

Ethel took the neatly folded, coffee-stained article about raising teenagers out of her purse, carefully unfolding it and handing it to him. "I know these headaches are caused by the stress I'm under because Carlton's daughter spends too much time with that no-good Gael Delaney. I'm sure you've heard about him. He's a juvenile delinquent whose parents sent him to Turtle Creek for his senior year because he was kicked out of school in California."

"I haven't heard about Gael Delaney. But I'm sure Carlton is aware of this friendship and he will discuss any concerns he has with Amanda."

"But he thinks she is perfect, and doesn't see the bad things that will happen if Amanda continues to spend time with this hoodlum."

"I understand how this upsets you, but you can trust Carlton's good judgment. I think the headaches might be triggered by menopause, as well as the accumulation of stresses you've had to deal with since you were young. Have your periods been irregular?"

Ethel didn't want to talk about menopause. Her periods were not regular anymore, but she'd heard enough women talking about the problems they had when going through their change of life, and she didn't believe there was anything that could be done about it anyway. She said, "I know I'm going to be fine once Amanda has gone to college."

"We need to talk more about the stresses you're experiencing. Your father's tragic death was difficult. These headaches sound like migraines, and one of the causes of migraines is psychological disturbances."

Ethel didn't like the sound of Dr. Olson's fancy words. "But those things happened long ago. I've been managing just fine all these years, if I do say so myself."

"I'm sure you have, Ethel. However, I'm giving you a prescription for the migraines. As soon as you see the first signs of a headache, take one of these pills. Is there anything else you are concerned about?"

"When Amanda's gone, I'll be fine. The Lord will get me through the next two years."

"Having a strong faith does indeed help us deal with things, however, I want you to fill this prescription. Medicine can also help," he said, handing it to her along with the magazine article.

When Carlton asked later how the exam went, she said, "Doctor Olson told me that my strong faith will help me deal with the headaches." She didn't tell Carlton about the prescription she had crumpled up and stuffed in her purse.

Ethel's headaches continued. She tried to ignore the dancing spots before her eyes, the nausea, the clamminess, the odor of her skin. After several hours of lying still on her bed, with the shades pulled, the pounding would diminish. Any sliver of light made the headaches worse. Even when she didn't have a headache, she was most comfortable in the darkness of her bedroom.

"I'm taking you back to Dr. Olson," Carlton said in December. "He needs to give you a complete physical. I talked with him the other day and he told me you refused to be examined. There are drugs that can help you with the headaches. I could write a prescription for you, but I want to be sure we are not missing something."

"I don't need to see Dr. Olson. I know what I need to do. Bright sunlight seems to trigger the headaches. I just have to lie down in darkness at the first sign of a headache. I can manage until Amanda leaves for college."

That night, after Ethel finished her prayers, she decided to add a postscript. "Thank you, Dear God, for giving me such a strong body that I don't need to see Dr. Olson. He refuses to admit that Carlton's blind spot regarding Amanda is the main problem. I know the headaches would get better if he would simply forbid her to see that Gael Delaney. You know what's best, dear God. I can hang on until she leaves, if that's what you want."

Ethel would often be in her bedroom with the door closed when Amanda came home from school, not because of headaches but because she didn't want to interact with Amanda. When she was up and about, she lacked the boundless energy she once had.

Ethel still kept the house spotless, but she performed her duties in a listless manner, no longer getting pleasure out of the shiny waxed floors or the stiff white shirts she starched and ironed for Carlton.

Amanda seldom returned home before supper because she was either working on the school newspaper or at Carlton's office, which relieved Ethel because, apparently, Amanda was not spending time with that California hoodlum. But it bothered her that Amanda was a reporter, as her mother had been in college.

"No good can come of it," she told Carlton one night, enjoying a second cup of coffee in the dining room when she was feeling pretty good. "I always wanted to be a teacher. It's such an honorable profession, and one a true lady should aspire to."

"I think it's wonderful that Amanda's a reporter," he replied. "We should be thankful that she has the confidence and desire to do this, especially after she found that letter."

The setting sun sent bright rays through the west window into Ethel's eyes. She got up and pulled the drape closed. "Does Amanda ever say anything to you?"

"About the letter? We don't talk about it," Carlton said with a heavy voice. "I'm just thankful that she's keeping up with her school work and enjoys being a reporter." He put on a brave smile. "It's natural for teenagers to want to spend more time with their friends."

"But Amanda's never had real friends, except for Joey. The only kid she sees is Gael Delaney. I don't know how much time she spends with him. She says she's going to the library to do research on Saturdays, but she's usually gone all day."

"Gael may have had problems in California, but I like him. And I've heard only good things about him around town. Mr. Wessel says Gael is by far the best physics student he's ever taught. He gives him extra problems to work on, very difficult problems, because he needs to be challenged. Gael's also a big help to Olav at the station. He's very polite. Every time he's pumped my gas, he always does the windows, offers to check the oil, puts air in the tires."

"Well, I'm glad to hear he's busy. Idleness is the devil's workshop. I still think you should forbid Amanda to see him, instead of encouraging that boy by inviting him to spend time inside our home."

Carlton gave her a stern look. "How can you say that? You don't want Gael in our home? Would you rather have Amanda sneak out to be with him. You worry about her doing it every Saturday. I happen to know that Gael works all day at the station on Saturdays because Olav hasn't been feeling well this winter."

"What's wrong with Olav?"

"You know I can't talk about that. I shouldn't have said as much as I did."

"Everyone but me in Turtle Creek probably knows what is going on with Olav, but never mind."

"You exaggerate the gossip in our town." Carlton was mad. "You're being foolish to get upset when Gael comes here to study. If you didn't always go to your bedroom and shut the door, you would see they're studying innocently at the dining room table!"

Carlton's anger crushed Ethel, yet she couldn't keep from saying, "Maybe so, but what do they do when they walk out to his car, and stay there so long before he leaves. My hearing is very good. I know when they go outside, and how long Amanda is gone. I wasn't born yesterday. The whole town is probably talking about what goes on right outside our front door." Ethel took a deep breath. "And then you let Amanda buy Coca Cola for them to drink when he comes over. I don't like having that in my refrigerator. It rots their teeth, and it stimulates teenagers too much."

Carlton's face turned crimson with anger. "What are you talking about? There's caffeine in Coke, but it's not hurting kids, not in moderation. We consume more caffeine in the coffee we drink every day."

Ethel weakly said, "But what about Amanda's teeth?"

At first, Carlton didn't respond. He stared at the bottom of his coffee cup. Then he looked up and said, "You may have a point. Too much sugar is bad for teeth."

Sensing an advantage, Ethel quickly added, "How I wish you would forbid Amanda to see that boy."

"I'm not going to do that." Carlton gulped the last of his coffee.

"I'm going upstairs to see if Amanda needs any help with her algebra." In the doorway, he stopped and turned. "Ethel, don't you think we've done enough damage to Amanda's self-esteem? I don't want you to say anything more about Gael to Amanda, or to me."

When Carlton knocked on Amanda's door Ethel carefully got up and tiptoed to the bottom of the stairs. She heard Amanda say, "What do you want, Dad?"

"Need any help with algebra?"

"No thanks. Gael's been explaining it to me much better than Mr. Wessel does."

Ethel retreated to her bedroom, lay down on the bed and folded her arms across her chest in prayer. "Dear God, I don't think I could bear another headache right now. Please lift this burden from me. I live in fear that it will come. I can tell no one about the things I see and the foul odor I smell before the headaches come. Dear God, I'm so ashamed. What have I done to deserve this? You judge my actions so harshly. I have always thought you understood why I've had to do the things I've done.

"From now on I will try to ignore the devil when he makes the flashing lights and the jagged lines, and I will wash my body in scalding hot water every day to prevent that odor of rot and decay from coming. I remain, as always, your humble servant, Ethel."

Waves of nausea rolled over her. "Oh no, dear God, don't let the devil torment me," she begged just as jagged lines began dancing on the ceiling and the walls.

13. Mr. and Mrs. Delaney

Amanda enjoyed working at her dad's office, but once in a while, someone would look at her suspiciously, as if they didn't know what she was doing there, which made it hard for her to be cordial. "The doctor will see you as soon as possible," she would say as politely as possible.

She quickly learned the difference between urgent phone calls requiring immediate transfer to her father, and calls he could return when he had time. Amanda was a good typist, which made clearing overdue bills from the slush pile a snap once she drafted a simple, direct form letter. The number of patients owing considerable amounts, some of them years overdue, upset Amanda. Her father approved, though Mary worried the gentle payment due reminder might offend some of the patients.

"Mary," said Dr. MacGregor, "Amanda's letter is not threatening. I like it, and it should be sent. You know I never refuse to see patients who are behind in paying their bills."

Amanda was aware of Mary's jealousy. She wondered if her ability to get work done well and fast made Mary look bad.

When Amanda arrived at the office, invariably Mary would say something like, "Don't touch any of the things I've been working on. It's been so busy, and since I won't be able to finish everything today. I want my desk left just as it is. I'll manage to finish somehow in the morning."

Amanda would usually nod and say, "I'll be careful, Mary." If there were three or more patients waiting to see Doc MacGregor, she couldn't resist adding, "I see how full the waiting room is." Mary would grab her purse out of the bottom desk drawer and leave without a response.

Amanda didn't get to see her dad as much as she had expected. He was always so busy. She came to realize more than ever before just how much people depended on him, which made her feel very proud to be his daughter. As she was instructed to do, Amanda pulled down window shades and locked the front door at five, though often someone with an emergency would pound on the door after closing.

Carlton never finished before six in the evening, sometimes closer to seven. Always, on the way home in his Ford, he said, "Thank you for helping, honey." Quite often, her dad remained quiet for the rest of the short ride. Amanda notice how tired he looked. Until she started working at the office, she hadn't realized how hard he worked, and what a big responsibility it was to be a doctor, with many people every day depending on him to make them feel better.

Amanda earned one dollar an hour, which seemed like a lot of money because girls who babysat only made twenty-five cents an hour. She put her earnings in the top drawer of her bedroom desk. Knowing she had money to spend for special things like Christmas gifts for Gael and her dad, or for emergencies, if ever she had one, made her feel grown up.

G ael and Amanda were inseparable. They met at her locker before school and after, they always ate lunch together, and they studied together a couple of times a week. On the evenings when Gael came to the house, Ethel would retire to her bedroom early, refusing to even say hello. In Carlton's presence, Amanda and Ethel spoke formally, but otherwise they ignored each other.

Gael's uncle Ole wasn't feeling well, so Gael worked most weekends. Amanda knew she couldn't just up and ask her dad what was wrong, but she wondered why Ole went to the doctor as often as he did. She also knew that patient charts were kept in file drawer in the examining room. She didn't have access to them, or she might have looked. Better not to be tempted.

Two weeks before Christmas, it was a Saturday, the phone rang while Amanda ate a late breakfast; ten o'clock and she still had on her flannel pajamas. "Hello?" Amanda answered briskly.

"Guess what," said Gael without even greeting her. "I don't have to be back at the station until four. Let's go to Carson City, have a hamburger and maybe catch a movie."

"When can you pick me up?"

"How about twenty minutes?"

Amanda finished her cereal, left a note for her dad on the kitchen table and ran upstairs to slip into blue jeans and her red sweater. She put some water on her hair to calm it down, and started to pinch her cheeks for color, which she realized she didn't need to do because her cheeks were flushed with anticipation. She grabbed her jacket from the front hall closet and ran outside just as Gael pulled up.

"Hi Amanda, worthy to be loved," he drawled.

"Hey," she smiled, adding breathlessly, "I can't believe we're doing this."

"Ole is feeling better today, and I think he wanted to get out of the house." He leaned across the seat and brushed her cheek with his lips.

"It feels so good to have privacy" she said, savoring the electricity of his affection. "Everyone at school is always watching us, and when you come to study at my house, I always feel my aunt is listening through the bedroom door."

"Yeah, I know what you mean." The strange smile he often had washed across his face. Amanda could never tell whether he was happy or sad when he smiled like that. Gael turned his eyes to the street and took off for Carson City.

Fresh snow, soft and pure, glistening in the sunlight, blanketed the ground. Taking in the beauty of the morning, Amanda said, "This is the busiest time of the year, but everything seems to slow down. Usually when we are together time speeds up. I love knowing that we will have five hours together in this still and peaceful world."

"You're right. This past week at the station, I've noticed more people rushing in and out of the Mercantile, and yet they stop to talk on the street in kind voices."

"I love Christmas. My favorite memory is of Christmas Eve when I was in first grade, when someone my dad called Santa delivered a little typewriter from the Sears catalog. I'd had my heart set on it. I was sure I wasn't going to get one, because we'd already opened all of the presents."

Cruising along the highway, Gael cast a brief, tender look at his girl. "I wish I could have seen that."

"I loved that little typewriter. I would peck out little stories on it about Boo the magical bear." Lost in the memory, Amanda twisted a curl around her index finger. "Auntie was certain the typewriter wouldn't last long, and you know what? She was right. By that summer, the keys were sticking and jamming, so I put it on a shelf in my closet. Auntie wanted me to throw it away, but I couldn't."

"Sometimes the things that are most precious don't last long, but they live on in our hearts."

"That's so true. The broken typewriter is still on that closet shelf." Amanda reached over and touched Gael's arm. "What was your favorite gift?"

Gael concentrated on the road and picked up speed. "I don't have one. Christmas wasn't a happy time at our house."

Amanda kept her hand on Gael's arm, feeling the muscles tighten, noticing his grip on the steering wheel like it had been glued there. Uncomfortable, she didn't know what to say, so she said nothing. She started to gently massage his upper arm, feeling the muscles relax, and then airbrushed his skin with her finger tips.

Gael slowed the car to sixty. "That feels good."

Traffic was heavy in Carson City. Gael slammed on the brakes when a car backed out of a driveway right in front of him. "Sorry," he said. "Let's find a parking space as soon as we get downtown."

"I'll help look for a spot," Amanda said as large snowflakes started to tumble down on the hood of the car. "I can see one a block from Bert's." Gael parked and grabbed her hand. She realized he had no gloves. "Your hands will get cold," she said.

Gael smiled tenderly. "Your hand will keep mine warm. I'll switch sides when my other hand gets cold."

They walked slowly down the length of the street, listening to Christmas music and greetings, and the lingering ring of the Salvation Army bell ringer. They stopped next to the pot-bellied black kettle. Gael let go of her hand, reached into his jean pocket, pulled out a fifty-cent piece and dropped it in the kettle. The coin made a pleasant, tingling sound. "God bless you," said the volunteer.

The ringing resumed as they walked away. "That was a good thing to do," said Amanda, "especially when you have painful memories of Christmas,"

"I don't hate Christmas. I hate what my dad did. He contaminated everything he touched; but I don't want to talk about him." Gael grabbed Amanda's hand. "Let's pretend we both come from normal families. We are Mr. and Mrs. Delaney, Christmas shopping for gifts for our children."

Amanda's heart skipped a beat. "Splendid idea, Mr. Delaney. Let's look at the toys in this window display. We have to find a red fire engine for little Johnny. That's all he wants, but I don't see one here. Do you suppose we'll have to place a special order?"

"I think we should order one from Germany."

"Of course. Only the best red fire engine for our little Johnny."

Gael dropped Amanda's hand and stepped closer to the window to look at an eighteen-inch doll with long, dark locks, dressed in a shiny red taffeta gown. "But what are we going to get for Cathy? Do you think she would like that beautiful doll, Mrs. Delaney?"

Amanda's heart skipped another beat, the way Gael said Mrs. Delaney. "I don't know, dear husband. Cathy doesn't play much with the dolls she has."

"As always, you are right, my dear wife." Gael scratched his head, mimicking concentration. "I know what would be perfect for our little Cathy. I saw one the other day in a catalog, a real typewriter, but for children."

"Of course, Cathy would love a little typewriter. You are such a good father."

"No, I'm not," Gael said, breaking the spell. "I don't know how to be a father." As soon as the words left his mouth, he regretted saying them. He grabbed Amanda's hand again. "I'm hungry. Let's eat."

She squeezed his fingers. "Should we go to Bert's?" Walking the remaining couple of blocks to Bert's, Amanda made small comments about things they saw, trying to cheer up Mr. Delaney. "Oh, look at that man with the long white beard. Do you think Santa Claus is trying to get his own Christmas shopping done?

131

Aren't the wreaths on the lamp posts pretty? All the stores have festooning over their doorways."

Gael smiled sadly, nodding his head as she prattled on. When they got to Bert's, he opened the door for her. "You're so polite," she said. "You have better manners than any of the other boys in Turtle Creek."

Gael wore an amused expression. "Do you really think there's not one other boy in Turtle Creek who would open the door for you?" They slid in the last booth that was available as he said, "You are so sweet, Mrs. Delaney."

Bert's was so noisy they could barely hear each other talking; but to Amanda, all the voices filled with the anticipation and excitement of Christmas were cheerful sounds. She noticed that Gael seemed to enjoy the atmosphere as well.

"Did you know that the first American satellite, Explorer One, is scheduled to be launched from Cape Canaveral in January?" he asked excitedly. "I would like to see Cape Canaveral someday." When they finished eating their hamburgers, he asked, "Would you like to go to a movie?"

"I don't know what's playing, do you?"

"No, but there are two theaters on Main Street. We can walk by both and decide."

Lake Theater had a Christmas cartoon special for children, Bugs Bunny, Daffy Duck, the Road Runner, Felix the Cat and Woody Woodpecker. "What do you think, Mr. Delaney?"

"Look at all the cars double parked to drop off kids, Mrs. Delaney," Gael said. "Johnny and Cathy can attend the matinee while we finish our Christmas shopping."

Amanda's heart did a little flip every time he called her Mrs. Delaney. "Splendid idea, Mr. Delaney. She stopped to look at the cartoons listed. "Who is your favorite cartoon character?"

"Beep beep, beep beep." Gael did his best to imitate the *Road Runner*. "The best made plans to capture him never work."

"He's my favorite too."

Gael grabbed her hand. "Let's go see what's on at the Rialto." The theaters were only a couple of blocks apart. *It's a Wonderful Life*, starring James Stewart, was showing at the Rialto. "I've never seen this, have you?"

132

"I have, but I'd like to see it again. It's a classic."

"Then we should definitely see it, Mrs. Delaney." Gael purchased two tickets.

Leaving the theater after the movie, Amanda asked, "What did you think?"

"Jimmy Stewart is perfect for the George Bailey part. Goodness radiates from him. And Donna Reed is perfect as his wife."

"Is that how Californians analyze movies?" Amanda teased. "I want to know what you think of this story, not how well you think it was cast."

"Well, okay then," Gael drawled. "It delivered a good message. George's life was small-seeming to him, but well worth living, even though his dream of becoming a famous architect was not going to happen. The guardian angel showing him the town being filled with crime if he had not been there to stand up to Mr. Potter, the evil rich guy, is a clever twist." After thinking about it a bit, Gael added, "But you know what? The ending feels fake, too easy a solution to George's problems."

"I know what you mean. How realistic is it that all George's friends lend him all this money to save the savings and loan business? These same people must have lost money when the employee screw-up at the bank led to missing funds. Why was everyone suddenly so generous?"

"It did get one thing right though. Having money solves lots of problems in our world."

"Do you really think so? It doesn't solve my problems."

"It will, Amanda, because your dad having money will make it possible for you to go to college, have a career and leave this town forever if you want to."

"Guess so. You know something else *It's a Wonderful Life* makes me wonder about? My grandpa was president of a bank that collapsed during the Great Depression. He committed suicide in the attic of my house. I wonder, was he a good man like George Bailey, or did he steal money from the bank like people in Turtle Creek think? Aunt Ethel is certain he is innocent, but my dad says grandpa liked to gamble, and that gambling may have gotten him in trouble that led to stealing money from the bank."

"That's hard to live with."

"Ethel thinks it makes our lives in Turtle Creek very hard, but Dad feels that the people in Turtle Creek don't blame us for what Grandpa may have done."

They walked slowly down Main Street. "I know one person I'm sure is a good man like George Bailey, your father."

Amanda picked up speed. "But I do wonder how Dad really feels about my grandpa. Can he respect him if he was a thief? I can't. But then, I can't forgive my mother either, for deserting us, but Dad does."

"Why don't you ask him about what his relationship was like with his dad, what he thinks of him now that he is an adult?"

"That's a good idea," Amanda said thoughtfully. "How can you be so wise?"

"I've had lots of experience." Gael smiled his sad smile before grabbing her hand and giving it a squeeze. "Remember, when you ask him, to be prepared for whatever answer he gives."

"That's why I'm afraid to ask. If he says he respects my grandfather even if he stole from the bank, I will think my dad is weak. Sometimes I think he's weak for putting up with so much after my mother left, especially with Ethel being so difficult at times."

"Amanda, your dad's not weak. You have to be very strong to be able to forgive." Gael stopped and turned her to face him, forcing shoppers on the busy sidewalk to walk around them. "I know, because I can't forgive my dad. It's not what he did to me that's impossible to forgive, it's what he continues to do to my mother. Now that I'm gone, I fear he might take out his anger on her."

Right there on Main Street, with people stopping to stare, Amanda hugged Gael. When they resumed walking, she quietly said, "Why didn't she take you and leave him? It had to pain her to know that he was robbing you of your childhood."

"My dad convinced her that we couldn't survive without him, that the world was so evil that it would destroy us if he wasn't there to protect us, and when he beat us it was for our own good because we had disobeyed him."

"But how could she stay with him after you were sent here to Iowa?"

134

"She was the one who sent me, Amanda. She feared he might kill me when he was in one of his rages. The week before our school was to start, we had a senior orientation day. I got into a fight and the principal called my dad at work. Dad was so angry that he beat me three days in a row, until I felt like a shapeless mass of mater, so Mom called her sister and made the arrangements for me to come to Turtle Creek for senior year."

Amanda couldn't erase from her brain the image of Gael's bruised and battered body. She pretended to look at a window display of brightly colored Christmas decorations. After taking several deep breaths, she resumed walking. "Aunt Ethel heard you were kicked out of school. I hate how the gossips in this town spread lies."

"Yeah, but I know how that started. I had to be pulled off the guy who kept clucking like a chicken every time he saw me. I was suspended for the first week of school."

Amanda was shocked. "I can't imagine you doing that. He must have been tormenting you for a long time."

"He was, but when I lost control like that, I became my father." Gael opened the car door for Amanda. He got in and started the engine. "I worry about my mom there alone with him, but she won't leave. She calls me every Sunday morning from the phone booth by the grocery store. We just talk for a couple of minutes because she only has a few quarters to spare, but at least I know she's okay. He seems to treat her better with me gone."

"What are you going to do after you graduate?"

"I don't know," Gael said. "I'm learning to like your Iowa winter." He revved the motor and turned the heater fan on high. "Enough about my problems. Would you like to go to the park before we have to head back?"

"Yeah, I'd like that." Hope took seed in Amanda's heart that Gael might stay in Iowa. It made her feel so excited that she felt she had to do something. She got out of the car at the park, reached down, made a snowball, stepped back a little and she threw it at Gael, hitting him squarely in the chest.

"Now you're asking for trouble," he laughed, packing a loose snowball to throw at her. He hit her in the back as she ran behind a tree for cover. She bent down to pick up snow and peeked around the tree. A snowball hit her on the head. "Sorry, I didn't mean to do that!" Gael ran to her. "I was aiming for your legs and then you ducked." He started to lightly brush glistening snow away with his hand when the hand behind her back dumped a scoopful of snow on his head. They laughed and hugged, their wet hair in their eyes.

Ice skaters glided on the frozen park lake. They admired them, and then decided to slowly walk down the path next to the lake, their arms around each other.

Amanda felt the strongest, most peaceful sense of well-being she had ever experienced. She wanted to continue walking down the path forever, but they hadn't gone a quarter mile when they realized it was time to turn around and head back to Turtle Creek.

14. Tinsel miracle

Ethel had always loved preparing for Christmas. She gave the whole house an extra scrub and polish before carefully placing Nativity figures and a stable on the dining room buffet. For as long as anyone could remember, she hung a wreath from Peterson Floral outside on the front door and set a poinsettia, also from Peterson Floral, dead center on the dining room table.

But Christmas 1957 was different. Ethel dreaded the work involved to get ready for the holidays, especially decorating a fresh-cut Christmas tree in the living room, which always was done on the Sunday closest to two weeks before Christmas Eve. Carlton and Amanda decorated the tree by themselves that year. Ethel spent Sunday afternoon in bed anticipating a bad headache. She could barely make out the conversation around the tree as her brother and her niece unwrapped ornaments and hung them on the tree without her.

Sunday evening, Gael came to study with Amanda as usual. When she heard the doorbell ring, both temples on either side of Ethel's forehead started to throb violently. She sat up in bed to hear what was being said in spite of her pounding headache.

"It's a beautiful tree and it smells so good."

"Dad bought it yesterday. We still have to put tinsel on the branches. Want to help me?"

"Yeah, I would. We never had a Christmas tree."

"Just as I thought," Ethel muttered vindictively. "He comes from a family of heathens. He shouldn't even be touching our tree."

Monday morning, after Amanda and Carlton left the house, Ethel removed each glittering, silver tinsel strand that took Gael and Amanda over an hour to carefully drape on the branches. Ethel spread them out, one strand at a time, and pressed them between the pages of an old *Look* magazine where she always stored them from year-to-year. After spending most of the morning to finish the task, after she was certain every strand had been removed, she took the old magazine to the attic and placed it on the bottom of one of the ornament storage boxes. Feeling deep satisfaction that the heathen Gael would not be decorating her tree next year, she went downstairs and poured a cup of coffee. Sitting at the kitchen table for the first time in many days, it occurred to her to throw the contaminated tinsel away and buy new. "But that's so wasteful," she mused. "Maybe I can find a way to cleanse the tinsel before we use it next year."

That night, Amanda and Carlton came home from his office later than usual. Ethel had a pot roast with onions, potatoes and carrots cooking in the oven, and had set the dining room table with the good dishes for their supper, something she had rarely done.

"Boy, does that roast smell good," remarked Carlton pushing shut the back door.

"Everything's ready," Ethel said. Pot holders protecting her hands, she pulled the roast out of the oven. "Let's eat. You've had a long day."

"Mondays are always busy. Having Amanda there really helps." Carlton entered the dining room with Amanda. A wooden arch separated the living room from the dining room.

Amanda walked over to the Christmas tree. "What happened to the tinsel?" she asked, her voice shaky.

Ethel cleared her throat and placed the roast on the table with a thud. "I had to remove it. Come and eat now, before supper gets cold."

Simultaneously Carlton and Amanda asked, "Why'd you do that?"

"It didn't look right. I carefully removed it, and of course I saved it. We'll put it on the tree again next year. Sit down now."

"It looked the same as every year. Gael and I worked hard hanging each individual strand carefully on the branches."

Ethel sat down and put a slice of the roast beef and potatoes on her plate. "There's no need to make such a fuss. The tree looks fine without the tinsel." She straightened her shoulders. "It's good to try new things. We have to say grace now, and eat."

Amanda continued to stand by the Christmas tree. "You never like to change anything. I know why you removed the tinsel. It's because Gael helped me put it on the tree."

Carlton took his seat at the head of the table. "You and Gael had done a good job. The tree was beautiful. We need to discuss this more, but right now we should eat."

"I'm not hungry," Amanda said, turning quickly and running upstairs. She slammed her bedroom door. Carlton jumped up from the table. "I'll eat later," he said, heading for the stairway. He stopped and turned around to confront Ethel. "You do understand why Amanda's upset, don't you?" He didn't wait for a reply.

Alone at the table, Ethel carefully chewed her food. "I must eat, even though the dinner doesn't taste good now because of Amanda's tantrum. She'll get over it." Ethel raised her head to stare at the Christmas tree. "I think it looks very nice without the tinsel. I wish Carlton realized why I had to remove it. I must spell it out to him later."

After a few tasteless bites, Ethel got up from the table and carried her plate to the kitchen, setting it in the sink. When Carlton and Amanda came back down stairs, she turned around thinking they were finally ready to eat. Back in the dining room, she couldn't believe what she saw. They were removing tinsel from the *Look* magazine and putting it back on the tree.

"You can't do that!" she screeched. "It's dirty! Don't you realize that Gael Delaney is a heathen?"

"What are you talking about?" Carlton asked.

"I always pay attention. Didn't you hear him say last night that his parents never had a Christmas tree? He's a heathen. He shouldn't be defiling our tree."

"You're being ridiculous, Ethel." Carlton flung a strand of tinsel onto a high branch.

"I'm getting a headache. I have to lie down." Ethel left the meal on the table and went to her bedroom. She knelt on the cold floor, her hands folded in prayer, elbows resting on the bed. "Dear God, please, please don't let the devil possess our home. I know you are stronger than the devil. Why, why can't Carlton see what is happening?" Her head hurt so severely she had to lie down on the bed, pulling her blanket up to her chin. Lacking the strength to remove her clothes first, she stayed that way all night.

In the morning, Ethel refused to set foot in the living room or to even look at the Christmas tree. She noticed that the dishes had been done. What was left of the pot roast was in the refrigerator. Apparently, the devil had given Carlton and Amanda an appetite. The roast was almost all gone and no vegetables remained. She decided that Carlton and Amanda could fend for themselves. She was going to take a cleansing bath and put on one of her clean, faded cotton housedresses.

Soaking in the tub, she decided that 1957 was going to be the worst Christmas ever. She had had a premonition about that tree the moment Carlton brought it into the house on Saturday. "I won't put my gifts under that tree. I won't even go into the living room, and that tree is being removed from the house the day after Christmas."

Ethel would not walk through the living room to answer the doorbell when it rang that afternoon. She listened to it ring three times, and peeked between the drapes of the dining room window to see a child walking away carrying boxes of Christmas cards. "It's just as well I didn't answer it, she thought. I'm not sending out any Christmas cards this year."

Ethel didn't get up early to make coffee again until Christmas. She stayed in bed until the house emptied. It bothered her greatly that neither Amanda nor Carlton seemed to mind making breakfast for themselves. She was furious that they appeared to do just fine without her fussing over them. Carlton would always peek in her bedroom to check on her before he left for work. Sometimes she pretended to be asleep. Other times she would feebly say, "I'm okay, just go tend to your patients. They are more important than I am."

Alone in the empty house, Ethel spent a lot of time trying to decide what she was going to do about Christmas gifts. Of course, she would buy a white dress shirt from the Mercantile, but didn't want to chance running into people who would ask her questions about Amanda. She finally decided to call the Mercantile and ask if a shirt for her beloved Carlton could be delivered to her back door, because she wasn't feeling quite up to her old self. She would explain that she had a bad cold that she didn't want anyone else to catch from her. God would understand why she had to tell this little lie, and would forgive her.

But what was she going to do about Amanda? She really didn't want to buy anything for her. Then she came up with the perfect gift. She would call the jewelry store and ask to have a certificate made out for Amanda, which they could mail to Ethel, stating that Amanda should bring her Bulova watch to the store for a cleaning and polishing. Ethel would wrap the certificate in white tissue paper when she got it. Amanda had been wearing it for three years, and Ethel was sure Amanda wasn't taking good care of it. It looked okay on the outside, but Amanda was a careless girl, kissing that hoodlum in public. Who knew what else she had been doing while wearing that watch?

The Sunday before Christmas, Ethel managed to get up and dress for church. Carlton found her drinking coffee in the kitchen. "It's good to see you up," he said, adding, to Ethel's great surprise, "You look so nice in your Sunday best." Ethel couldn't remember the last time he had paid her a compliment. She also couldn't remember a time when Carlton was as distant with her as he had been since she removed the tinsel. As she walked down the hall she quickly glanced in the living room. The tree did look nice, with the tinsel glistening on the branches.

During the church service she decided that God enlightened her, as she thought he had done several times in the past. She realized that God must have cleansed the tinsel after she took it off and put it between the pages of *Look* magazine. Otherwise, it would not have looked so pretty this morning. She would throw away the contaminated magazine and use a new one when they took the tree down. Feeling one hundred percent better, at the end of the service she walked out of the church with her head held high, holding on to Carlton's arm. Of course, she didn't talk to anyone, and was annoyed when Amanda stopped to chat with Thor's Italian wife.

When they got home, Ethel immediately started to set the dining room table. Amanda said, "Let me help."

"No, I can do it," Ethel snapped.

Carlton grabbed silverware out of the drawer and said, "I think the three of us should do this together."

"Why Carlton, how nice of you to offer," Ethel responded. She decided she could put up with Amanda as long as Carlton was right there. "The tree looks so pretty," Ethel said. "You did such a nice job when you put the tinsel on the branches."

Remembering his broad smile after her remark about the tinsel helped her get through the Christmas Eve service two days later, the gift exchange that night and the holiday meal the next day. Her prayer the evening of December 25th included an addendum to the Lord. "If I do say so myself, Dear God, didn't I do a good job of being civil to Amanda throughout the holiday festivities? Of course, it was done for Carlton's sake. I know my mission on this earth is to take care of my beloved Carlton, even though it is extremely difficult because of his blindness regarding Amanda." She was sure there would be many stars in her crown when she got to heaven, one for each time she was civil to Amanda when she really wanted to scream at her instead.

The following evening, Gael picked up Amanda right after supper. "What would you like to do?" he asked as he opened the door for her.

Amanda settled into the warm car, realizing that she felt deep contentment for the first time since they had spent that day in Carson City before Christmas. She had a package, wrapped in white tissue with a red ribbon around it, curled at the ends. She slipped it between the seat and her door. "I'd like to see what the lake looks like in the moonlight. Let's go to Carson City."

"Great idea." Gael smoothly pulled away from the curb. "How was your Christmas?"

"It wasn't too bad. Ethel even thanked me for the handkerchiefs with the initial 'E' embroidered on, which I found on a back shelf at the Mercantile, gathering dust."

"Sounds like the perfect gift for her. I can't picture her grabbing a *Kleenex* when she needs to blow her nose."

Amanda laughed. "She always has a handkerchief tucked in a pocket of her apron or her housedress."

"Does she always wear a dress?"

"Oh yes. I've never seen Ethel in slacks. The dresses she usually wears are cotton, most of them faded, and in the winter she wears thick cotton hose called snuggies to keep her legs warm." She laughed again, "They're gross, kind of a dead flesh color, and baggy, with lots of wrinkles."

When they got to the park there were no other cars there. Gael slid close to her and got a small box out of his pocket. "Merry Christmas," he said as he handed it to her.

Amanda opened the white cardboard box. Between two pieces of cotton bunting was a gold chain with a heart on it. Amanda tried to read what was engraved on the heart, but there wasn't enough light from the lamp pole by the edge of the lake. Gael said, "Give me a kiss and I'll tell you what it says." She gave him a long, sweet kiss. Catching his breath, Gael took the heart and traced the engraving. "It says 'My heart belongs to you.'" He put the chain around her neck, fastened the clasp, and kissed the tender spot on the hollow at the back of her neck.

"I'll never take it off," she said, reaching down for the gift she had for him. Gael slid the ribbon off the soft tissue. Worried that her gift didn't have the special meaning of Gael's gift, she apologized, "Hope you like it. It just some practical things."

A pair of black leather gloves lay on top of a plaid wool muffler. Gael put the gloves on and slowly wrapped the muffler around his neck. "Every time I wear these I will remember holding hands with you, and your arms around my neck." He removed one glove and caressed the other glove. "The leather is so soft. I've never had anything this elegant." Then he grinned as he said, "But I won't want to get these wet with snow. I'll be defenseless next time you ambush me with a snowball."

"That's my plan," Amanda said, happy that he liked her gifts. She put her arms under the muffler around his neck. He kissed her on the forehead, on the nose, and then he kissed her lips. She didn't want the kiss to end, feeling an ache deep inside as his hands moved from her shoulders to her ribs, to her waist. Then he pulled away. Amanda's voice quivered. "You will never be defenseless. All you have to do is kiss me anywhere to make me melt." She slid closer to him, returning his kiss with intensity, wanting him to continue to explore her body.

Gael ended the kiss, taking a deep breath and bumping open the car door. "Let's walk down our path. I want to test drive my new muffler and gloves."

"I love you, Gael Delaney," whispered Amanda. They walked slowly, arms around each other's waist, their feet and bodies synchronized.

The rest of that winter passed smoothly for Amanda thanks to Gael. They spent as much time as they could together at school. Amanda especially liked Rebecca's newest tactic of ignoring them, looking right through them with a blank stare as if they didn't exist. She and Ethel kept the truce they arrived at during Christmas. When Carlton was home, they were polite to each other. When he was gone, they had little to say. Amanda spent a lot of time in her bedroom. Ethel stayed in bed with a headache for several days at a time every couple of weeks.

Amanda loved working at her dad's office after school two days a week, and on the school paper the other days. If there wasn't work to be done for the *Turtle Creek Trumpet*, she often stayed after school to do some homework in the Trumpet newspaper staff office.

15. Natalie

Spring of 1958 arrived early. The sun's rays seemed to Amanda to be kinder, softer, yet more penetrating than the brittle sunlight of deep winter. They felt cozy, like a flannel blanket. By early April, small patches of snow that remained on the ground turned soft and slushy.

Amanda yearned to spend more time alone with Gael. She wanted him to do more and more when they were necking, to kiss every inch of her body, to touch her in the secret places she had never wanted to be touched before.

One Saturday in mid-April, Gael called. "Want to go to a movie tonight?"

When he came to pick her up, she got in the car, slid over, kissed him on the ear and said, "Let's not go to a movie. There's nothing showing I want to see. I want to park on a deserted country road and feel your arms around me."

Gael squeezed her hand. "Believe me, I want that too. But we need to talk." Gael pulled away from the curb.

"Is something wrong?" Amanda asked. "What do we need to talk about?" Gael rolled down his window. Damp early spring air penetrated her body.

"Don't worry. You haven't done anything wrong." He quickly found a place to park on the edge of town, down by Turtle Creek, and turned off the motor. But he did not take her into his arms. "I need to tell you something, Amanda. You are lovelier than any girl I have ever known. You're beautiful in such a fresh, innocent way. You don't know how beautiful. You also don't know how a girl like you can take over a guy's mind. I have to tell you something that will forever change the way you think about me."

Amanda blurted out, "Nothing you can say will make me stop loving you."

"Please just listen." Gael took a deep breath and let it out slowly, delaying the words that had to come next. He took another breath and in a tight, controlled voice said, "I dated a girl last year. Natalie Andrews. She wasn't at all like you, but she bewitched me like you do. My parents didn't know I was seeing her. I wanted to tell my mom, but didn't because she couldn't keep anything from my dad, and I didn't want him to know about Natalie. I worked that summer at a restaurant we never could have afforded to eat at. Started out washing dishes, but was promoted to waiter after filling in for someone who was sick and the owner liked my work. That's when I first met Natalie and became obsessed with her. She was having dinner with her parents, eating lobster, drinking champagne from her mother's glass, and flirting with me." Gael shook his head, trying to understand how it all happened. "Her parents thought it was cute, their daughter seducing a poor, dumb waiter. Before she left, Natalie gave me her phone number, and for the next two months I spent a lot of time at the Andrews' home.

"I'll never forget the first time I walked up the long driveway to their mansion, just off Rodeo Drive. I felt like I was playing a part in a glamorous movie, and the audience, her parents, loved watching the movie over-and-over. They would have cocktails on the pool deck while Natalie and I swam in their huge pool. They had home theater, and always begged me to stay to watch movies. I couldn't, because my parents thought I was working at the restaurant. I didn't want them to know about Natalie."

"Was she beautiful, Natalie?"

Gael stared out the window. "Not as beautiful as you. But yes, she was very pretty. One afternoon, Natalie's mother asked me if I could come early the next day and arrange to stay longer because they had some business in San Diego. Natalie hated to be alone. So the next day, I called in sick. Natalie was wearing a bikini when I arrived at eleven, a lot more revealing than other swim suits I had seen her wear. She walked up and kissed me. We'd kissed before when her parents weren't looking. I knew she was more experienced than me. When we embraced in the water, sometimes she would pull my hands to places on her body. Well anyway, that day we ended up in her bed."

Amanda's head drooped. She couldn't look at Gael. "Natalie tricked you."

"It wasn't all her fault. I was stupid. I didn't stop to think about the consequences. Natalie got pregnant."

Amanda turned her face away from Gael. "I don't want to hear any more."

"You have to listen. I'll never be that irresponsible again, Amanda. Natalie's parents said I betrayed their trust. They thought it was all my fault. They said they would take legal action unless I promised never to see Natalie again."

Amanda felt dizzy. "What happened to the baby?"

"Her dad came to the restaurant to talk to me. Smog was thick around Los Angeles that day. He said Natalie was going to have an abortion. He wanted money from me. I didn't have much, just some I'd kept from tips. The rest I turned over to my dad. I told Natalie's dad I could give him two hundred bucks. He laughed and said, 'You have no idea how expensive your little fling was, young man. I'll be back tomorrow for the money." I felt like worthless scum. The next day, he came for the money. He said, 'If you ever try to contact Natalie again, you'll be sorry!' I didn't want to see her again anyway. I felt relieved that the nightmare was over. But now, when I think about it, I feel sick inside."

Amanda reached out and put her arms around Gael tenderly, as if comforting a child. "Thank you for trusting me enough to tell me this. I understand why you've been trying so hard to be responsible, and from now on I'll do the same."

It wasn't easy for Amanda. She was ready to give herself freely to Gael. She wanted to be his, and at times, before she drifted off to sleep, she fantasized about Gael kissing every inch of her body.

Graduation day grew closer. Gael turned moody. "I don't know what to do," he said one day in the cafeteria a couple weeks before graduation. "I need to go back to Los Angeles to see how Mom is doing." He reached across the table and brushed Amanda's arm, his touch lighter than the wings of a lingering moth. "I wish I could take you with me."

"I wish I could go with you," she said, "I want to be wherever you are, always."

That night, sitting on the front steps after finishing their homework, Gael said, "My mom didn't call last Sunday, or the Sunday before that. I need to get home right away. I'm leaving on Saturday."

Amanda panicked. "But you can't go yet."

"Don't worry. I'll be back as soon as I can. Olav is letting me take the car."

"You've made these plans without talking to me. It's not fair to run off like this! You're my life." Amanda had never felt so badly betrayed.

"I'm sorry. I wanted everything in place before I told you. I'm taking two final exams early." He put his arms around her. "Please, please understand. I have to go. When I called home Sunday night my dad answered the phone. All he would say was that Mom was sick, and couldn't come to the phone. He didn't even ask how I was doing, or when I was coming home."

"Maybe your mother just has the flu. She's probably better now."

"She has never been sick. No, something is going on there. I have to go."

"Call her right now, from here. Dad will let you." Amanda was desperate.

Gael looked frantic. "I called from the phone booth by the station before coming over. No answer. Frieda called after supper and no one answered. Amanda, I have to go."

"We only have one more day. We have to spend it together. Let's skip school."

"I have two finals to take. Besides, you'll get in trouble if we skip. Your dad would be furious."

"No, he won't. He'd understand. Let's skip," Amanda begged. When she saw the look of despair on his face, she said, "I know we can't ... I know."

"We'll be together tomorrow night."

Amanda sat alone on the step after Gael left wondering how she was going to get through the next day, the next month What if Gael didn't come back to Iowa? When she finally went inside, she went directly to her bedroom, but couldn't sleep.

Gael couldn't eat lunch with her the next day because he had to take one of his exams. Amanda spent the afternoon in a trance, unaware of time passing until the bell rang at the end of each period and she walked to her next class dazed.

At the end of the school day, Gael met Amanda at her locker.

"I've got to run down to the station to change oil in my car and get ready for the trip."

"I'm going with you. *The Trumpet* will have to manage without me today."

"I know how hard this is for you," Gael said. "Believe me, it's just as hard for me." He took her hand. "I'll write you as soon as I know what's going on in California."

"But we've got tonight, don't we? Don't say goodbye yet."

They walked to the gas station hand-in-hand. "Prolonging this isn't going to make it easier. In fact, it will make it harder. I'm thinking I should leave tonight."

"What?" Amanda silently watched Gael lift the hood and change the oil.

When he finished, he wiped his hands on a shop rag and sighed. "I'm all packed. Everything's in the trunk. Let me drive you home."

Amanda got in the car, tears welling in her eyes. "You knew all along you were going to do this," she sobbed.

Gael stopped in front of her house, reached over and held Amanda in his arms. "I am not worthy to be loved," he said. "You are the best thing that's ever happened to me. I wish I could have been more direct." He released her. "I thought I was trying to make it easier for you, but I know now I was really trying to make it easier for myself."

"When will I see you again?"

"I promise you, I will do all I can to be with you. I don't know how or when, but it will happen." Gael's goodbye kiss filled Amanda with sadness and longing. A big hole in her heart filled with silent tears, the kind of tears that never dry up because the sorrow can't be released. "I'll write you as soon as I get to California."

Amanda watched Gael's car disappear down the street, continuing to stare long after he'd gone.

16. Love letters in flames

Ethel knelt on the bare floor next to her bed. "Thank you, Dear God, for answering my prayers! Now that that California hoodlum is gone, our lives can return to normal. I realize, because I have always been very perceptive regarding how others are feeling, that Amanda is miserable right now. I know that you want me to do what I can to cheer her up. But it will not be an easy task. She has always been rebellious, a trait she inherited from her mother. Her mother. I will never understand what Carlton saw in Sarah. Of course, I realize men have needs that women don't have, but I can't imagine how my dear Carlton allowed those physical needs to get the best of him when it came to Sarah. I remain, as always, your faithful servant, eager to do your bidding."

Well satisfied with her nightly supplication, Ethel got into bed and drifted off into the most peaceful sleep she'd enjoyed in months.

After Gael left, Ethel quickly grew frustrated. She found it nearly impossible to talk to Carlton without Amanda listening nearby. She also had misgivings about Amanda working fulltime over the summer at Carlton's office. "I'm convinced he's creating work for her, little jobs to just to keep her busy," she muttered over morning coffee. "That has to be driving poor Mary crazy. How can she get any work done with Amanda there, looking like a sad Cocker Spaniel because her boyfriend is in California? Amanda no doubt depresses everyone who comes in. Maybe Carlton could create a job in the storeroom, dusting off old files or scrubbing the floor. Hard physical work is just what Amanda needs now." Ethel sipped lukewarm coffee. "Carlton's a saint to spare me her daily misery," she mused.

Amanda sulked at the supper table, casting gloom over Ethel's meals. "I'm not hungry, Dad. Can I be excused?"

"I'm worried about her, Carlton," Ethel interjected. "Amanda, you're not eating enough to keep a bird alive," she said in what she was sure was a kind voice.

"I said I'm not hungry!" Amanda snapped, poking at her untouched plate with a fork.

"Ethel, please don't nag her. We had a big lunch at the Chat and Chew." said Carlton. "Sweetheart, you're excused."

Fuming, Ethel gathered dishes and began washing them. "I must talk to Carlton tonight. I'll stay up until Amanda goes to bed."

Father and daughter had grown closer. Besides working in the same office all day, summer evenings allowed them to take long walks together before returning to the living room, sitting together, reading the newspaper, magazines and books. Carlton always stayed up until Amanda went to bed. From her room, Ethel could hear Carlton and Amanda's conversation, though they usually didn't say much.

Amanda finally went upstairs at 11 p.m. When Ethel heard Amanda's bedroom door close, she intercepted Carlton before he reached his bedroom. "I need to talk to you about Amanda."

Carlton suppressed a scowl with a crooked smile. "Let's do this in the kitchen, that way we won't disturb her."

Ethel rested her elbows on the kitchen table and folded her hands together. "Amanda needs our help to get over that boy, that Gael Delaney." She could barely spit out his name. "What does she do at your office all day?"

"She runs errands, gets the mail, picks up lunch at the Chat and Chew when I don't have time to leave the office. She's organizing the files in the storeroom, typing up my notes. If I can ever convince another doctor to join my practice, they'll be able to read my notes now."

This was the first time Ethel had heard about Carlton's interest in bringing a second doctor to town. The news offended her. *What other secrets is he keeping from me?*

"I've sent a notice to medical schools around the Midwest, but so far no inquiries about coming to Turtle Creek. We're a small town, but that doesn't stop my medical practice from growing. Even with Amanda's help, we have trouble keeping up."

"I'm not sure it's a good idea to have two doctors in town," she said, "but we can discuss your practice another day. I have some ideas on how we can help Amanda."

152

"I'm glad to hear you're concerned. She misses Gael a lot. She's been talking a lot about him on our walks. He's a fine young man. I know they're young, but I hope it works out for them."

"You know the chances of her ever seeing him again are slim. Instead of encouraging her to talk about him, I think we should find something else to talk about."

"And how do you propose we do that?"

"Why, by finding something new for her to do."

"That's what I'm doing at the office, Ethel."

"I know you're trying, but she needs more physical work. She could scrub and polish the floors in all the rooms once a week, and wash and iron the curtains and throw rugs? They will have to be replaced sooner because they will fade faster, but it is money well spent. You will keep Amanda's mind from wandering to thoughts of that boy." Ethel stopped to catch her breath. A wonderful idea came to her. "And I will teach her how to wash and iron properly. She needs to learn those skills before going off to college."

Carlton shook his head and smiled broadly. "She gets plenty of physical exercise on our daily walks. If that's not enough, she walks when she runs errands. It won't be necessary for her to be scrubbing floors and ironing. Besides, Mary's sister cleans the office every Saturday afternoon."

Why was it, Ethel wondered, that whenever she felt great pride in an excellent plan, Carlton rejected it? She would go from feeling on top of the world, like a balloon floating freely in the sky, to getting a sharp pin prick, which deflated her, sending her crashing to the earth. She cleared her throat in disapproval. "Mary's sister is getting old. Are you sure she's doing an adequate job?"

"I'm sure, Ethel. The best thing you can do for Amanda is to be kind to her."

"I know that, Carlton. I'm really trying. But she's always so sullen. When I compliment her she barely mutters a thank you, and without looking at me." Ethel was exasperated. Carlton didn't get it. "Sometimes she ignores me completely, like I'm not there, even when I've given her a compliment!"

"You know why that is, don't you, Ethel? If you could find it in your heart to realize that Gael Delaney is a decent kid; if you would let her know you've had a change of heart about him, and about her; if your attitude improved, even a little, your relationship with Amanda would improve five hundred percent."

Ethel knew she could never change her opinion of Amanda's indecent obsession with Gael Delaney. She also knew she could never convince Carlton that Gael Delaney was a hoodlum. So she just nodded her head and said, "I will try harder," believing that God would forgive her for the little lie she just told.

In mid-June, the first letter from Gael arrived. Ethel would never forget it. She had worried that Gael would try to contact Amanda. Ever since he left, she'd watched like a hawk every day for the mailman. Then her fear materialized. There it was, a standard size white envelope addressed to Amanda in careful block letters. Ethel did not hesitate for one second. She grabbed the box of kitchen matches out of the cupboard and walked briskly outside to her flower garden. In a back corner of the perennial bed, she dug a little hole with her fingers, tore the envelope into tiny pieces without opening it, and struck a match. The letter quickly turned from threat into ashes. Then she smothered the ashes with rich, black soil and compacted it with her heel.

"I need to wash my hands," she stammered, not so much concerned about dirt under her fingernails, but instead to purify her hands after touching the evil letter. She filled the kitchen sink with scalding hot water and submerged her hands until she could no longer stand the heat, then rubbed them with homemade lye soap and rinsed them again in hot water. She repeated this until the water had cooled.

The next morning, Ethel felt like her old self. She woke early, eager to begin the day. When Amanda entered the kitchen for breakfast before work, Ethel already had egg coffee perking and oatmeal cooking. "It's good to see you up and about," Ethel said, pouring coffee into Amanda's cup. "I'm so sorry that you have had to go through so much. I know it was hard to have Gael Delaney leave." Ethel drew a cautious breath. "Your father says that he was very smart."

"He is very smart."

Ethel knew that Amanda looked at her with utter shock because this was the first time she had said anything remotely nice about that hoodlum. Suddenly, she realized it might be useful to do this more often. No harm could come of it because Ethel was doing everything in her power to make sure Amanda would never hear from him or see him again. "You look nice today. You're so lucky to have natural curly hair. And how pretty your brown eyes are," said Ethel, thinking all the while that her niece had the sad eyes of a cocker spaniel. "I agree, Amanda, Gael is smart, and so are you!"

That night, kneeling in prayer, Ethel asked God to forgive her for the lies she had told. She knew God understood, but she wanted to be sure that He knew that she knew.

Ethel found that lies improved Amanda's attitude, which improved her life immensely. She started lying at supper, making up conversations, like one in which she implicated Gunnar Larson. "Oh, Amanda, I was buying groceries today and Mr. Larson told me that he really misses Gael Delaney at the gas station because Gael evidently knew so much about fixing cars."

"What was wrong with Gunnar's car?" asked Carlton.

Fearing her brother deliberately intended to catch her in a lie, she stammered, "I don't remember exactly what he said the problem was."

Carlton knocked on Ethel's bedroom door that night after Amanda went upstairs. "Come in," she said, pleased to see Carlton.

"I just want to tell you, Ethel, that I'm really happy that you're trying hard to be kind to Amanda. She's having a hard time. We both have to continue to do all we can to help her. Even her appetite is improving, judging by how much she orders for lunch at the Chat and Chew."

"Are you sure you can afford to spend all that time off eating?"

Carlton laughed. "Actually, it's good for me to take a break. Amanda and I are having good conversations about college and career plans."

"What about Mary?"

"Mary eats at her desk like she always has. She watches the office, answers the phone, seats patients. If an emergency comes up, she calls the Chat and Chew. With Amanda working late, Mary gets to go home early in the afternoon, or to do whatever she likes. Amanda takes over at the office."

"Isn't that foolish to allow her to take off early? I hope you're not paying for time off."

"Mary has worked hard for many years. I would never reduce her salary because she is not working as many hours this summer."

Ethel didn't sleep well that night. Daily lunches at the Chat and Chew bothered her almost as much as the thought of Amanda discussing college and career plans with Carlton did. "Amanda evidently has an appetite at lunch but barely touches the food I slave all day to prepare for supper!" She decided to phone Mary at home the next afternoon, sure that Mary could not possibly be happy with what was going on.

Mary answered right away with a cheerful greeting. "Hello?"

Ethel said, "I just called to see how you're doing. It must be hard for you to have Amanda at the office all the time."

"You know what? I love having so much time off every day. I've been watching *As the World Turns*. Do you watch it, Ethel?"

"What is it?"

"It's a soap opera. It's on TV every afternoon."

"Well, we don't have a TV. Carlton has said many times that he'd like to get one, but I'm sure I'd never have the time to watch it, especially in the middle of the day."

"Sometime I'll tell you more about it, but it's on right now, so I have to say goodbye."

Ethel hung up the phone. "What is this world coming to? Oh well, I can't let this bother me. I have much work to do."

After Gael Delaney left town, Ethel had only one headache and it lasted just a few hours, not a few days. She took that as a sign. She was defeating the devil, with God's help of course. As always, she kept the house spotless and her flower bed meticulously weed free. Every day, down on her hands and knees, she examined the garden and ruthlessly uprooted any tiny weeds. That felt so good.

Another letter from Gael arrived on a Monday at the end of June. Ethel repeated the earlier ritual of tearing up the unopened envelope and burning it in the garden. She felt more uneasy the second time because Amanda had repeatedly asked if any letters from Gael had been delivered. Ethel would say, "I didn't see any letters addressed to you," convinced she wasn't lying because she had only looked at the envelope, not the actual letter.

A few days later, a third letter arrived. Ethel decided the time had come for extreme measures. She again destroyed the letter without reading it, but this time she jotted down the return address in California. And that afternoon, she carefully penned a letter to Gael in handwriting that could have passed for Amanda's. It was brief and to the point.

> *Gael, I've decided it is best for me never to see you again. Do not write any more letters. I will just destroy them without opening them. Amanda.*

Ethel examined the fraudulent letter carefully. "It does look like her hand writing, if I do say so myself." She folded the page and put it in an envelope with no return address. Then she walked to the post office and mailed the letter. Indescribable satisfaction washed over her as she slipped Amanda's letter into the mail slot.

17. Sweet Daisy

Gael's departure of course left Amanda feeling numb and friendless. The only person she could talk to was her dad. He understood how much she missed Gael. When Ethel started saying nice things about him – after he had gone – she felt slightly less alienated, but Ethel was still Ethel, and Amanda could barely speak to her. Days filled with chores at the office helped take her mind off Gael, and so did eating lunch with her dad. Still, she couldn't understand why Gael hadn't written. Did he make it to California? Was he okay? What was going on between his dad and mom?

During one of their evening walks, she said to her dad, "I'm worried about Gael. He hasn't written. What if something bad happened to him on the way to California?"

"Honey, there is a simple way to find out if Gael made it safely. Why don't you ask his aunt if she's heard from her sister?"

"I couldn't do that, Dad. I can't drop in and tell her I need to know about Gael when I've never even said hello to her before."

"Call her then, and tell her you're worried about Gael. Frieda is a kind woman. I'm sure she'll tell you what she knows."

Amanda started walking faster. "Gael will write. I know he will."

Technicolor visions of Gael's mangled body trapped in a crushed car on a deserted highway in the desert began to torment Amanda. First she lost her appetite, then she couldn't sleep.

Early one evening, Carlton said, "Sweetheart, you've got dark circles under your eyes from fretting over Gael. Now, we're a block away from Frieda and Olav's house. Let's walk over there together."

Amanda stopped. "I'm afraid to."

"When I have to do something I'm afraid to do, I ask myself, 'What is the worst thing that could happen?'"

"But that's just it, Dad. What if Gael's aunt says that something terrible happened to him?"

"I don't think that is likely, sweetheart, but even the most terrible news is better than not knowing. It's hard to go on with your life when you don't know."

"But Dad, that's what happened to you. You don't really know how Mother could have deserted us. But you went on with your life."

"Yes, and that's why I believe it's so important for you to talk to Frieda."

"Oh, Dad!" Amanda hugged him. "All right, let's go to Frieda's."

When they arrived at Frieda's house, Carlton asked, "Do you want me to go to the door with you?"

"No, I can do this by myself. You go on home." Amanda walked rapidly to the front door and knocked. The door opened quickly, as if someone had been watching. There stood Frieda wearing a faded cotton housedress, just like the ones Ethel wore. Her tightly permed hair sat like a pincushion on top of her head. Amanda was certain Frieda had probably been to church every Sunday, yet she couldn't remember ever seeing her before. "You don't know me, but I'm a friend of Gael's."

"Amanda MacGregor," said Frieda. "I'm so glad you stopped by. Ever since I heard the news, I've been meaning to talk to you."

"News about Gael? Is he all right?"

"He's fine. Why don't you come in and sit down? I'll do my best to explain." Frieda ushered Amanda into the living room, gesturing for her to sit on a large sofa. Frieda sat in a straight chair across the room. "You and Gael spent a lot of time together. You need to know what's happened."

Amanda perched on the edge of the sofa. When she realized she was nervously rubbing her hands together, she folded her hands and rested them on her lap. She leaned closer to Frieda. "Did he have an accident? Is he okay? Did something happen to his mother?"

"Evelyn's okay. In fact, she is feeling very good now that Gael is home. This isn't bad news, Amanda, but it may be hard for you to hear." Frieda cleared her throat. "I don't know where to begin. Did you know that Gael had a girlfriend in California?"

"He told me about a girl named Natalie."

"Did you know she had a baby? Gael is the father."

Amanda couldn't speak and barely managed to shake her head *No.*

"Gael's parents didn't know either," Frieda explained. "They didn't even know about Natalie until her parents showed up at their home in a gold Cadillac with Natalie and the baby in the back seat. Evelyn said that she and Bill were very upset at first to learn that Gael was a father, but the baby – it's a boy – looks just like him. Evelyn said Natalie's parents seemed like nice people; they obviously have lots of money, but they raved about Gael and seemed genuinely thrilled to meet his parents. Naturally, they hoped that Gael would want to do the right thing, marry Natalie and raise his son. They said they wanted to help Gael and Natalie get a good start, and would pay for Gael's college education."

Amanda wanted to cry and laugh at the same time. "He's going to marry her?"

"Evelyn says that Natalie is very sweet. As soon as she knew she was pregnant, she knew she wanted to keep the baby. She loves Gael very much. She's thrilled to have Gael back in California. And Gael is happy to be a father. They're getting married in August." Frieda paused to give Amanda a chance to respond. Amanda's eyes remained glued to her knees, so Frieda nervously continued. "Evelyn couldn't get over the fact that Gael's dad wasn't furious. Bill has a temper. But once he saw that the baby was the spitting image of Gael, and Natalie called him Billy, Bill accepted Natalie. I've never known Evelyn to be so happy."

Amanda, sick to her stomach, started for the front door. "I can't hear any more."

"You must try to be happy for them," said Frieda. "Gael has a wonderful opportunity now by marrying Natalie." As Amanda was going out the door, Frieda added, "Amanda, you have so many opportunities also, being a doctor's daughter."

Amanda slammed the door. She didn't know where to go, but she wanted to run away and never return. After sprinting until she couldn't breathe, Amanda walked blindly up and down side streets, putting one numb foot slowly in front of the other. She stumbled through dim-lit neighborhoods long after the sun sank in the sky. Dark, heavy air closed in on her. She felt a hand on her shoulder and screamed.

"Amanda, I've been looking everywhere for you!"

"Dad!" Amanda fainted in her father's arms. She came to on the examining table in her dad's office, her blouse was loose around her neck and her head slightly elevated. Carlton sat beside her. "Do you want to tell me what happened?" he asked.

"No."

"Okay. Just lie there as long as you need to."

Amanda lost track of time. When she finally sat up, her dad was at his small desk writing patient notes. "Dad! Gael's getting married to his old girlfriend Natalie; he has a son."

"What?"

"According to Frieda, everyone is thrilled, even Gael's awful dad, because his girlfriend Natalie's parents have tons of money." Tears ran down her cheeks. "Gael's mother says the baby looks just like Gael."

Carlton cradled Amanda in his arms, gently rocking her back and forth as she sobbed. "Honey, I know it's hard, but it's important that you know this."

Amanda buried her head in his shoulder. "Gael said I was the best thing that ever happened to him," she moaned. "Why didn't he have the guts to let me know he's getting married?" She raised her head. "I know he doesn't love Natalie. Everything he told me, Dad. It couldn't all be lies."

Carlton continued to hold his daughter, tears streaming down his cheeks. "I'm sure he meant what he said. But he had to go back."

"I've got to talk to Gael, Dad. I want to call him. Shit, I don't even have his phone number!"

"We can get the phone number from information, but let's talk more about this before you call."

"He's being forced into the marriage, Dad. Natalie tricked him. Gael told me he felt terrible about getting her pregnant. Natalie's dad wanted money from Gael to help pay for an abortion! Gael felt awful. He was always so careful that we didn't go too far. He loves me!"

"Having a baby complicates things, Amanda. Maybe it's best to not contact him right now. He'll write you once his life settles down. The Gael we both know would do that." Carlton held her tight. "I know it's hard, but you need to honor Gael's decision."

"But he doesn't love Natalie! How can marrying her be the right choice?

"Give him a chance to explain why he's done what he's done." Carlton took a deep breath. "You know that most people will say he is doing the right thing by marrying Natalie."

Amanda broke away from Carlton. "No!" She slid off the exam table and bolted for the door. "I hate how calm you are. You're not helping at all. I'm not you! I can't just go on with life after being betrayed."

"Hold on, young lady. You're all worked up again. No more fainting spells. Let me drive you home."

"I don't ever want to go home again. I hate this town. I'm sure Frieda has told everybody about Gael's baby. Everybody is laughing at me."

"I know how hard this is for you, honey. I believe Gael will write you, just as he promised, and maybe you'll have the closure I never had."

Amanda hated Turtle Creek and everybody in it more fiercely than ever, including her dad. "He is so weak," she fumed, alone in her bedroom "I don't want a dumb letter from Gael begging me to understand why he married Natalie. How could that help?" Walled in behind her anger was the hope that if Gael never came back for her, at least he would have the decency to write.

The next morning, Carlton knocked on Amanda's door. "Time to leave for work, sweetheart."

"I'm not going to the office with you anymore," she announced. "You don't need me there, and I don't want to be there."

"Amanda ..."

"... leave me alone!"

For the next three weeks, Amanda stayed in her room. She read *War and Peace*. Getting lost in Tolstoy's world helped her, but she couldn't stop hoping that Ethel would bring her up a letter from Gael. After *War and Peace*, and still no letter, she stopped listening for Ethel's footsteps after the postman delivered the mail.

Ethel became Amanda's servant, cooking her favorite foods, carrying meals on a tray to her room. Ethel went to the library for Amanda to get the books she requested. Daily, Ethel brought fresh flowers to Amanda's room, which only fueled Amanda's anger and deep sadness. She knew Ethel was only being considerate because she was overjoyed that Gael was gone forever, forever out of her life. She refused to let the flowers stay because she cried when she looked at them.

Despite Ethel's best efforts in the kitchen, Amanda had no appetite. One evening, Ethel tried to spoon feed her. "You have to eat something."

"This hot dish is too salty. I can't eat it," Amanda said after one bite. Ethel brought a new dish. Amanda took several bites, but refused to eat more. "Take it away."

When Carlton got home from work, he always went first up to her bedroom. "Let's take a walk, honey. Please?" he begged.

"Not today." Amanda felt like her legs wouldn't hold her up if she tried to take a step.

Carlton tried to engage her in conversation. She gave minimal responses to his questions, usually just saying either yes, no, or I don't know, unable to make eye contact. When he gave up trying to talk to her, she was glad she wasn't looking at him because she could hear the defeat in his voice. She had no desire to do anything except wait for as long as it took for Gael's letter to arrive.

During Amanda's reclusive period, Ethel fussed the most on Sundays because her niece refused to go to church. Amanda vowed she would never set foot in Saint Olaf Lutheran again, even though there was a new minister. Her dad would tell her how good his sermons were, and how he was very open minded. Amanda was curious, but she knew everyone would stare at her like she was a freak. "I won't go. Stop asking." Every night before sleep, Amanda took a long hot bath, steaming, soaking, visualizing

Gael seeping out of her pores. "I need to get rid of him," she muttered. Exhausted, she slept without dreams.

One evening toward the end of July, it was so hot and humid she couldn't bear the thought of punishing herself with another hot bath. Instead, she took a cool shower. Wide awake, she looked out her window with longing as the sun slipped below the horizon. Remembering the spotlight tag she and Joey used to play, she decided to take a walk. She slipped on some shorts, a blouse, and tennis shoes.

Downstairs, Carlton stood in the archway to the living room. "Change your mind about taking a walk? It's cooling off a little. Mind if I join you?"

"I need to be alone," she said, brushing past him rudely on the way out. Amanda remembered, when they played spotlight tag, how the front steps used to be the prison. Feeling freer than she'd felt since Gael left, her mind speeding, she headed for the creek without slowing down. "Got to figure out how I can get through the next year. He didn't have the decency to write. Everything he said about me was a lie. I'm never going to be such an idiot again. Never!" When she got to the creek, she tore off the locket Gael had given her at Christmas, tossed it in the water and watched it sink. Part of her wanted to grab the locket before it disappeared into the muddy bottom of Turtle Creek. "How could you lie like that? You said your heart belonged to me."

Stumbling blindly along the creek bank, she eventually ended up at Joey's house without realizing it. Yellow light shone through the screen door. She saw Daisy folding clothes on the worn wood table in the center of the room that served as kitchen, dining room and living room. Amanda watched Daisy a long time before hesitantly walking up to the screen door and gently knocking.

Daisy looked up. "Why Amanda! How good it is to see you. Come in, come in."

Amanda didn't speak. Time passed in a blur. Daisy gently patted her arm. "Let's sit. Would you like a glass of ice tea?"

Amanda nodded and sank into a soft, well-worn sofa. Daisy poured two glasses of tea, handed one to Amanda and sat in an old wooden rocker close to Amanda. She didn't say anything, just rocked slightly, slowly, back and forth and sipped ice tea.

Humid July air wrapped itself around Amanda, almost smothering her. "My life's been smashed to pieces." She took a long sip of chilled tea. "Somehow I've got to pick them up and glue them back together. I don't know how to do that."

"What happened, Amanda? Do you want to tell me?"

"I'm sure you've heard all about Gael and me."

"I knew you were friends, but I don't pay attention to gossip. If I did I wouldn't have been able to survive in this town." Daisy reached out and caressed Amanda's hand. "I've discovered that I can turn my back on the winds of gossip. They come and they go, empty words. Most people, once they stop blowing hot air, are decent."

"I don't have the energy to worry about what people think. Gael broke my heart. That's all that matters." Amanda sat up straight. "He probably knew he was getting married before he left. Did you realize that he took off before graduation? I should have suspected something when he left in such a hurry. Why didn't he have the guts to tell me the truth about the baby? I didn't realize until just tonight that I could hate someone as much as I hate him," said Amanda in an icy voice.

Daisy got up and sat next to Amanda. "Gael is marrying the mother of his baby?"

"Yes." Amanda said with brittle finality. "How will I ever be able to trust anyone again?"

"I know from my experience, that in time you will realize there are many people you can trust." After a long silence, Daisy added, "I know that sounds easy to say, but it's true. You're wise to know that your job now is to pick up the pieces and glue your young life back together."

Amanda stared at the floor for a moment then raised her eyes and spoke with authority, "There's nothing I can do about Gael."

Daisy smiled. "Probably not, Amanda."

After a long silence, Amanda smiled back. "Can I ask you something else? Did you know that my mother abandoned us, me and Dad?"

Daisy got up and started pacing. Amanda had never seen her look so uncomfortable. "I know your dad wasn't happy for a long time after Sarah left. He didn't smile for ages unless it was at you.

Sarah's family disowned her, you know, when she married your dad." Daisy stopped pacing and faced Amanda. "Shortly after your mother left, your Aunt Ethel came to the Red Owl one morning right after I opened for the day. I was surprised because Ethel usually shopped at the other grocery. There was no one else in the store. She said to me, 'I have a favor to ask.' Ethel had never been friendly to me; always very formal and superior. 'I have some bad news. Carlton believes Sarah went to New York to care for her ill mother.' I told her that I'd heard. 'Well,' she said, 'I just received a letter from Sarah's father.' Ethel unfolded the letter and handed it to me. 'The day she arrived in Buffalo, Sarah took a walk. She was hit by a car and killed.'" Daisy's eyes got big.

"Ethel told you this? Why you?"

"I asked her that exact question. She looked me square in the eye and answered, 'Daisy, you're not a gossip. You see almost everyone who lives in Turtle Creek at least once a week. I'm entrusting this important information to you to pass on.'"

"In the form of gossip!" shouted Amanda. "Gossip ruined Ethel's life, and she was using your good nature to destroy my dad's life!"

"Amanda, Sarah had decided to file for divorce from your father before she abandoned you and went back east. And if that wasn't enough to destroy your dad's life, his in-laws didn't notify him about Sarah's funeral until after she was buried. That's what the letter was about, her decision to leave Turtle Creek and her sudden death crossing the street in Buffalo. I'll never forget the last paragraph. Sarah's father wrote it, and it was shockingly cold. He stated that he understood you'd been born and that Carlton was your legal guardian. I'll never forget his hideous ending statement. 'Sarah's mother and I want nothing to do with you, Carlton, and nothing to do with the baby girl.' I handed the letter back to Ethel in a state of disbelief. Ethel said Carlton had asked her to destroy it, which she intended to do, but she felt that it was important for the people in Turtle Creek to know the truth."

"What about me? Nobody told me the truth, not Ethel, not my dad, not you! I found by accident last fall that my mother didn't want me in her life. She never wanted a baby in the first place!"

"I'm sorry, Amanda. I always thought you knew. That morning at the grocery, Ethel promised me, "Of course we'll tell Amanda

167

the truth when she is old enough to understand the truth.' I remember asking her, 'Are you sure you want me to tell people that Sarah left Turtle Creek to get away from Carlton and Amanda?' She buttoned up her coat. 'I want you tell people that Sarah was struck by a car and died. As for the rest of it, use your best judgement. I know I can trust you to explain what happened. If it came from me, people would believe I was making it up out of spite. Everyone in town knows Sarah never belonged; I never trusted her.' On her way out of the store, Ethel turned and said, 'Carlton would be furious if he knew I showed you this letter. He needs to get on with his life, not constantly be reminded of Sarah's unfortunate death. Please ask people to avoid reminding Carlton of this tragedy by expressing condolences. Yet he needs sympathy. My brother is a doctor. His job is to heal others, not to worry the good people of Turtle Creek with his personal problems. Ask people to be especially kind to him.' Ethel leaned toward and whispered, 'Lord knows, only through the process of healing others will Carlton be healed. I will take it upon myself to care for Amanda and raise her as a good Christian.'

Amanda wore an expression of sorrow tinged with disgust. "Be especially kind? Daisy, I started hearing awful rumors about my mother when I was in first grade."

Daisy bowed her head. "Amanda, Ethel was right about one thing, I never spread rumors. You're the only person I've told about that letter. I thanked Ethel for her trust, but explained I would only bring up Sarah if someone asked. No one ever asked, so I never said a word. Somehow the story spread like wildfire all over town.

"Ethel."

"She didn't come back to the Red Owl again for many weeks, and when she finally did, she was distant, like she always had been, like she didn't know me, like she had never shown me the letter."

"You know what haunts me most? It's that Sarah rejected my dad and me before she died. I think Ethel made her life miserable when she was here, and drove her away."

"How did you learn about this?" Daisy stopped pacing and sat next to Amanda.

"I went up into the attic where my grandpa hanged himself. I found a trunk covered in dust, opened it. Inside, there was my mother's wedding dress and some other clothes, and a letter she wrote to Dad. I know Dad had carefully wrapped the dresses in tissue. It broke my heart. But I was mad too, and confused, because he had always pretended that my mother loved me."

Daisy said softly, "Don't judge your father too harshly."

"I know he's never stopped loving Sarah." Amanda paused, remembering word for word the letter her mother wrote. "You know what? I'm going to visit my mother's grave in New York. I want to meet my grandparents. They can reject me if they want to, but I have to try."

"You need to discuss this with your father."

"You're right, I do." Amanda got up. "I feel somewhat better. Thank you."

Daisy walked Amanda out. "Please come back often. I miss the days when you and Joey played here."

"How is Joey? I haven't seen him for ages."

"He's busy. Can't come home much. He has a job in a lab at the university during semester breaks and summer vacation. The rest of time, he plays basketball."

"How do you stand not seeing him?" Amanda searched Daisy's face. "Don't you miss him terribly?"

"He writes me weekly. The letters are my lifeline." Daisy gave Amanda a wide, warm smile. "I've taken the bus to Iowa City to see him play several times this year. I'm so happy for him, Amanda. He will graduate in two years with a degree in chemistry and not much debt thanks to basketball."

"What does he plan to do?"

"Joey hopes to get a grant to do graduate work. He's not sure if he wants to be a pharmacist or do research." Daisy hesitated, then said, "You know, he often asks how you're doing."

"It would be good to see him. I knew he'd do well in college. He's so smart, so organized." Amanda tried to keep the sadness out of her voice. "Joey was like a brother when we were kids." She looked at Daisy's silhouette in the screen door. "I'll talk to Dad and let you know my next move."

Summer rain fell lightly on Amanda as she walked home, "Fairies dancing," she whispered, "Each satin drop soft as a dream."

A man walked toward her carrying a big black umbrella. Amanda was not surprised to make out her dad's handsome face under the streetlight. "Wanna share?" he asked.

"No, Dad, the rain feels so good."

Carlton folded the umbrella and lifted his face to the sky. "You're right, it feels good," he said, falling in step beside her.

"Dad, I want to go to Buffalo. I want to see where my mother grew up, and I want to try to contact her family."

"Sweetheart, your mother's family refused to have any contact with us years ago. I've long hoped they would have a change of heart and contact us. But I haven't heard a word from them after your mother's dad wrote to say she'd been buried. They don't want to have anything to do with us."

"Then at least I can see her grave, Dad. We could go together You've never taken a vacation. Who knows, maybe they'll talk to us. What if we just showed up at their door? Maybe they have mellowed with time."

"Slow down, honey. If any of your mother's relatives want to see us, they know how to contact us. There's a good possibility that her parents are no longer alive."

Amanda bent her head down and walked rapidly ahead without saying another word. When she got home she went directly to her room.

Carlton knocked on her door an hour later. He handed her a slip of paper. "This is your grandparents' address. Why don't you write them? Tell them you want to meet. If they agree, we'll go to see them."

Amanda broke into tears and hugged him. "Thank you, Dad."

18. *As the World Turns*

Ethel stared through her bedroom window at the garden. After Carlton told her that Gael Delaney was engaged to be married in California, she had slept very well. Ethel did something she had never done before, she spontaneously opened her arms and raised them in benediction. "I lift up my hands to praise you, dear God, for answering my prayers in the best possible way. I can hardly imagine the good to come from this. The devil incarnate, Gael Delaney, is no longer a problem. As you know, I continue to do all I can to help my niece Amanda. If she becomes a lifelong recluse, I will care for her to the end of my days, ensure that her daily needs are met. You are all wise. I am thankful she's kept herself chaste. I pray she will continue to be clean. Lord, I have one small request. Will you change her heart regarding the bouquets I bring to her room daily? As you know, my garden has never been more beautiful, but she refuses my flowers. I realize that once a heart is hardened you cannot change it, but I also know it is my duty to try to cheer her up with fresh flowers. True, I have never liked the smell of flowers in my own bedroom, too cloying, like almonds, but Amanda loves the fragrant blossoms. I believe flowers could brighten her outlook if she would let me leave them in her room."

Ethel lowered her gaze to the bright colors that stood out: the sunny yellow day lilies, blue, purple and white bachelor buttons, and the deep pink, velvety hollyhocks. "Your creations are glorious, dear God. Thank you for all you've done to answer my prayers. Your faithful, and if I may be so bold as to add, joyful servant, Ethel."

Ethel enjoyed eating breakfast and supper while Amanda brooded in her room. Carlton was talkative during meals, which warmed her heart. He thanked her daily for demonstrating patience with Amanda. "This is a difficult time for her. Your care is excellent, as always, and your cooking is delicious, even if Amanda doesn't want to eat."

"I'm glad you're happy. At least we know Amanda is safe in her room, not out running in that boy's car."

"Yes, well," Carlton stammered. "What about you?"

"What about me?"

"You haven't had a bad headache for a while now. But you work so hard. I'm just concerned, is all, that you don't overdo it taking care of Amanda. We don't want to bring one on."

"I get plenty of rest. I always get my nap in, and I have only had two headaches so far this summer." Ethel paused, debating if she should say what she knew he would want to hear. "The next time a headache starts, if you feel it would help, I'll take one of your pills. After all, you're the doctor," she smiled, knowing God would forgive her a small fib if she later decided not to take medication.

Carlton never mentioned his walk in the rain with Amanda, or that he'd urged her to write her grandparents in New York. But after she visited Daisy in August, he began spending a lot of time in Amanda's room each evening. Ethel would stand at the bottom of the stairs, straining to hear what they were talking about. But they talked so quietly, she only heard bits and pieces. One evening she clearly heard Amanda say, "New York."

"New York," Ethel repeated with alarm. "What's going on now?" It wasn't long afterward, a couple of weeks before school started, that Carlton bought a television set and Amanda left her room on Saturday night to watch the *Lawrence Welk Show*. Alarmed as ever, Ethel started talking to herself. "Can this be a good thing for Amanda? Somethings they did on that show are morally questionable! I have to admit, however, that the Lennon sisters seem innocent and ladylike. And that Lawrence Welk is a real gentleman." Still, she worried about Amanda. Sunday, before church, she took breakfast on a tray up to Amanda's room only to discover the room empty. Ethel hurried downstairs shouting, "Carlton, Amanda's not here."

Carlton wasn't upset. "She went to visit Daisy. It's Daisy's only day off."

"Do you think this is wise? Amanda should be going to church, not visiting with someone who never attends church."

"Ethel, I'm glad Amanda's getting out again. When she's ready, I think she'll attend church. In my opinion, Daisy is a better influence on her than many of the church faithful. You know I'm right."

"Better eat while the food's warm," Ethel said as she sawed off a huge mouthful from a stack of pancakes and chewed vigorously.

Initially, the television frightened Ethel. She was concerned about wasting time watching all the foolishness on TV. At first, she only watched the *Lawrence Welk Show*, which she had to admit she found uplifting. But a few weeks after they got the TV, Carleton suggested, "Next time you're at the store, why don't you buy some frozen TV dinners. We could watch the evening news while we're having supper. Won't that be fun?"

Ethel put her foot down. "Fun? Eating in the living room, fun? What is the world coming to?"

"Ethel," Carlton chuckled. "Please?"

Ethel reluctantly purchased half a dozen assorted TV dinners, but they stayed in the freezer. Then, one afternoon, she tuned into *As the World Turns*. "For heaven's sake, why did Mary think this was so wonderful?"

Deciding it was her duty to give *As the World* Turns a try, Ethel brought her lunch into the living room the following afternoon and watched the popular soap opera while eating a bologna sandwich, apple and a cup of coffee off of a green metal tray decorated with brightly colored flowers. These were the same fancy trays she served desert on when she hosted the Knit and Purl Club. Balancing the tray carefully on her lap, she relaxed when Dan McCullough announced, "And now, for the next thirty minutes, *As the World Turns*."

"Thirty minutes?" she complained. "The radio soap only lasts fifteen minutes, and I can be scrubbing the floors or putting together a hot dish while listening to the radio. She took a bite of sandwich and watched skeptically. Against her better judgement, the psychological study of families headed by legal and medical professionals hooked her from the start, a rare guilty pleasure for Ethel MacGregor to watch the Hughes family deal with personal and professional problems. More than once, Ethel felt like a window peeper into the fictional lives of the residents of Oakdale,

Illinois. But most of the time, she was grateful to get the inside scoop.

Adultery and other immoral behaviors did not go unpunished, which she approved of. She also loved the slow pace, like real life, when actions and consequences take time to unfold. The intricate plot twists and turns taken by the core family fascinated her. Best of all, in the end, justice always prevailed, just as it had with Amanda. "Hopefully she has learned her lesson after her foolish, improper behavior with that Gael Delaney."

Ethel held her head high whenever she walked downtown to shop. People would stop her to ask how Amanda was doing. In her kindest voice, Ethel liked to say, "I'm so worried about the poor girl. It's a lot of work to take care of her, but I do all I can. I bring her meals up to her bedroom because she is so ashamed of what she did. She can't leave her room. I pray to God daily that He will forgive her for refusing to attend church."

Rebecca Nelson's mother went so far as to say, "You are a saint, Ethel. You've had so many difficulties, but this has to be the hardest of all."

"Why, thank you," replied Ethel, thinking that that was the nicest thing Mrs. Nelson had ever said to her. She glided through the rest of the day. "If Mrs. Nelson thinks of me as a saint, no doubt everyone else in town must feel the same way."

19. *The Trumpet*

The first draft of Amanda's letter to her New York grandparents ran more than 800 words. She showed it to her dad. "I think the message will be more powerful if you can keep it as simple and direct as possible," he said with a loving hug.

The next night, when Carlton came to Amanda's room to talk, she read a revised letter. "I cut it to a hundred seventy-one words.

> *"Dear Mr. and Mrs. Rosenthal. My father has always loved your daughter very much, so she must have been a wonderful person. I would like to know more about her. What was she like as a child? What were the traditions and beliefs of her religion? Why did she choose to attend the University of Wisconsin? I would like to see where she was born and where she is buried. I am enclosing a recent picture of me. I will graduate from Turtle Creek High School this coming spring. My senior year will be challenging and exciting because I am the editor of our school newspaper, the Trumpet. I plan to attend the University of Wisconsin and major in journalism. I have always loved to write. My father says that I remind him of my mother, both in my looks and my personality. If you will write me, we can begin to get to know each other. I can't tell you how much this would mean to me. Sincerely, Amanda MacGregor."*

"That's my girl," said Carlton. "I think it's perfect."

Amanda showed the letter to Daisy, who read it out loud so Amanda could listen to how it sounded. "What do you think?" asked Daisy.

"I like it," replied Amanda.

"I do too."

The next morning when Amanda showed up in the kitchen early, Ethel asked, "Why, my goodness, what are you doing up and about?"

"I'm going to mail a letter."

"You can leave the letter here for the mailman to pick up."

"I'd rather take it to the post office. Besides, I want to go for a long walk."

"May I be so bold as to ask what's so special about this letter?"

"It's personal."

"My dear child, I hope you're not writing to that Gael Delaney."

"I'd rather not talk about it." Amanda felt good walking to the post office. But when she slipped the letter into the slot, for a brief moment, it was hard to let go. She worried about how the Rosenthals would react. Then the concern passed. She dropped the letter, walked to her dad's office and approached Mary. "When my dad has a free moment, I'd like to talk with him."

"It's good to see you, Amanda. I'm sure he can talk with you as soon as he's finished with his patient. How have you been?"

Amanda smiled, knowing Mary probably knew all about why she stopped coming to the office. "I'm good, Mary. Thanks for asking." Amanda thumbed through *Life* magazine until the patient her dad had been seeing left. Mary arched her eyebrows in the direction of the exam room.

"Hi sweetie," said Carlton when Amanda poked her head into the room. "Did you mail the letter?"

"I did, but I'm scared about what could happen. I'll feel more rejected than I already do if they want nothing to do with me."

"It's good that you have the courage to face this, Amanda."

"I'm glad you said it was okay to put your office as the return address. Ethel was so snoopy about me going to the post office. It's none of her business."

"I respect your need for privacy, but you can't blame Ethel for being curious."

"She thinks I'm writing to Gael. She can just stew over that."

"Is it okay if I tell her not to worry about the letter?"

"Yeah, I suppose. I know I shouldn't be mean to her."

"No you shouldn't. Ethel loves you. So what are you going to do for the rest of the day?"

"I'm going to stop in at the Red Owl to say hi to Daisy. Then I thought I'd make an appointment for my graduation picture."

"That's a good idea. When school starts, you'll be busy. You're editor of the *Trumpet* this year. Have you thought about what you want to put in the first issue?"

"I have some ideas. Maybe I can run them by you sometime."

"That would be great, sweetie. I have to get back to work now. Thanks for stopping by." He gave her a brief hug. "I'm so proud of you."

Several people greeted Amanda on her walk to the grocery store. They acted genuinely glad to see her, asking with sincere concern in their voices how she was doing. She couldn't remember people being so friendly before, not just walking down the street. They probably know about Gael, she thought. They're trying to show me that they care. It made her feel good inside.

At the Red Owl, Amanda found Daisy on her knees unpacking a crate of Campbell's soups and stacking them on a shelf near the front of the store. "Guess what, Daisy? I just mailed the letter," she said.

Daisy put her index finger to her mouth and whispered "Hush," just as Mrs. Nelson walked to the checkout counter. Daisy hurried to the cash register. While Mrs. Nelson paid for her groceries, Amanda pretended to debate which can of soup she wanted, Cream of Mushroom or Cream of Chicken?

Mrs. Nelson walked past. "Why Amanda, it's good to see you out and about. Your aunt's been worried sick about you."

Amanda made eye contact. "I'm fine, Mrs. Nelson."

"That's good to hear because you're going to have a demanding senior year, editor of the school paper and all."

"I know. I'm making arrangements today to have my senior picture taken before school starts. At least that's one thing I won't have to think about when September gets here."

"Are you having it done locally?"

"Of course. My father says we should support the businesses in our town, and Bjornson's Portraits does good work."

"They do take an adequate picture. But you only graduate from high school once. Rebecca will have several poses taken, wearing different outfits, at Golden Memories Photographic Studio in Carlson City."

"It's not that big a deal to me."

Mrs. Nelson started to leave, then turned to look at Amanda. "I hope things work out for you this year, Amanda. You know that being editor of the *Trumpet* is a big responsibility."

"I welcome the challenge, Mrs. Nelson."

After Mrs. Nelson left, Daisy hurried over to hug Amanda. "You're going to have a great year."

Amanda began helping out mornings at Carlton's office as a pretext for checking the mail. One afternoon before school started, she borrowed her dad's car to shop for new clothes in Carson City. She bought a long-sleeve white blouse and a straight, dark wool skirt that she felt made her look professional. She also bought a pale blue sweater to wear for her graduation picture. One morning, she expectantly knifed open mail from a stack larger than usual, sorted the letters and passed them to Mary. At the very bottom of the huge pile, she discovered her letter to the Rosenthals stamped, "Return to Sender, Address Unknown". Amanda stared at the envelope, unable to touch it, wanting to pretend it wasn't there. Finally, she picked it up and headed to the front door.

"Mary, I have to go."

"Thanks for sorting the mail," called Mary.

Amanda hurried out of the office and started walking blindly once again to Turtle Creek where she promptly ripped up the letter and tossed pieces in the slow-moving water one at a time, each shred floating for a moment before sinking to the bottom.

When Carlton came home after work, he raced up the wooden stairs and knocked on Amanda's bedroom door. "Sweetheart, you there?"

"Come in," she said in a muffled voice, her face buried in a pillow.

Carlton sat on the edge of her bed. "Mary told me you left suddenly this morning after sorting the mail. Did you get a letter from Buffalo?"

Amanda turned her tear swollen face to Carlton. "Not the letter I wanted. Mine came back marked 'Return to Sender'."

"How stupid of me to think Sarah's parents would still be at an address from seventeen years ago."

Amanda sat up. "We need to do some detective work to find out where they live now. Do you think the librarian knows where we can get a Buffalo phone book?"

"First of all, honey, we can't assume they're still alive. Sarah's mother was forty-two when Sarah was born. She'd be in her eighties."

"Did Mother have any brothers or sisters?"

"I know so little about your mother's family." Momentarily lost in thought, Carlton finally said, "She had an older brother, Aaron. We could also try to find his address, but I'm not so sure we should. Sarah's family has never tried to contact me." Carlton's voice had a bitter quality Amanda hadn't heard before.

"We don't have to do anything if you don't want to, Dad. But you told me it's better to know the truth, no matter how painful, than to spend your life wondering."

"Honey, I've been thinking a lot about your mother since I gave you her parents' address. I have to admit that Sarah's mind was made up She left not long after you were born. I was away at a medical conference in Des Moines. To come home and find out she'd gone to New York was a staggering blow. I felt guilty. I've always wondered whether she would have stayed if I'd been there helping her care for you. I left her alone to adjust to a small Midwestern town far from her family and community. I should have seen the signs. I was too busy putting all my energy into being the best doctor I could be to see that your mother was so unhappy, so alone."

Amanda realized that she was opening old wounds. "Dad, I don't have to pursue this. I don't need confirmation that her relatives want nothing to do with me. I need to get on with my life? I need to think about something else besides Gael."

"School starts next week. You'll have lots to think about. Besides the demands of senior year and being editor of the *Trumpet*, you'll need to decide soon about which colleges to apply to."

"I want to go to your alma mater, the University of Iowa. You're right, I have a lot to focus on this year. I want each issue of the Trumpet is the best it can be."

Making the first issue of the *Trumpet* the best it could be turned out to be a big job. Assigning stories to reporters, ensuring they met deadlines, editing copy, each step took a lot of Amanda's focus and time. At the end of September, as publication of the first issue neared, Amanda stayed after school for several hours every night. She had to supervise a staff of 48 students from grades 10, 11 and 12.

Once the *Trumpet* was distributed, Amanda was anxious to hear what kids thought about it. Unfortunately, the first remark she overheard came from Rebecca Nelson talking to Suzy.

"Did you read Amanda MacGregor's dumb editorial about the differences between large and small schools?" she asked loudly, the pair walking a few steps behind Amanda to their first class. "Who does she think she is? Lecturing the administration about the lack of accelerated courses? Lecturing seniors, that if they easily keep up with their assignments, we should do extra work to better prepare for college? Our school doesn't prepare us for college? Amanda's always thought that she's better than everybody else."

When Amanda had heard all she could take, she turned around, clutching her math book tightly to her chest. "You must not have read the whole article, Rebecca. The emphasis was on the great opportunities for students in a small school, especially the individual attention kids in big schools don't receive from teachers with large classes."

"I wasn't talking to you." Rebecca lifted her chin and marched into her homeroom with Suzy.

Unable to move, Amanda suddenly wondered if anyone who had read her editorial liked it? Other students stared at her. She couldn't enter the classroom. The first period bell rang. Amanda slowly walked to the room with business machines where the *Trumpet* was typed and reproduced. She sat at the editor's desk staring at a large green mimeograph machine stained inky purple. She suddenly hated that old, temperamental machine. So much work went into publishing the school paper. First, she had to edit the articles written by reporters. Then the work of typists and stencil-cutters had to be checked. A final proof edit, the next step was very important. That first issue, Amanda had to be right there making sure that the mimeograph machine was working properly.

She then oversaw stapling all seventeen pages together to make sure pages were collated properly and that they lined up correctly without leaving anything out, which happened quite a bit.

So much work. Writing, editing, typing and assembling. Did anyone appreciate it? Did they even read her editorial pointing out both the advantages and disadvantages of small schools? Her dad had read it and approved. The *Trumpet* faculty advisor, Mr. Olson, told her it was excellent. The next eight months were going to be difficult and long. How would she survive when she couldn't even put out a paper the students liked? Amanda got up, left her books on the desk and walked out. Classes were underway. The hall was empty. She passed Principal Johnson's office, where the door was always open.

The secretary, Mrs. Williams, looked up wearing a worried expression. "Amanda, where are you going?"

Amanda ignored her. She left the building. Cool fall air chilled her. Shocked by how easy it was to walk away from school, Amanda had no idea where she wanted to go, just that she needed to get out of Turtle Creek. On the east side of town, she walked along the shoulder of a blacktop road. A car whizzed past.

"I could step in front of a car and end it all," she muttered. "But what if I didn't die? What if I ended up paralyzed and had to be taken care of by Ethel for the rest of my life? Ugg."

Amanda moved off the road to the upper edge of the grassy ditch. An approaching truck stopped. Ivan Christopherson's dad rolled down the window. "Everything okay, young lady?"

"I'm ok. Just needed a walk."

"Aren't you Doc MacGregor's daughter? You should be in school. Not skipping class, I hope?" He leaned over and opened the door. "Let me give you a ride back to town."

Amanda felt the warmth of a blush. She realized Ivan's dad would immediately tell her dad if she refused a ride back to school. "Thank you," she mumbled.

Mr. Christopherson dropped her off at school. She noticed he didn't drive away until she entered the building, which she did, walking straight to the principal's office, her stomach churning over what she would say.

The principal's secretary looked up. "I called your aunt. I

worried you were ill. She called back later and said you had not come home. So I called your father. He's very upset." Mrs. Williams looked at her watch. "I'll let them know you're back. I'm sure they're worried sick. You do realize you've been gone for almost an hour without permission?"

Mr. Johnson appeared in his office doorway.

"Amanda, what's going on? Come on in." He gestured for her to step inside. She entered. He closed the door and sat behind his big desk, crossed his arms and waited for her to speak.

"I don't want to be editor of the *Trumpet* anymore," she blurted out. "It's a lot of work. Besides, all I heard about the first issue was how awful my editorial was."

He lifted his hand and rested his chin on it. "I read the first issue last night Both the content and the format really impressed me, Amanda. As for your thoughtful article, I thought it was outstanding. Good job. Now, what exactly did you hear?"

"Rebecca Nelson said my editorial was a dumb lecture. She said I was critical of the administration for not offering advanced placement courses. But I wasn't, Mr. Johnson. Just because I suggested kids do extra work to prepare for college doesn't mean I think our school doesn't do a good job. We have a great school."

"I'm glad you think so, Amanda. You're living proof of that."

"Rebecca said I think I'm better than everybody else."

Mr. Johnson leaned forward and clasped his hands together. "I'm not offended by your observations. Students need to be challenged to do more. And believe me, I know that a small school can't offer all the courses a larger school does. But can you see how a student might misinterpret that to mean that our school isn't good enough?"

"Rebecca has always hated me. She's always trying to find fault with anything I do."

"What comments have you heard from other students?"

Suddenly embarrassed, Amanda realized she had probably overreacted. "I haven't heard any other comments," she said, her eyes focusing on a pattern in the linoleum.

"Would you like to hear what I've heard?"

"I guess so."

"Several students said that your editorial made them think. Made them think! That's one of the highest compliments a person can give after reading an editorial. Amanda, you asked students to write to the editor with suggestions, comments or complaints. That really impressed me. This is the first time we've put a box in the commercial room for letters to the editor of the *Trumpet*."

Mrs. Williams knocked on Principal Johnson's door. "Dr. MacGregor is here."

"Please come in, Doctor."

Carlton leaned down and hugged Amanda. "Sweetheart, you scared me. I asked Ethel to go out to find you. I wondered if I should report you missing to the Sheriff. I'm glad you're safe." He took a deep breath before he added, "Where've you been?"

Amanda stared at her shoes. "I'm sorry, Dad. I was upset about a comment Rebecca made, so I didn't go to class. Mr. Christopherson picked me up on the blacktop and gave me a ride back here." She looked into her father's eyes. "I've decided to tell Rebecca that I understand how the written word can have different interpretations and thank her for her comment about my editorial. Her comments will help me to express myself more clearly."

"That's a good idea," said Carlton with a quizzical smile for Principal Johnson.

The second period bell rang. "I'll give you an excused absence for the first period, but you, young lady, had better get to your next class."

20. Buddy Holly

Ethel slumped over the kitchen table, head resting on her arms, lips moving in angry pantomime.

"Amanda always finds ways to bring disgrace to the family, just like her mother. The whole town knows she cut class and walked away from school. Thank God she's back in class, but I'm upset because Carlton expected me to roam the streets to find her. Carlton knows the whole town would pity me just like when dear Daddy died. Thank goodness Carlton didn't call the police."

Amanda pushed open the back door. "Auntie? Are you having another headache?"

Ethel painfully lifted her swollen eyes to meet Amanda's worried expression. "What do you think you're doing? The whole town is talking about you again. You're an embarrassment!"

"So what if they are? Who cares about gossip? I skipped first period. Big deal!"

"People gossip when the town doctor's daughter is truant! I want to know why you skipped class," Ethel demanded.

"I was upset, Ethel, if it's any of your concern. Rebecca made a snide comment about my editorial in the *Trumpet*. I cut first period to get some air. I talked to Principal Johnson. He excused the absence. Dad was there. My first period teacher gave me a make-up assignment that's due tomorrow. I'd better go up to my room and finish it."

"If you want to know the truth," Ethel yelled as Amanda rushed upstairs, "Principal Johnson wouldn't let any other student off. You don't know how lucky you are, Amanda, that your father is so well liked and respected." Ethel moved slowly, groping a cupboard door open. She grabbed a handful of chocolate chips from a canister and shoved it into her mouth, tasting metal. She muttered to herself, "A bad headache is coming. I should take one of Carlton's pills. I don't want to be bedridden when he gets home. I want to know exactly what Principal Johnson said."

Ethel stood at the kitchen sink peeling potatoes when Carlton came home. "How was your day, sister?" he asked, intentionally more cheerful than usual. He hoped to avoid any discussion of Amanda's behavior.

Without greeting him, Ethel turned and poked the air with a wet paring knife. "I've tried so hard to be a good mother to Amanda. Why does she continually humiliate me?" Deep in her heart, Ethel believed she'd been a better mother than Sarah ever could have been.

"Ethel, Ethel," Carlton scolded, waving for her to put down the knife. "This is not about you." His voice sank with deep sadness. "No one is judging you for what Amanda did this morning. She realizes she shouldn't have left school without permission. She's a good girl, a good student and a hard worker. Principal Johnson understands why she left. He and I had a good talk after Amanda left his office. She's editor of the school paper, Ethel. She's an honor student."

Ethel set her knife on the counter. "If Amanda is so smart, why did she leave school when she was supposed to be in class? Everybody knows you can't do that."

Carlton sat at the kitchen table. "She was upset. Rebecca said something nasty, as usual, about her editorial."

"Well, getting upset is no reason to be irresponsible. She can't run away from nasty comments." Ethel sat down. "Where did she go?"

"Mr. Christopherson picked her up on the blacktop east of town. Look, Ethel, Amanda is exhausted. Putting out the first issue of the *Trumpet* took a lot of work. She wasn't thinking clearly. She discovered the truth about her real mother, Ethel. Then she lost her boyfriend over the summer. You've been a loving aunt, but Amanda is going through a phase of missing her mother."

"What exactly are you saying, Carlton?"

"I'm saying, Ethel, it's fortunate that Mr. Christopherson found her walking out there and drove her back to school. I repeat, she wasn't thinking clearly" Carlton rose slowly out of his chair. "Is she in her room? I'm going to tell her how proud I am she's decided to take the high road and thank Rebecca for her comment."

Ethel attacked the remaining potatoes with a vengeance. "How can he be proud of her? I thank God that next year at this time she will be gone from our lives!" Peeling too fast, Ethel cut her thumb, a slip-up that rarely happened. She stared at the bright red blood streaming out of the wound. The sight of her own blood made her feel sick. A long-buried memory quickly surfaced, a memory of blood on clean white sheets after her father left her bedroom the first time. She forced the memory back to the deepest part of her mind, taped a Band-Aid on her thumb and resumed peeling potatoes.

Amanda's senior year passed quickly. Autumn turned into Thanksgiving, then Christmas. Ethel was unprepared for gift giving. Fortunately, what Amanda wanted was a portable phonograph she could use in her bedroom until it was time to take it to college in the fall. Carlton would buy that. The phonograph seemed like a foolish expense to Ethel, but she decided to save her energy for the big battles, relieved that at least she did not have to shop for her ungrateful niece.

Naturally, the compact phonograph in the pink and blue case thrilled Amanda. "This is one of the best gifts I've ever received, Dad!" she squealed. "It definitely ranking right up there with the typewriter Santa gave me in first grade." She spent most of Christmas vacation in her room listening over-and-over to a recording by Buddy Holly.

On New Year's Day, Carlton was reading the newspaper in the living room, Ethel knitting in her chair, Buddy Holly singing in Amanda's bedroom a refrain that had imprinted itself in Ethel's memory: *That'll be the day when you say goodbye. Well that'll be the da-a-ay when I die.*

Ethel shoved yarn and needles into a large, straw knitting basket. "How can it be good for Amanda to spend hours in her room listening to words that come straight from the devil's mouth? Who is Buddy Holly anyway? He should be put in jail."

"Ethel, think of the songs that were popular when we were young. Singing about separation from loved ones, that it's like dying, is a very common theme for teenagers."

"But Amanda is not a stable person like you and I are. What if she decides to kill herself because of what that Gael Delaney did to her?" Ethel retrieved her needles and started knitting furiously.

"I could never show my face again in this town if that happened."

The newspaper fell from Carlton's lap to the floor. "Amanda's fine." Carlton climbed the stairs and knocked on Amanda's door. "Honey, can I come in?"

Ethel picked the newspaper up off the faded oriental carpet, then stood at the bottom of the stairs trying to overhear Amanda and Carlton. But even with the volume turned down, Ethel couldn't make out what they were talking about. Satisfied that her brother had asked Amanda to lower the volume, Ethel decided the kitchen floor needed a good New Year's Day scrubbing. "I wish I shared Carlton's assessment that Amanda is doing fine," she mumbled, down on her hands and knees attacking the kitchen with scalding water and a stiff bristle brush.

By the time school resumed, Ethel had grown sick and tired of listening to Buddy Holly. But then, Amanda bought more records with her Christmas money, all Rock N Roll. "Awful devil's music," is what Ethel grumbled to herself every time Amanda played Buddy Holly, or worse, if that was possible, Elvis Presley. "Every Rock N Roll song comes straight from the devil!"

She discussed Rock N Roll with the new minister one morning, cornering Reverend Halverson at the grocery store. "I've been meaning to ask, what do you plan to do about that awful Rock N Roll music? I haven't heard you preach a sermon condemning it yet." Ethel looked young Reverend Halverson up and down. "I'm waiting for you to forbid teenagers to listen to it. Remind them every Sunday that they are headed straight for hell if they listen to the devil's awful music."

"Miss MacGregor, Rock N Roll music is about love. Some are about loss, losing the one you love, just as popular music has always done. Perhaps the rhythm has changed, but not the message. Young people fall in love, so it's understandable that they listen to love songs."

"Precisely! I don't understand why you're not concerned about the temptations facing our young people today."

"There are temptations." The Reverend cleared his throat. "Since the earliest history, these same temptations have existed. To forbid teenagers to listen to the popular music today would only make the music more attractive to them, forbidden fruit if you will. We have to pay attention to how and why the music speaks to our kids."

Riding home from church with Carlton the following Sunday, Ethel turned to her brother nonchalantly and said, "I suppose it's alright that Amanda doesn't attend church with us. She isn't going to hear from that Reverend Halverson the message she needs to hear anyway."

Carlton had taken to watching morning news on the television before leaving for the office. On February 3, 1959, the morning news anchor reported that just hours earlier, a plane crashed shortly after takeoff from Clear Lake, Iowa. Carlton rushed upstairs to tell Amanda that Buddy Holly, Richie Valens and the Big Bopper were killed after performing at the Surf Ballroom.

Ethel knelt in front of the TV during a commercial break and prayed. "Thank you, dear God, for answering my prayers by removing that Buddy Holly and those other singers from this earth. Maybe now Amanda will realize that Rock N Roll music is pure evil." Ethel pretended to pick a piece of lint off the rug and to look for more when Amanda and Carlton came downstairs. She noticed that Amanda was crying. "Oh," she said, "I left oatmeal cooking on the stove!" On the way to the kitchen, she asked Amanda, "Can I bring you a cup of coffee or hot chocolate?"

"Coffee would be good. Thanks," Amanda muttered, immersed in the TV news. "I wish I'd been at the Surf to see Buddy Holly, Dad. I can't believe he is dead."

"Honey, it's over three hours to Clear Lake from here. At least you got to see him perform on the Ed Sullivan Show."

Amanda whispered, "Ethel spoiled Buddy Holly's performance for me last Sunday, leaving the room in a huff." She struggled to keep from crying. "Life is so damned unfair, Dad. How do you make any sense out of it?"

In a calm, soothing voice, Carlton said, "There are many things we don't understand. We have to continue to do the best we can each day, to go on after bad things happen."

"I don't want to go to school today, but I suppose I should."

"That's my girl. You should go."

Ethel brought coffee. She'd of course eavesdropped on the entire conversation, and feared Amanda would again cut classes.

Every time the phone rang that morning, Ethel was sure the school secretary was calling to report Amanda truant again.

Ethel found support for her strict attitude from other women, women of a like mind that Rock N Roll was the devil's music. They often complimented her for doing a good job of putting up with Amanda's rebelliousness at church and school, and of course spending all of her spare time in the bedroom listening to infernal Rock N Roll. Mrs. Nelson, Rebecca's mother, often expressed sympathy, which especially pleased Ethel.

The rest of winter was tinted sepia for Amanda, but she managed to keep up with her class assignments and editorial work on the *Trumpet*. Each day she crossed off the date on her calendar before she went to bed, glad to be one day closer to graduation. Carlton decided to take Amanda to visit the UW Madison campus in April.

Of course, Ethel was upset because Carlton wouldn't be going to church with her. "I guess I'll have to walk there and sit alone. I hope God understands why you two are doing this on His holy day."

They left early that morning, with high spirits. The first thing they did was to explore the campus. "You never told me how beautiful this is," she said as they walked up Bascom Hill. "The trees look like they've been here forever and have seen so much. Don't you wish they could talk?"

"I'm sure they'd have many interesting stories to tell." When they got to the bottom of the hill he said, "Let's eat lunch at the Memorial Union. Then I'll take you for a walk on the path along the lake." His voice sounded sad as he said, "Your mother and I often walked there."

"This is hard for you."

"Yes, but it's also good. I've never been back. Those were wonderful years, and meeting your mother the last year of med school was the happiest time of my life."

After they ate they walked out to the Union Terrace and looked at the sailboats and canoes on Lake Mendota. "This feels more like a resort than a school," she said as they started to walk along the lake.

"It is beautiful. There are so many opportunities for intellectual growth. It has a proud tradition of being a liberal campus."

"I know it's not a resort when I look at the students, who are everywhere; carrying books, and so many looking like they are having intense conversations as they walk together."

They continued on in silence. When they came to a spot along the lake path where there was a fork Carlton said, "Let's take the path going up to some of the dorms. Then we'll walk along Observatory Drive." When they came to the Carillon Tower Carlton said, "This is where I first kissed your mother. It's a tradition for lovers to kiss beneath the bell tower."

Amanda squeezed his hand as she said, "Thank you for telling me this."

Carlton seemed embarrassed as he led her away from the Carillon and said, "Let's spend some time on State Street."

"What a neat place to hang out," Amanda said as they walked along State Street. "There are tons of restaurants, book stores and coffee shops, and I've never seen so many unique stores." She stopped by a shop where the large window was filled with hats of every style and shape. She was amazed because it looked like the only thing sold there was hats.

Carlton looked down the street and thoughtfully said, "There also are a lot of bars, and here the legal age to drink beer is eighteen. You will need to learn how to drink wisely if you decide to indulge."

"I don't like the smell of beer," she said as they walked by a bar with an open door. "I don't think I'll be eager to try it."

On the drive back home Amanda said, "I've been thinking about your comment about how liberal UW is. How could you go back to Turtle Creek to practice?"

"A liberal campus has many professors challenging you to find new and different ways to look at problems. Once my mind was opened up it never closed. You can live among very conservative people and, respecting their beliefs, gently encourage them to try new things when old ways no longer work."

"You are so wise, just like the trees on Bascom Hill."

The trip to Madison was a turning point for Amanda. It made real the fact that she would be starting college in five months. She walked with a lighter step.

The month of May excited Ethel. "The end is in sight!" she said under her breath each lovely spring morning. "Of course, we'll host a fancy graduation party for Amanda. The whole town will rave about what a good mother I've been to that child." And so it happened, one day when Amanda came home from school, Ethel announced, "We need to start making plans about your graduation party. Your father told me you will be the valedictorian. You know, he was class valedictorian too. I think an open house on Sunday after graduation would be appropriate."

"I don't want anything like that. I don't want to have to think about anything but my valedictorian speech. Nothing else."

"But everyone celebrates graduation. It's not normal to do nothing."

"You can explain to your friends that I insisted on doing nothing."

And that's what Ethel did, pleased to receive so much sympathy from the other women about how inconsiderate and difficult Amanda could to be. Mrs. Nelson said, "I know you would have put on a grand graduation party. I hope you are at least making a graduation cake. You are so good at baking."

"I have an excellent idea," Ethel replied, "If Amanda doesn't want a cake, would you like me to bake one for Rebecca?"

"Would you really do that? It would be fantastic to have one of your beautifully decorated cakes to serve at Rebecca's graduation party!"

"As I think about it, I'm sure Amanda won't want a cake. Ask Rebecca what kind of cake she would like, and what decorations, and call me."

"I'll do that. Rebecca will be thrilled."

21. Beautiful Yolanda

Editing the last issue of the *Trumpet*, Amanda already felt nostalgic for high school. Being editor had taught her a lot about working with others. She wasn't going to miss all the hours, but she was glad for the experience.

Strangely enough, her feelings about Rebecca had changed from anger to pity. One morning in the middle of May, Amanda approached her locker and overheard Rebecca talking to Suzy. In a loud voice she proclaimed, "I'm so excited about my graduation party. You will never guess who's making my cake."

"One of the bakeries in Carson City?"

"Guess again. Ethel MacGregor is baking and decorating my cake."

Amanda couldn't believe her ears. What was going on? She grabbed her books and took off in a huff for home, where her first words were, "Ethel, why are you making a cake for Rebecca's party? Isn't that a little odd?"

"It's not odd at all. Rebecca's mother and I have become very close."

Amanda stared at Ethel in disbelief. "Seems odd to me." She left the kitchen and went to her room. There she put Elvis Presley's *Heartbreak Hotel* on the turntable and left her door open. She looked over her valedictorian speech knowing that Principal Johnson wanted to see her first draft. "I hope he'll agree talking about Dad being my hero is an appropriate opening topic," she mused. Inspired by her campus visit to Madison, she wrote about the opportunities available to the class of 1959.

"You know, about half of your classmates will not be going to college," remarked Carlton after he read the speech. "They will still have opportunities to learn and grow. The love of learning often fostered in college can also be encouraged in many other ways."

"You're right. I need to point that out."

One morning, Ethel interrupted Amanda in her bedroom sorting through clothes to take to college. "A letter came from the University today. I thought you'd want to see it right away," she said.

"Thanks." Amanda opened the envelope and began reading, a big smile taking over her face. "It's the name and address of my roommate. I'm going to write her now." She took out stationery from her desk and exclaimed, "Yolanda is from Mississippi."

"Yolanda is an unusual name," Ethel said, peering over Amanda's shoulder.

"Isn't that great? I requested a roommate from outside the Midwest. I want to get to know people who come from other places."

"I just hope, young lady, that you don't get in over your head. I've always found it easier to understand people who come from Turtle Creek."

"And you've never lived anywhere except this house."

"I've done very well here. You know your father would never be where he is today if I hadn't been there to take care of him." Ethel left the room and marched down the stairs.

When a letter from Yolanda Jones addressed to Amanda arrived, Ethel delivered it to her niece, busy polishing her shoes in the kitchen. A picture fell out of the envelope when Amanda eagerly slit it open. "Oops."

Ethel snatched up the photo. "Something is wrong with the color," she said, holding the wallet size print up into sunlight streaming from the window. "She appears to be black."

Amanda grabbed the picture back. "Yolanda is black, Ethel. I can't wait to show this to Dad. I can't believe my good luck!"

"How can you say this is good luck? It's a disaster. I'm going out to work in my garden. When your father comes home he'll talk some sense into you. Hopefully you'll be able to get another roommate."

Amanda sat down and examined the picture. Yolanda was beautiful, with high cheekbones and large dark eyes. Amanda thought that she looked like a queen.

Her letter was friendly, but brief. She was excited about attending the University because she had never been outside the rural region in the Mississippi delta where she was born and raised. She also looked forward to getting to know Amanda, and hoped to hear from her soon.

Amanda immediately went upstairs and started to compose a letter. *We both come from small towns, she wrote, and are excited about all the new experiences we will have. I am so happy that you will be my roommate.* That afternoon Amanda walked to the post office and mailed her letter.

As soon as her dad came home she told him the good news. They were in the kitchen, and Ethel had to add her two cents. "You have to contact the university and say it is unacceptable for Amanda to have this Yolanda Jones for a roommate."

"I know this is hard for you to understand, Ethel. It's a wonderful opportunity for Amanda."

"You think I don't know anything because I've never lived outside Turtle Creek. You mark my words, Amanda will regret having a Negro roommate."

Soon, another letter from Yolanda arrived.

> *Dear Amanda, I want you to know more about me. Where I live, the population is eighty percent black. The white kids go to private schools and the black to public. Half of the black students don't graduate from high school. My mother only finished the eighth grade. She had to quit school after she was raped and became pregnant. She was only fourteen when I was born. She is the strongest person I know, and very smart. She taught me to read before I started school.*
>
> *"She has always worked as a maid at the same mansion. The white children she nursed, and comforted after they were disciplined by their mother, loved her until the beauty, sophistication and charm of their mother took over their hearts. My mother knew all the family secrets. The matron, Mary Sue, would tell her about the frustrations she had trying to keep her children pure and innocent; and complained about how hard it was to always pretend everything was perfect when she was with her girlfriends, and when her husband was present.*

"I know this sounds like my mother had a hard life, but she always felt lucky because she worked for a family who liked her and depended on her. Of course, when we were in town we always had to step into the street whenever a white person approached us on the sidewalk, and we could never look a white person in the eye when we were in a public place. My mother would give me any books she could borrow from the white children, and always wanted me to leave the South as soon as I could. I'm on a full scholarship at the U, and plan to be a teacher. When I get a job, I will have my mother come north to live with me.

When you wrote that you are eager to know me I decided that the first thing you need to know is about my past. I look forward to hearing from you again. Love, Yolanda."

Sunday morning, when Carlton and Ethel attended church, Amanda visited Daisy, eager to show her Yolanda's second letter. After reading it Daisy said, "It took a lot of courage for Yolanda to be so open and honest. I wish I could be as brave as she and her mother are."

"So do I. My life seems easy by comparison."

22. Discouraged servant

Ethel helped Amanda prepare for college. She initialed all of Amanda's underwear and told her never to wash her clothing with Yolanda's because there had to be a good reason why the Negroes were not even allowed to sit at the same lunch counter as the white people. She also instructed Amanda to be aware of wolves in sheep's clothing, and to always keep a dollar bill in the inside of her right shoe for emergencies. Her Knit and Purl group had given Ethel this advice to pass on. When Amanda couldn't hide a smile as Ethel was telling her this she said, "Get that smirk off your face. I wasn't born yesterday you know."

When Carlton took Amanda to college there was a pole hooked across the back seat filled with hanging blouses and dresses. Amanda said, "I'm sorry there's no room for you to come along. I'm bringing lots of clothes because I don't know what I'll want there. Some time I want you to see how beautiful the campus is."

"I saw it when Carlton graduated," declared Ethel. "I took the train to Madison. It's a shame that we don't have a train stopping at Turtle Creek anymore." She proudly added, "I would take it to Carson City at least once a month when I was a young woman, to buy the things I couldn't get here."

"I didn't know you did that, Auntie. It's a shame that you can't now, but you'll be able to come along with Dad some time."

Ethel was glad that she wasn't going along. She would give Amanda's room a good scrubbing, and of course she didn't want to miss "As the World Turns." As she washed the walls and the floor, with bleach added to the hot water, she felt Amanda's presence fading. It was such a good feeling. Now she would have Carlton all to herself. Of course, she told herself that the reason she was so happy Amanda was gone was because Carlton wouldn't worry so much. His hair definitely had more gray in it because of the strains caused by raising a teenager the last four years. The gray hairs were hard to see in his blond hair, but she knew they were there. Thank goodness she had such a strong constitution. Of course, the bad headaches had been a problem for a while. The past year she rarely had one, and she had to admit that Carlton was right. It helped to take a pill when she felt one coming on. Her sweet Carlton was so smart.

The first Sunday after Amanda left Ethel prepared one of Carlton's favorite dinners. You could smell the roasted chicken as soon as you entered the house. "Now you sit down and read the paper while I mash the potatoes and cook the peas," she said.

Wasn't Reverend Halverson's sermon excellent?" Carlton said as he removed his hat and suit coat.

"He's still too highfalutin for me, but he did make a good point when he preached about how the greatest virtue is to love one another."

After the meal, which Carlton said was delicious, with the best gravy he'd ever tasted, he said, "I'm going for a walk."

"You go ahead while I clean up the kitchen. It will help you digest your food."

She took a nap when she was finished. When she woke up she saw that it was already three o'clock. She got up and went to the living room to be with Carlton. He was not there. "Carlton?" she called out. He never took naps, but she looked in his bedroom just to be sure he wasn't there. She put her hat on, deciding she'd better go look for him. What if something bad had happened? Men younger than him had had heart attacks.

Which way should she go? Toward the cemetery and the creek of course. After she'd gone a block she saw him coming toward her.

"Why Ethel, how good to see you out walking," he exclaimed.

"I was worried about you being gone so long."

"I'm sorry. When I passed Daisy's house she was working in the yard, and I ended up having a cup of tea with her."

"I've been frantic, thinking you had a heart attack."

"I'm really sorry," he said as he looked at his watch. "I didn't realize so much time had passed."

"What did you find to talk about for two hours?" Ethel asked.

"We talked about Amanda, and about Joey of course. We also had some interesting conversations about politics. Both of us

198

hope the war in Vietnam won't last long. She's a deep thinker; a very spiritual person."

Ethel didn't say anything more until they got home. As they entered the house she said, "I don't have time to sit and talk. I have work to do."

That night she added an addendum to her usual prayers. "Dear God, you know how much I've had to put up with in raising Amanda. Now that I don't have to deal with that every day I want some peace. I was looking forward to having Carlton spend his free time at home with me. Please help me convince him that this is what he should do. Your faithful, and as usual, exhausted servant, Ethel."

When she woke up in the morning, the answer came to her. Carlton obviously wanted to talk about Amanda, so she would do that. "Thank you, Dear God, for answering my prayers so fast," she said as she put on her faded, cotton housedress. Every morning, and every evening, she made a point of saying something about Amanda. "I wonder how she is doing. I hope all is going well for her. I'm sure she is not having trouble with her studies because she is so smart, just like you are."

Carlton always responded with enthusiasm. One time when they were sitting in the living room he said, "I think you miss her as much as I do."

She didn't know how to respond. She couldn't lie by saying he was right because, of course, she didn't miss Amanda, so she pretended she hadn't heard him. She purposely made some uneven stitches. "This has to be done over," she complained as she ripped them out.

Ethel's efforts were not enough. Every Sunday afternoon that fall when she got up to clear the table Carlton would say he was going for a walk. "Don't worry about me. I may stop in to talk to Daisy," he would add as he left.

The first Sunday in December Ethel asked Carlton to take her shopping in Carson City. "I want to get some special gifts for Amanda, and I need your help."

"I don't think there is much that she wants. Her letters sound so happy."

"There has to be something special we can get. How about some records for her phonograph? You know what music she likes."

"I guess we could go for a couple of hours."

In the car on the way there Ethel said, "I'm so anxious to have Amanda with us for Christmas vacation. I've read the few letters she has sent many times. I was hoping she would write more about all the experiences she is having at the University. The cost of mailing a letter is so reasonable, even though it has gone up from three cents to four cents. I'm sure the increase means that some people don't write as often as they would like to."

"She's busy studying. The academic pace is so much faster than it was at high school. It's a big adjustment."

"I wouldn't know about that."

"I'm sorry, Ethel. I forget how much you had to give up so that I could go to college."

At the music store Carlton bought a new Elvis Presley album, and an album from a group Ethel had never heard of before called the Kingston Trio. "I think you will like the folk songs of the Kingston Trio," he told Ethel. "They are talented musicians, and sing some breath-taking ballads."

On the ride home, Ethel talked about how she was going to prepare all of Amanda's favorite meals, and was very anxious to hear the Kingston Trio.

Her mood darkened when Carlton said, as soon as he drove into the driveway, that he was going for a walk.

The day Amanda's vacation started Carlton asked if Ethel would like to go with him to pick up Amanda. "That would be wonderful," she exclaimed. She was looking more forward to the ride up than she was to the ride back. It was always good to have Carlton as a captive audience to hear her words of wisdom. "I'm curious about what Amanda will have to say about her black roommate," she said as they turned on to the highway. "I wonder how the poor girl is doing. She must feel so out of place."

"From what Amanda has written, Yolanda is having a very positive experience. Remember when she wrote that Yolanda had straight A's at midterm?"

"I know, but that doesn't mean she is being accepted socially. You have to admit, Carlton that she doesn't really belong."

"Don't say that to Amanda. She'll be furious."

Ethel was hurt that Carlton didn't think she had more sense than that. "I know I can't be as frank with Amanda as I am with you, but I still am concerned that there will be problems. Yolanda will never fit in."

Carlton didn't respond immediately. Finally, he said, "I'm sorry that you feel that way."

The ride was not as pleasant as Ethel thought it would be, and when they picked up Amanda, Ethel couldn't believe her eyes. Amanda had stopped smoothing out her curls. Her hair looked like an unruly mop, and she had on white lipstick. With hair flying every which way and lips that looked like there was no life in her, Ethel didn't know what she wanted to do when Amanda greeted Carlton with a big smile and a hug. Ethel didn't want to touch her. She was stiff when Amanda hugged her, but she did manage to give her two little pats on the shoulder with her right hand before she backed away.

"Would you mind sitting in the back on the way home, Ethel?" Carlton asked. "It will be easier for me to talk to Amanda if she's in the front seat."

"Of course, Carlton. I'm very flexible."

The two weeks Amanda spent at home were dreary weeks for Ethel. She got tired of hearing Carlton and Amanda talking about how awful segregation was, and about something they called women's lib, which Ethel thought was unnecessary, maybe even silly. Didn't they realize that if women weren't there to take care of men and children the world would fall apart? It was best to let men think that they are the strong ones. Why couldn't Carlton and Amanda appreciate how strong she has been all along? Of course, they didn't know about all the things she has had to do.

Sometimes she wondered exactly what that Gael Delaney had written in those letters she had burned, and how it probably would have hurt Amanda more to read them. At times, she wished she hadn't destroyed them, and yet, if Gael had written that he will always love her Amanda would cling to that for the rest of her life. It was good that she had burned the letters.

There was one faint ray of hope. The folk songs of the Kingston Trio were easier to listen to than Elvis Presley or Buddy Holly. Carlton was right. Many of their songs sounded nice. She even found herself humming along with some of them.

When it was time for Amanda to go back to the university Ethel didn't go along because she knew she'd be asked to ride in the back. When Carlton arrived home that day she cornered him to vent her frustrations. "Sit down at the table and have a cup of coffee," she said when he came in the back door. She poured two cups and sat down across from him. The first thing she said was that Amanda didn't eat very much. "I made all her favorite foods. She's not eating red meat now, and says my vegetables are overcooked. Where does she get such highfalutin ideas?"

She also told Carlton she was concerned because Amanda never wanted to talk to her. "It's a repeat of her last year of high school. The only way I knew she was even home is because that phonograph was always on. I think she has a problem. Why couldn't she leave that fancy machine at school?"

"Ethel, I was glad she brought it home. Don't forget that we gave her record albums for Christmas."

Ethel didn't respond to that comment. She took a deep breath before she said, "My main concern is that Amanda says that Yolanda is her best friend. How could you tell her it was a good idea when she said she was going to ask Yolanda to come to Turtle Creek for spring break? The whole town will be talking. I've had to put up with so much gossip through the years because of Amanda, but this takes the cake."

Carlton was frustrated. "I'm sorry you feel that way. There has not been that much gossip. I never realized it was that hard for you to help me raise Amanda." Carlton got up, and then said, "I'm going for a walk."

The thought that Carlton was mad at her scared Ethel. *What if he stops loving me?* "It's almost time for supper. Don't be gone long," she begged.

"I think I'll ask Daisy to join me at the Chat and Chew. Don't wait up for me." He left before she could think of a reply.

That night she was knitting in the living room, with the TV on, when he came home. The ten o'clock news was on. He sat down to watch it, making no apology for being so late.

When a commercial came on Ethel said, as she set her knitting needles in her lap, "What did Daisy have to say?"

"She was thrilled when Amanda visited her last Sunday, and told me she was looking forward to meeting Yolanda." Carlton turned to look at Ethel. "You know, when she closes up the store at 6:00 p.m. Daisy comes home to an empty house. She says she doesn't mind because she deals with people all day, but I think we should invite her to join us for supper some night this week. Of course, Saturday wouldn't work because the store is open until 8:00 p.m. then. Did you realize that Daisy puts in as many hours as I do every week?"

"How can you compare what she does with what you do?" When Carlton frowned she quickly added, "Of course we can invite her over some time this winter. I'm sure Daisy will appreciate a home-cooked meal. I'd rather not do it this week if that's all right with you. My knitting group meets here Thursday, and I have to finish putting away all the Christmas decorations before then."

"That's fine. I'll ask her to join me at the Chat and Chew Wednesday night. Then you won't have to make a meal for me as you're preparing for your company."

"It's no work to cook for you, Carlton. That has always been my pleasure."

"I appreciate that, Ethel," said Carlton gently, "but you'll have enough to do on Wednesday."

I n her wildest dreams Ethel never imagined that she would be so blue when Amanda was gone. She was losing Carlton, and that broke her heart. He didn't ask her again to have Daisy over for supper. Instead, in February and March, he took Daisy to the Chat and Chew every Wednesday night, as well as spending Sunday afternoons with her. When he was home he was pleasant to Ethel, but didn't seem to notice how quiet she was. He was acting like a love- sick teenager. What would Ethel do if Carlton wanted to marry Daisy?

One night in early March Ethel knelt on the cold floor by her bed for some serious praying. "Dear God, what is happening? This was supposed to be the happiest time of my life. Instead, I now see that I will never be free of Amanda. No matter where she goes or what she does she will always have the number one spot in his life.

"I believe I could adjust to that, because it's no different than what I've had to put up with the past eighteen years. The problem is that I can't put up with his falling head over heels in love with Daisy. What does he see in her? She's spinning her web, pretending to be so interested in Amanda. For a man who is so smart how can he be so dumb when it comes to women?

"Please let me know, Dear God, what you want me to do. As you know, I always carry out your will. Your faithful, but discouraged servant, Ethel."

23. The confession

The first Wednesday in April Ethel awoke to a steady rain pounding the house. It made her feel like she was going to drown. She pulled the heavy weight of her body out of her bed, slid her robe over her shoulders and staggered to the kitchen. Sinking down on a chair she saw a note from Carlton. "You were sleeping so peacefully when I left, so I didn't want to disturb you. The coffee is made. I didn't make it as strong as you do. I like the way Daisy makes it. Hope you don't mind. Have a relaxing, peaceful day."

"How can I feel peaceful and relaxed after that remark about my coffee?" Ethel muttered to herself. "Carlton is blind. He has no idea how much I've been struggling throughout this bone chilling winter. He hasn't noticed the film of dust on the furniture, nor the dust balls underneath everything. He never asks me about how my day went." Ethel shook her head vigorously, as if she were talking to another person. "I no longer want to keep busy. Now I don't even have enough energy to get up and pour myself a cup of that weak coffee."

Then she decided that it was better than nothing, but when she tried to get up her legs shook so much she couldn't stand, even when she placed her hands firmly on the table and pushed with all her might. She collapsed on the chair and buried her face in her arms. Then she started to tremble all over. "Why am I being punished?" she repeated, over and over, to the empty room. "It's not fair to punish me for the letters I had to write. On the surface, they looked like they were filled with lies; but deep in my heart I know that the fibs told real truths." She lifted her head and the trembling stopped. She cautiously got up and poured herself a cup of coffee. She took a sip, made a face and set it down on the counter. "I need to write another letter, the most important one I will ever write," she decided.

A sense of purpose gave her strength. She strode to her bedroom, where she got her onionskin stationery, her fountain pen and her bottle of black ink from the bottom drawer of her dresser. Her dear daddy had given her the stately black pen. He told her it was just like the pen he used to sign all of his correspondence at the bank. She never used it when she wrote the other letters because everyone else used a ballpoint pen. But this letter would come from her, not from anyone else.

She sat down at the kitchen table and unscrewed the lid from the bottle of ink. She dipped the tip of the pen in the ink and slowly filled it. Then she lifted the bottle to the light and she could see that the ink was almost gone. "It's just as well," she thought. "Probably the Five and Dime no longer sells ink for fountain pens. She took a sheet of the onionskin paper out of the stationery box and posed the pen above the paper. "This will be the unvarnished truth. I can't repent for the things I had to do, but I can try to explain then to Carlton. I owe him that much."

The words came unexpectedly easy, as if she always knew that someday she would have to write this letter. "Carlton will understand what I had to do and why. God understands also. When she was finished, she held up the translucent onionskin and looked it over, admiring her elegant flourishes and embellishments. She put it in a matching envelope, calmly sealed it, and addressed it to Carlton. She placed it next to the stationery box on the edge of the table.

As she grabbed the edge of the table, for support while trying to rise, she accidentally nudged the stationery box over the letter. She wobbled across the kitchen and grabbed a flashlight from the cupboard next to the cellar door. As she opened the door she almost choked on the musty air. The flashlight guided her down the dark stairs. At the bottom, she placed her bare feet on the cold, damp cement and pulled the string hanging down from the bare light bulb. Except for the huge furnace the cellar looked empty. With her flashlight, she searched along the walls and corners, knowing what she was looking for. In the far corner was the thick rope, coiled like a snake. She shivered as she picked it up and carried it upstairs. It felt good to place her bare feet on the warm kitchen floor. Grasping the rope firmly in one hand and grabbing the kitchen stepstool with the other, she proceeded up the stairs to the second floor; and then up the creaking stairs to the attic.

At the same spot where her daddy hanged himself, the beam in the middle of the attic roof, she stopped. She felt like her soul was struggling to leave her body. She threw the thick rope over the beam, made a noose and secured it. Placing the stepstool right under the noose she climbed to the top step and slipped the noose around her neck. She was only four feet off the floor; but it was enough. She kicked the stool out from under her. Her last thought was "This is as it should be. I will be with my daddy."

C arlton was exhausted when he got home at 6:15. He wanted to collapse in the overstuffed armchair and read the paper. He walked in the back door, slipped his raincoat off and threw it on the kitchen chair closest to the door. "Ethel?" he called out. There was no answer. He called again, louder. There was not a sound in the huge house. He looked down at the table and noticed her fountain pen and ink bottle in the middle, and her stationery box at one end. "Maybe she was going to write a special letter," he mused. "She must not be feeling well," he decided as he went to her bedroom. The door was wide open and the room looked the way it always looked; nothing placed there purely for the pleasure of looking at it.

Carlton's mind raced. "Where on earth is Ethel? She never leaves when she's expecting me home. She's got to be here somewhere. Maybe she fell and hurt herself." He looked in every room on the main floor, and then admonished himself for wasting time looking in rooms he knew she had no reason to be in. He went upstairs to Amanda's bedroom. "I bet she was getting it ready for Amanda's Easter vacation," he decided as he climbed the stairs. "I hope she didn't try to carry the folding cot we talked of setting up for Yolanda, down the attic stairs." A quick glance at the room showed him that neither Ethel nor the cot were there. "She must have fallen in the attic when she went to get the cot. Why didn't I think of this right away?"

Carlton rushed up the wooden stairs, taking two at a time, not stopping to turn on the light. From the muted sun faintly shining through the attic window he saw Ethel's body suspended in the air. He frantically rushed toward her, reaching out and touching her body. It swayed back and forth. Carlton's legs gave out as he fainted. When he came to he was lying on the attic floor, close to her body. "This can't be," he sobbed, over and over. He wanted to lower her body and gently carry it downstairs, but he knew he shouldn't touch it. He must call the police station.

Carlton stumbled down the stairs and made the call. The town cop, Gunnar Nelson, answered the phone after two rings. "What can I help you with?" he said. It was his standard greeting. Carlton had known Gunnar for at least twenty years and, as with almost everyone else in Turtle Creek, he always doctored with him.

"There's a disaster at my home, Gunnar. You must come as soon as you can." Carlton sounded much calmer than he felt. For a moment, by habit, he had slipped into his professional voice. But after Gunnar hung up Carlton continued to stand in the kitchen, dumbly holding the phone next to his ear until he heard a brisk knock on the door. Carlton numbly put the phone back on the receiver and opened the door. He couldn't even greet Gunnar. "The attic," he moaned and pointed to the stairs. Gunnar firmly grasped Carlton's shoulders before Carlton turned to lead the way, giving him the message that he would be by Carlton's side for whatever was ahead.

"What on earth is this about?" he wondered as he followed Carlton up the creaking attic stairs. When Carlton pulled the cord for the ceiling light Gunnar gasped as he saw Ethel's limp body suspended in the air. "I'll call the mortuary," he said as he reached out again and patted Carlton's shoulder. "Let's go down stairs." Both walked cautiously, stiffly, down the two flights of stairs. When they arrived at the kitchen Gunnar gently asked, "When did you last see Ethel alive?"

"This morning Ethel was still sleeping when I left," Carlton reported with a catch in his throat. "I didn't want to disturb her. Usually she is up long before me and has coffee made. I made it today, and I see that she must have poured herself a cup, but she didn't drink much." He picked up the cup on the table and examined it. "I don't understand why she took her life. I know she was having a hard time adjusting to Amanda being at college, and it was difficult for her to accept the fact that Amanda has a black roommate. Yolanda is wonderful according to Amanda, and she planned on bringing her home for spring vacation. Ethel was concerned about that, but I thought she would get used to the idea. She's always had such a strong constitution. She has been able to learn to put up with things she could not accept initially.

As I look back I realize that it often must have been hard for Ethel to do that." He sat down, folded his arms on the table, and bowed his head.

Gunner again patted Carlton's shoulder as he said, "Don't blame yourself for this." He then called the mortuary and two men arrived shortly. Carlton observed them efficiently carrying Ethel's body out of the only home she had ever known, but he kept hoping this was a bad dream he would awake from soon. When Gunnar asked if he should call Reverend Halverson Carlton said, "Yes, please do."

Gunnar was thankful that the Reverend answered after the first ring. "You need to come to Dr. MacGregor's as soon as you can. Ethel has died." Gunnar opened the door when he heard the pastor knock. "It's good that you were able to come quickly. Ethel's body was just removed. She hanged herself in the attic, just as her father did."

Reverend Halverson immediately walked over to Carlton, who said, "Please sit with me for a bit. This is a nightmare."

As the pastor sat down across from Carlton Gunnar said, "I think it's best for me to leave now. Don't hesitate to call if there's anything I can do."

When they heard Gunnar's car pull away Carlton started to talk rapidly. "I can't believe this. I should have seen the signs. She was depressed and I failed her, just as I failed to see that my beloved Sarah must have been depressed. I can't forgive myself. I don't deserve to live."

Reverend Halverson reached across the table with his hands open. "You must not be so hard on yourself. Hind sight always makes us regret that we didn't see what seems like obvious signs once a tragedy has happened."

"Ethel was always there to care for me, ever since I was born. You know, our mother died when she gave birth to me. I took so much for granted. I can never forgive myself for that, but I don't understand why she took her life. How could things be that bad, Reverend?"

"Please call me John," the pastor softly said. "Did she leave a note?" he asked as he looked at the box of stationery.

"I ... I haven't seen one. This was here when I came home. It's stationery she always saved for special occasions." He lifted the box up to show it to Joe, and there was the letter. Carlton placed it in front of himself and stared at it. Then he carefully opened it, afraid to read it. The cream-colored onionskin sheet was filled with Ethel's elegant, flowery script. "This was not written in haste," he said, choking on the words. "Will you read it to me? It's too painful for me to be looking at her beautiful handwriting."

John took the letter and started to read it out loud.

> *My Dearest Carlton,*
>
> *Don't weep for me. Wherever Daddy's soul is, that's where mine will be. Bury my body next to his lonely grave. He is the only one who needs me.*

Carlton interrupted. "Did you know, John, that our father killed himself during the great depression? It was rumored that he stole money from the bank. People blamed him for the bank collapsing. Everyone knew that he loved to gamble, so he may have been blamed for something he didn't do. Then again, he may have taken money before the bank collapsed."

"I don't put much stock in rumors. I know that a lot of people respect you highly, Carlton," replied John before continuing to read.

> *No one will ever love you as much as I do, but I can see the handwriting on the wall. I know that Daisy will jump at the chance to be your wife. I pray that she will take adequate care of you. At least Daisy is tolerated in our town, even though her standards are not up to ours. I'm sure she was never brought up right. She never attends our church, and Joey was not even confirmed."*

John set the letter down on the table and said, "Everyone I know has respect and admiration for Daisy. She runs the Red Owl efficiently, and is always so pleasant and helpful. She also has done a wonderful job raising her son. I understand that she has not been active in our church because her husband wasn't allowed to be buried in our cemetery. I think Ethel would have found fault with any woman you dated."

"I've never dated anyone else," said Carlton. "I must admit that I've thought about asking Daisy to marry me, and I know that

Ethel would not have liked the idea at first. I always would have provided for Ethel. This big house was getting to be too much for her to take care of. I planned on buying a smaller, newer home for her. She would have been upset at first, but she has always eventually adjusted to change. You understand that losing our mother when I was born, and then our father when she was fourteen, made it difficult for her to accept any change."

"You are absolutely right. There's a lot more in this letter. I think your relationship with Daisy was not the main reason Ethel committed suicide." John resumed reading.

> Now I have to write about something it will be hard for you to understand. You know, deep in your heart, that Sarah was not accepted in Turtle Creek. She had to leave because she would never fit in. You do realize that, don't you? I had to help her leave. She was miserable in our beautiful town. The arsenic that I used to improve my complexion worked very well. I put one large dose in her coffee. The sweet almond flavor must have tasted good to her because she gulped it down. I did not let her suffer long. When she was leaning over the toilet vomiting I put her out of her misery. I was ironing at the time, so I dropped the hot iron on her head. Then she was at peace.

Shocked, John stopped reading. He could see the shock on Carlton's face. "Should I continue?" he asked.

"How could her mind be so twisted? I can't believe she could do that." His face paler than a white sheet, he said, "I need to hear it all."

> I poured the rest of the arsenic down the drain. Since that day, I have never used it to improve my complexion. I will always remember those Indian summer days that fall of 1941. Amanda had just been born, and you went to a medical meeting in Des Moines. It was unusual for you to be gone overnight. I seized the opportunity. You probably don't remember that I had the ground dug up for my flower garden a few days before you left. The earth was soft, and I was able to dig a deep hole in the middle of the garden plot the night she died. I know that God approved my actions because it was a miracle that none of the neighbors saw me

211

drag the gunny sack containing her body to the garden. The
flowers I planted the following spring have always been so
beautiful, proof that God blessed my actions."

John had to stop again. He couldn't understand how she could
be so sick that she believed she actually was doing what God
wanted her to do. He didn't say this to Carlton because he didn't
think it was a helpful thing to mention. After a brief pause he
resumed the reading.

I've had to carry this secret with me all these years. It has
been a heavy burden. It was hard for me to see you so
distraught when I told you that Sarah was gone, but I knew
I had done the right thing when you so easily believed the
web of lies I had to spin. Of course, the important things I
wrote in the letter you thought was from Sarah were true.
She was never happy living with us, and she was
overwhelmed trying to take care of Amanda. She never
would have managed if I hadn't been there to help her. I
only had to lie about how she left us. It has been a great
comfort to me that God understands why Daddy and I have
had to do the things we've done. After our mother died I
had to take her place in the bedroom, do what Daddy
thought a wife should do. Most people would never
understand, but God did. It was hard for me, but I've
always done what I had to do.

Carlton stood up and shouted, "Why didn't I realize what was
going on when Dad was alive?"

Reverend Halverson said, "You were a child. You must not
blame yourself for not knowing. He stood, walked over to
Carlton, reached out and put his arms around Carlton's shoulders.
"How old were you when your father died?" he gently asked.

"I was seven." Carlton laid his head on John's shoulder and
wept. After several minutes, he relaxed his body and lifted is head.
"Please finish," he said.

I worried that Sarah's parents would be a problem, even
though they had disowned her when she married you. I wrote
them a letter saying that both Sarah and the baby had died
in childbirth. I had to sign your name to it. I know you will
forgive me for that, and that you understand why I had to

212

write that. I didn't want them ever to try to contact us. Of course, I had to write one more letter, the one from Sarah's father, saying they wanted no contact with us. This must have been true; otherwise they may have tried to get in touch with you, even though they thought both Sarah and Amanda were dead.

My life has never been easy. It was hard for me to raise Amanda because she is so much like her mother. You need to realize that I did the best job I could. I tried so hard to make her fit in. Do not be upset if she disappoints you. As you have always done, you must focus on your work as the town's only doctor. That has always been God's plan for you. That sums up everything you need to know. Ever since our dear daddy died you have been my whole life. I hope you understand why I had to do what I did. Your faithful sister, who has always loved you more than anyone else ever could, Ethel.

Carlton was in shock. "This is the hardest thing I have ever had to deal with. How could my sister do such evil things? Amanda needs to know that her mother didn't run away, but how can I show her this letter? I always knew that Ethel had a hard time raising Amanda, but I didn't know that she hated her because she looks like Sarah."

John responded immediately. "I bet Amanda has known all along that Ethel didn't think she belonged here. What Ethel wrote about her probably won't be a shock to her. The brutal death of her mother is a horrible shock, but it also sends a powerful message to Amanda. Her mother didn't run away."

"I need to call Amanda tonight," Carlton said firmly. But after placing the call, he got nervous as he waited for the phone to be picked up.

24. The kiss

Amanda sat at the desk in her dorm room writing an essay on the dynamics of the small group when the hall phone rang. Someone yelled, "Mandy, It's for you." She got up from her desk, wondering who could be calling.

In a voice so shaky Amanda could barely recognize it, her dad said, without even greeting her, "This is very sad news. Your aunt committed suicide."

"What?" was all that Amanda could say.

"I know this is a terrible shock. It happened sometime today. You have to come home. I'll pick you up tomorrow morning." His voice continued to shake. "The funeral will probably be in a couple of days." There was dead air over the phone. Then he stammered, "Reverend H-H-Halverson is with me now."

It was hard for her to believe that this was her dad talking. "Can I speak with him?" There was a pause before a man with a deep voice said he was Reverend Halverson. "Please tell me what is going on," she said. "I don't think he sounds well enough to make the trip tomorrow."

"I'm going with him, Amanda. In fact, I will drive. He found her in the attic when he came home from work today. She hanged herself." He paused before he added, "You need to understand that she was not well."

"Oh my God. It's my fault. I have never been really nice to her. I always just put up with her. When I was home for Christmas vacation I hardly talked to her. She wanted to know what college is like. I barely answered her questions. I listened to records in my bedroom instead." Amanda started to cry. "She was always so stubborn, so old fashioned. She must have been hurting a lot. I never realized it," she said through her tears.

"She was mentally ill. Her letter will explain a lot."

Amanda tried to respond. She couldn't make her voice work. Finally, she said in a hoarse undertone, "She left a letter? I don't know if I want to see it."

In a gentle voice the Reverend said, "Reading it will help you deal with this tragedy. You must not blame yourself." Then he raised his voice. "Your father wants to talk to you again."

"I just want to let you know that I'm okay," Carlton said in a more controlled voice. "You must talk to the dean first thing in the morning. The funeral most likely will be on Saturday. Can you be ready to leave by eleven?"

"I can. I love you Dad."

"I love you too, Amanda."

After hanging up the phone Amanda had to concentrate on taking a step with her right foot, and then very carefully, her left foot. Her numb body would not move without this effort. When she got to her room she collapsed on her bed. As she lay there an odd thought crossed her mind. Everyone here calls me Mandy, but at home I'm Amanda. It doesn't matter. I know I 'm not really the carefree Mandy.

She didn't know how much time had passed when Yolanda came back from the library. "Hey, what's wrong?" she asked. "You're staring at the ceiling like you're in a trance."

Slowly, with great effort, Amanda responded. "I don't understand what happened. Ethel is dead."

"What? You mean something happened to your aunt that you told me those funny, yet sad stories about?"

Amanda sat up. "She killed herself, just like my grandfather did, hanging from a rafter in the attic. The minister was with Dad when he called. He said Ethel was not well."

"Oh, my dear friend, I'm so sorry to hear this." Yolanda sat down next to Amanda on her bed.

"The tears, which had been near the surface, came streaming down Amanda's face. "I wish I had been nicer to her," she sobbed.

Yolanda gently pulled Amanda up as she said, "Let's walk. You need to keep moving till you're so exhausted you can sleep." With her arm around Amanda's waist they walked up and down the long dorm hall until Amanda said, "I have to stop." Yolanda led her to bed, removed her shoes, and gently tucked a soft blanket around Amanda.

When morning came, Yolanda asked, "Have you slept? You haven't moved."

"I don't know. I think I slept a little. She sat up, and with great effort she swung her heavy legs over the side of the bed."

"Can I bring you coffee, or juice, or rolls?"

"Maybe coffee. I have to shower, pack some clothes, and talk to the dean."

"While you shower I'll get your coffee."

The morning passed without Amanda realizing it. By 11:00 she was carrying her suitcase down to the dorm entrance. A white car she didn't recognize pulled up and her father got out. They clung to each other without saying a word. Then Carlton stepped back, still keeping his hands on her shoulders, and stared at her as if he couldn't believe it was her. Finally he said, "It's so good to be with you." He put her suitcase in the trunk and opened the door for her; then walked around the car and got in the back seat with her. "This is our pastor, John Halverson."

"Thank you for driving Dad here," Amanda said as she moved closer to her dad.

John reached across the seat and shook her hand. "I'm glad to do it. Your father is a good man."

"I know," Amanda said as the tears started to come. Carlton put his arms around her and she buried her head in his shoulder. He gently rubbed her back. Nothing more was said as they drove out of the city. In the safety of his arms Amanda fell asleep. She woke up when they were approaching Turtle Creek.

As John pulled up to their front door he said, "Would you like me to come inside?"

"Yes," Carlton said, "Come with me." He pointed to the overstuffed armchair. John sat on the edge of the comfortable chair, leaning forward, his hands clasped on his knees. Then Carlton said to Amanda, "The letter is on the kitchen table."

Amanda walked slowly to the kitchen. She could feel her dad's presence directly behind her as she carefully picked up the translucent, ivory-colored sheets. She went to the living room and primly sat on the davenport. Her dad sat next to her, watching her carefully as she slowly read the letter, each heavy word suspended in her brain, and then, sinking to the bottom of her heart.

When she got to the part where Ethel described how she killed and buried Sarah she jumped up, the letter dropping to the floor. Amanda said, "This is evil. How could she do this?" She ran for the bathroom, saying "I'm going to be sick." Carlton and John could hear the retching sounds as she vomited.

When she stumbled back to the living room and collapsed on the sofa Carlton said, "My poor darling. Do you want to lie down and rest?"

"No, Dad, I want to finish the letter." She continued to comment as she read. "I'm getting angrier with each sentence I read. Grandfather started the evil. How could he do that to his daughter? It doesn't excuse what she did, but it helps explain why she was so evil." Then she came to the end of the letter. "I always knew that she didn't like the fact that I reminded her of mother, but I never knew she hated me. When I was little I used to think she loved me. I remember times when she rocked me, and let me snuggle up to her cozy robe. But she must have hated me to make it look like my mother never loved me, and to say that you, Dad, should not be upset if I disappoint you." Amanda bowed her head. "I was a burden to her all these years."

Pastor Halverson stood up and walked over to her. "Ethel was so damaged that she was not able to love anyone in a healthy way. She had to have complete control, and could not tolerate anyone unless they did exactly what she thought they should do. If you had never been born, Amanda, she still would have had these distorted beliefs because, in order to convince herself that what her father did was normal, her whole view of the world was distorted, making her extremely rigid and self-righteous. " Amanda and Carlton got up from the davenport. The Reverend reached out and grasped both of them by the hand. "The most important thing the two of you must always hold close to your heart is that Sarah loved both of you. Ethel was so sick that she was extremely threatened by this love. It is very sad, but neither of you should blame yourself for what happened to Ethel. That would be an even greater tragedy."

Clinging to what Reverend Halverson said about her mother, Amanda was able to sleep more that night. The next morning she got up early and made coffee. Her dad entered the kitchen when it was ready. "That smells good," he said as he sat down at the kitchen table.

In the bright morning sunlight Amanda saw the dark circles under his eyes. "I hope you got some rest. This is so hard."

"As I tried to sleep I remembered the times I rolled my eyes when Ethel was worried about what people would think. Now I realize why she was so easily threatened by so many things." He took a deep breath before he said, "We'll get through this together. Today we have to meet with Mr. Olson, to choose the casket and plan the funeral. I talked with him briefly Thursday morning. We'll keep things simple."

As Amanda sat down Carlton continued. "When my dad died only a few people were present at the burial." He paused, lost in thought. "My teacher was there. That meant a lot to me."

"So, what are we going to do?"

"Pastor Halverson told me we should honor Ethel's life with a Christian service and burial. Our merciful God knows what she did, and how sick she was. It is not our duty to decide her fate. As she requested, Ethel will be buried next to our father."

But what are we going to say when people ask how she died?" Amanda thought about what she had just said. "Maybe that's a dumb question. The whole town probably knows all the details already."

"Only Pastor Halverson knows about her letter. It's not necessary to tell people about that. The town people know she had died at home because the hearse picked up her body shortly after I found it, and that it was sudden and unexpected." Carlton reached across the table and held her hand. "You're right. The whole town probably has figured out that she committed suicide, but I believe that they will be kind to us during this difficult time, just as they were when my father hanged himself."

Amanda absorbed Carlton's words before she said. "But why didn't we have some clues about what was going on in her mind?"

"I can't answer that either. I will always wish I had known what Ethel had to go through when she was a teenager. The person I can't understand is my father. How could he sexually abuse my sister? He was my hero when I was a child. It will take time for me to forgive him. Maybe I never will forgive him for what he did. But I do know one thing. My mother died giving birth to me. Both you and I must not blame ourselves for the problems that happened when we were born."

Mr. Olson was professional when he explained to Carlton and Amanda what they needed to do. Choosing the casket wasn't hard because both agreed that Ethel would want it to be modest, yet well-constructed.

Choosing what clothes Ethel would be buried in was more difficult. When they got home after meeting with Mr. Olson Carlton asked Amanda to select the outfit because, as a woman, she would know more about what would be appropriate.

When Amanda opened the door to Ethel's closet she saw faded, cotton housedresses. There were several "Church" dresses in pleasant floral prints, neatly hanging on one end. All had sleeves, either elbow length or wrist length. "She must have been hot during the summer services; refusing to wear a sleeveless dress, or to fan herself with a church bulletin with accordion folds," Amanda mused. She chose the most cheerful dress. It had a soft gold background that was covered with daisies.

When she brought it to the living room to show her dad she said, "I hope this one meets your approval. I wish there was some jewelry for her to wear with it."

He got up from his comfortable chair and said "Ethel never wore jewelry. She always wanted things plain and simple." He paused, then added in a voice heavy with sadness, "I wonder if she would have worn a necklace and earrings if I had thought to buy them for her. Why didn't I pay more attention to her? Maybe I would have realized how sick she was."

Amanda laid the dress on the sofa and walked over to her dad, putting her arms around him. Don't blame yourself. She hid her sickness with a robe of twisted righteousness. I want to put it on the front page of the *Turtle Creek Tribune* that my mother did not abandon us. I know I can't do that." She hugged her dad tighter.

"After we've had time, I think it would be helpful for both of us to tell Daisy the whole story. She will understand."

"That's a very good idea," Carlton said softly.

A manda found the visitation that Friday night exhausting, but she was touched by how kind people were. Most of them simply expressed sorrow over Ethel's death. When Mrs. Nelson talked about what a pillar of strength Ethel always was, both in the church and in the community Amanda had to keep her face in a frozen blank stare. She couldn't respond, "If you only knew."

After most of the people had left Amanda saw Frieda Johansson, signing the guest book. Amanda started to leave, but Frieda followed her, saying, "Amanda, wait. I need to talk with you."

Amanda stiffly said, "I was just leaving. It's been a long day."

"I know, but I have a message for you from Gael. I called him today because I thought he'd want to know about your aunt's death." She reached up and nervously adjusted her pillbox hat perched on top of her hair. "After all," she added, "he did spend a lot of time at your home."

With immediate regret, because she didn't want to care, Amanda said, "How's he doing?"

"School's going okay, and the baby is over a year old now." Frieda paused, and then added in a puzzled voice, "He asked me to tell you that he's getting a red fire engine for Billy next Christmas." More comfortable, she added, "He also wants you to know how sorry he is about how things ended between you two. He understands how upset you were about the way he left. He didn't really expect you to answer his letters."

"Letters? He wrote letters?" The words made no sense. It took a long minute for Amanda to regain her composure. She finally said, "Tell Gael I'm okay, and I love college." She started to walk away; then stopped and slowly turned around. "I wish him luck, and tell him I know that he will be a good dad to his son."

"I'll be sure to tell Gael that. His mother says that it gives her so much pleasure to watch how good he is with his son." Frieda reached out and lightly patted Amanda's arm. "It was good to talk with you." Then she turned around and left in a hurry, as if she was embarrassed.

Amanda slowly walked out of the funeral parlor. Everyone had left. Carlton was waiting in the car. As soon as she opened the door she said, "Do you think Ethel would have destroyed any letters Gael sent? Frieda told me that he wanted me to know that he understands why I didn't answer his letters." Amanda's whole body started to shake involuntarily.

Carlton reached out and hugged her. In a voice filled with sadness he said, "Knowing what we do now I'm sure that Ethel was very capable of doing that. We both know that she never liked Gael, and I believe him when he told his aunt that he had sent letters." He continued to hold her until she stopped trembling. "He would have no reason to lie about the letters. Gael is a good person. How evil it was to destroy his letters and not even mention it in her confession." Then he started the car and drove slowly home.

When they entered their home, Amanda turned to Carlton and said, "You know what Dad? I no longer feel guilty. What I feel is a deep sadness for Ethel because she was so sick, and relief knowing Gael must have been writing to explain his actions and apologize to me." After pausing, because she was deep in thought, she added, "I think Auntie didn't confess to burning Gael's letters to me was because she didn't believe she'd committed a sin."

"I feel the same way about Ethel, and I no longer respect my dad. Looking back, as I get older, I realize that Donald Wallace MacGregor was grandiose. It was both his charm and his nemesis. But how could he sexually abuse his daughter? He was so narcissistic that he had no conscience. At least my grandfather, Carlton Lewis MacGregor, was a good man. That I know, and I will try to be as good a person as the man I was named after."

Reverend Halverson's sermon focused on how much God loves and forgives all of us, and how Ethel had to take on a lot of responsibility from a very young age. He added that it would be difficult for many people to deal with the challenges she had to deal with. He also announced that the fence separating the three graves from the rest was being removed. He said, "Who are we to judge who should be buried in the cemetery?"

When they exited the church after the service there was a watery sun trying to shine, while a light, thinly-scattered rain was falling. Amanda stared straight ahead, knowing she would break down if she looked at any of the faces, which now seemed to be filled with pity. As the casket was being lowered into the ground she lifted her eyes and saw Joey standing directly across from her. He was looking at her with tenderness that filled her with courage. You can get through this, he seemed to be silently saying to her.

As they left the cemetery he came over to her and grabbed her hand, like he used to do when they walked to school together. "I have to leave because of a meeting with a visiting professor regarding my research." He added, apologetically, "He's leaving for France tonight. Can I take you to the church before I go?"

Amanda turned to her father, who was standing near her. "Is it okay with you if I ride to the church with Joey?" He nodded his head.

Joey led her to his car, a beat up black Ford. "This looks like a wreck, but it's dependable," he said as he opened the door for her. It actually looked a lot like the car Gael had fixed up. Amanda didn't want to think about that.

The ride to the church, where lunch was being served in the basement, only took a few minutes; but before they got there it was raining in earnest. "Wish I had an umbrella," Joey said as he pulled over to the curb.

"It's okay. My hair just gets curlier when it's wet."

"I like the way you're wearing it now, the soft curls framing your face."

"Thank you," Amanda said formally. "It's easy to take care of." She started to reach for the door, then turned and said, "Thanks for coming. It's like I have my brother here."

Joey grabbed both of her hands and pulled her close. "I'm not your brother," he urgently said. "I've always wanted to kiss you. After all these years, I still dream about it."

Amanda lifted her lips to his. She didn't want the kiss to end. Finally, she pulled away, breathless. "I have to go," she said, and then added, "When will I see you again?"

"Soon as possible. I've loved you since your first day of school, when I walked you home."

"I'll never forget that day," Amanda said as she got out of the car. She watched Joey drive away. Then she walked to the church, not caring that she was getting soaked by the rain.

Acknowledgments

I want to thank Shipwreckt Books managing editor Tom Driscoll for his excellent guidance and belief in my story. I also want to thank the professors at the University of Wisconsin Writers' Institute for the inspirational classes I took there.

Finally, I want to acknowledge my beta readers: Betty Benner, Karen Brezicka, Anita Giuliani, Joyce Goetz, Kris Graf, Jim and Mary Herrick, Karen Lewis, Mimi Lilly, Pat McClean, Carolyn Meier, Gale Pifer, Pat Radecki and Kathleen Vellenga. They have inspired me with their enthusiasm and helpful suggestions.

About the author

Judi Bergen has a master's degree in social work from the University of Wisconsin. She has worked as a therapist in inpatient and outpatient mental health settings for over forty years.

For the ten years before she retired, Judi also worked with Hospice patients and their families.

Writing has always been an important part of Judi's life. Her short stories have been published in literary journals. Her 2005 essay about a hospice patient was published in a rural life magazine and placed in the top five in the National Writers Association that year. *Longing to Belong* is her debut novel.

She lives with her husband in Austin, Minnesota, where they have enjoyed raising their three children.